Nothing LEFT BUT Dust

A NOVEL

To Michelle

Thanks for your support!

MELISSA GEISSINGER

ARKEN PRESS

Library of Congress Control Number: 2023902165

Cover design by Melissa Geissinger
Select artwork components courtesy of Vecteezy.com
Original maps by Nat Case

FIRST EDITION

ISBNs:
978-1-960440-01-3   Paperback
978-1-960440-00-6   Hardcover
978-1-960440-02-0   Digital eBook

To my mother, Nancy,
who gave me the heart to tell this story.

And to my son, Apollo,
who gave me the strength to see it through.

THE GOLDEN GATE

FORT MASO

RUSS

THE PRESIDIO

LONE MOUNTAIN ◆

M

Fulton St

Haight St

GOLDEN
GATE PARK

◆ BLUE MOUNTAIN

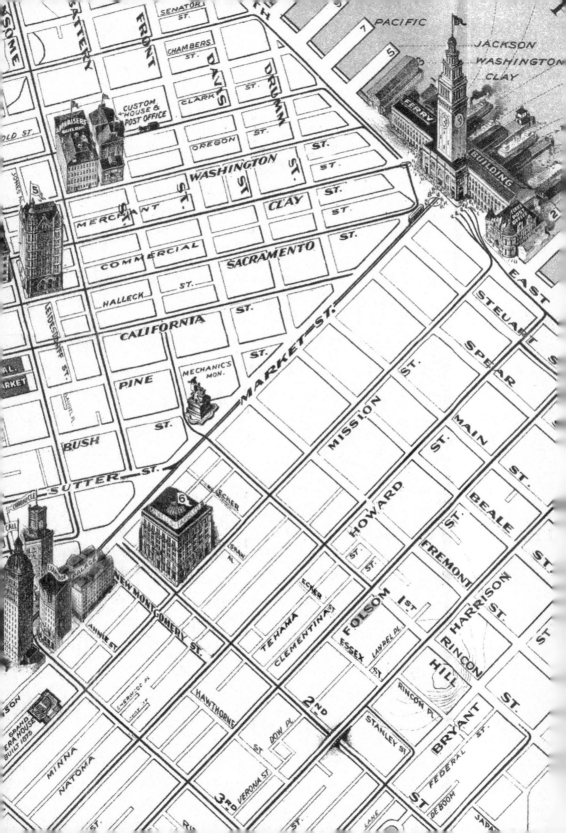

Chapter One

San Francisco, Tuesday, April 17, 1906

he corner of a well-worn map draped over Jo's legs and bounced in the warm breeze from the open window. Jo repeated the details of the lithographic transfer process aloud. "The wax drawing repels the water. The water repels the ink." She needed it memorized to the letter. It had to be perfect. *How can so much resistance be responsible for creating something so beautiful?* Her attention strayed to San Francisco's growing industrial center churning and coughing outside her second-story sanctuary at Minna and 2nd Streets. The rhythmic clunking of the presses running on the ground floor below was loud enough to block out most of the clamor of horse-drawn carriages while providing a persuasive reminder for her to concentrate.

Mrs. Tucci's empty desk rested prominently in the center of the room. Jo sat cross-legged on the floor behind it as she watched the early evening sunlight dance past the open curtains. Fog would typically have begun to roll into the bay by now, causing her to shut the window and light the lantern, but tonight was different, and oddly so. With each passing hour, it seemed to grow warmer instead of colder. *Earthquake weather*, Papa used to call it before Mama slapped the back of his head and told him not to be superstitious.

Crack!

The noise sent icicles careening through Jo's veins and thrust her mind back three years to relive that night. A gunshot, a scream, and a moonlit whirl—her father was ripped from existence, the accident that left her world forever changed. She slammed her eyes shut. *Stay right here. Focus.* She couldn't afford to lose herself. Not when she was this close to getting what she wanted.

Jo heard the tapping of footsteps on the floorboards. "Jesus, Mary, and . . . Josephine! Dear, you're crying!" Jo struggled to catch her breath. She opened her eyes and watched as blurry Mrs. Tucci marched toward her, an elaborate, wide-brimmed picture hat with iridescent plumage bouncing with each step. The door had swung open so hard upon Mrs. Tucci's return that it had hit the wall. "Oh, lamb. Are you okay? I didn't mean to startle you."

Jo pushed through the resistance of frozen fingers and dropped the map. She reached up to rub tears from her eyes and fought the impulse to throw herself into Mrs. Tucci's arms. Even though she trusted the woman with her life, she wasn't a little girl anymore. She couldn't help but cringe at Mrs. Tucci still calling her "lamb." She was almost sixteen.

"I'm f-f-fine, Mrs. Tucci," her teeth chattered. "S-s-sorry."

"You all right?" Mrs. Tucci's eyes widened. "Child, you're shaking."

"Y-y-yes," Jo wrapped her arms around herself and fought to keep steady. She knew if she just waited, the icy tremors would pass. They always did.

But instead of asking a million follow-up questions as she usually would, today was all about business. After years spent looking over her shoulder at the shop, Mrs. Tucci had finally agreed to test Jo's worthiness of an apprenticeship. If she proved she was ready, Jo could move into the spare room and study under her all day, every day, instead of a couple of hours here and there. She would no longer be stuck working for her loathsome uncle at his fruit and vegetable cart. Tonight could finally be the night she would tell him she was leaving.

"All right, Josephine. I've got a misprint for you." Mrs. Tucci got straight to the point. She didn't like to dillydally. She revealed a freshly rolled document and set it on the desk. Jo stood up, and Mrs. Tucci handed her a handkerchief she had stashed in her bosom. Jo wiped her eyes and then began to unroll the print.

All her anxiety dissolved as soon as she smelled the sweetness of the fresh ink. Unveiling a freshly printed map was like peeking through a window to a private Victorian parlor in Pacific Heights. It was intoxicating. This map wasn't just the newest addition to her collection. It was permission to dream of *what-ifs* and *somedays*.

Jo held the map up in front of her at arm's length. "Paris," she whispered. She could hear the accordion music and smell the sweet *chocolat*. *"Louvre, Arc de Triomphe, Notre Dame,"* she read aloud in the best French accent she could muster as she touched each illustrated landmark. She spread the map on the desk, using stray books and the oil lamp to hold the corners. She nearly forgot the purpose of the exercise as she ran her fingers over the pale blue path that the Seine carved through the city on its way to the English Channel. Studying the patterns of blocks and memorizing street names gave her a strange solace.

"Thanks to Fitz, the buffoon, you have what you've been asking for. Can you spot the error?" asked a droopy-eyed Mrs. Tucci. "I'll be in the shop if you need me, cleaning up another one of his messes."

As Mrs. Tucci retreated downstairs, Jo snapped into reality. *This is it. The test.* Her insides surged upward in anticipation. Seeking reassurance, she thrust her hand into the right pocket of her frayed dress in search of her pearl. She found the precious bead, closed her eyes, and gently rolled it between her fingertips. She took a deep breath and forced herself to swallow, pushing her heart and stomach back down where they belonged. *Forget daydreams.* The test gave Jo the chance to prove she had the skill required to become Mrs. Tucci's official mapmaking apprentice. She wanted it more than anything in the world.

She stared at the document and tried to think of everything she had learned from Mrs. Tucci. For half her life, Jo visited the shop nearly every day. It lay across the street from Papa's restaurant, so it was the best place for her to go—nearby and still out of the way. When Jo was nine, Mrs. Tucci caught her playing with some copper plates from one of the old hand presses. Instead of scolding her, Mrs. Tucci sat her down and taught her how to print her name by carving it in reverse.

"Excellent, little lamb," Mrs. Tucci would say. "Like a duck to water."

Jo searched the circular grid of Parisian streets voraciously, remembering tips she had learned about the mapmaking process from her mentor. Lithographic printing errors were hard to spot with an untrained eye and even harder on maps of places she had never seen before. Mrs. Tucci taught her to look for evidence of errors such as misspellings in the stamps, weak impressions, or broken lines. These subtle errors indicated mistakes in the production tools, such as not enough wax buildup in certain areas or chipped engraving wax, which meant the hair-thin layer had the wrong balance of ingredients.

Come on. It should be instinct by now. Find it. She looked at the symbols used to indicate cities, the colored lines used for tinting, and the spelling of landmarks, but she couldn't find it. Frustrated, she stopped. She forced herself to think of the primary lesson that Mrs. Tucci had cemented into her brain:

With perspective comes opportunity by design.

In other words, if Jo changed her perspective, she could find a solution she would never have seen before. She rose from the desk and stepped up onto the chair. She gasped. The colored pigments were out of alignment with the black lines toward the ends of the print. "There it is!" she announced to the empty room. Everything was aligned perfectly in the center of the map, but the farther out the pigment went, the more off it became, so the lines appeared fuzzy. Jo blinked to make sure she was focusing on it correctly. It appeared that the plate that made the image had shrunk.

"Mrs. Tucci!" she shouted toward the open door. "I found it!"

Mrs. Tucci's familiar footsteps clopped up the stairs again, and she appeared in the doorway, hands on her hips.

"So you think you've spotted it, hmm?"

Jo connected three corners of the map in the air with an open-palmed gesture. "The color layer, it's offset by about an eighth of an inch at the edges."

Jo's mentor paced around the room with her arms behind her back. Jo searched her face to indicate whether she had answered correctly, but Mrs. Tucci's stare was locked ahead of her. With each slap of sole to floorboard, Jo's throat tightened. *What if I got it wrong?*

"And what does this offset indicate?" asked Mrs. Tucci, still without meeting Jo's gaze.

Jo cleared her throat. "Well, it means that the plates weren't kept at a constant temperature."

Mrs. Tucci stopped pacing. A relaxed smile stretched across her face, and she nodded in approval. "Well spotted, dear."

"Thank you, Mrs. Tucci," Jo threw her shoulders back with pride. "I didn't see it at first."

"And then you changed your perspective, didn't you, lamb?"

"Yes. And then it was quite apparent."

"Of course it was, dear. Good instinct. But you would think Fitz would know better by now than to let the damn plates cool off too long before going to print." Mrs. Tucci's voice gained an octave. "If I see him make one more run out of register, I'll wring him by the neck!"

"He tries his best," Jo chuckled. There was no way Mrs. Tucci would see any real harm come to poor old Fitz. He meant well, and he had worked for her for ages. He just had a way of getting her goat.

"You've got an eye on you, Josephine. You'll be taking over for me one day, bet your boots! Maybe someday you might even inherit the shop."

One of Jo's hands clutched her chest while the other landed on her belly. "Really?" she cooed. "Oh, Mrs. Tucci, I couldn't possibly." Jo shrugged and tried not to seem over-eager. Mrs. Tucci and her late husband never had any children of their own, so this outcome was entirely possible. She had never considered it before.

It was truly exceptional that a woman ran the print shop. Jo especially admired her, for Mrs. Tucci was an Italian who, like her father, had built a business out of nothing. A job in printing was one of the most prestigious a woman could have because it required a good education. Mrs. Tucci had made a point of teaching Jo everything she knew, not just about printing and typesetting but also English spelling and grammar.

And, as Mrs. Tucci had taught her, printing was one of the only industries with a long history of supporting women in the field. The Women's Co-operative Printing Union had worked for over fifty years, and now women were paid as much as men. A position like this was practically—no, completely—unheard of, and Jo would not risk losing this opportunity.

"Now, the job is yours. Are you sure you can make this work, dear? You still have your commitment to your uncle. He must agree to your leaving."

Jo deflated. She hadn't known what Mrs. Tucci was expecting. As much as she wished she could vanish in the middle of the night and never hear from her uncle again, she had to confront him. "Mrs. Tucci, Uncle Giuseppe won't let me do anything but work for him until I pay my debts. According to him, I still owe him another year of my life."

Mrs. Tucci snorted. "If you ask me, your uncle is the one that could use a change of perspective. Your father's debts are not yours to carry." She took one rolled-up map and smacked it into her palm a few times.

With the mention of her uncle, Jo remembered that it was Tuesday, which meant she had to be home by 5 o'clock. She stretched her neck to read the carriage clock on the top shelf of the bookcase. 5:35 p.m. She was late. Again.

"There's a lot you can learn from maps, child," Mrs. Tucci droned on.

Jo rolled her eyes and let out a long breath. She saw the familiar speech coming from a mile away. "Yes, I know. Precious perspective." Mrs. Tucci was always using cartography as a medium for life lessons. Sometimes it was a bit of a stretch.

"You mock me, lamb, but recall what you did just now to find the error in the misprint. You switched your point of view, didn't you? What do maps teach us about perspective?"

"Yeah, I know," Jo shrugged off the lesson.

"With perspective comes opportunity by design," Mrs. Tucci couldn't help but repeat the phrase. "Josephine, you are a young woman now. It's time you face your fears instead of marinating in them like a day-old cutlet."

Jo sighed in frustration. "But what am I to do? You know how he gets. He won't listen. Whenever anyone stands up to him, they get the belt, or worse." She caressed the back of her left shoulder where the memory of a recent lashing still stung.

"Child," Mrs. Tucci glanced at the location of the hidden welt and reached for her hand. She pulled it toward her and leaned in closer.

"There are countless forces in this world that are set to work against us. Forces that push against us on account of our age, our heritage, and on account of us being members of the supposed weaker sex. Hell, forces of God and nature way bigger than we can even imagine push and pull on us for just being living, breathing souls trying to make our way through this dastardly world. Your Papa knew this all too well. We must push back. And when we cannot push, we must find a way to pull."

"But it seems so hopeless sometimes." Tears began to well up in Jo's eyes at the mention of Papa's struggles. "Ever since Papa died, my insides feel deader than a sardine in sturgeon season. Uncle Giuseppe is convinced I need to stay with him and work off this crazy debt that Papa owed him when he lost the Oyster House. There's no changing his mind. Believe me, I've tried."

"Perspective, darling. What is it that motivates your uncle?"

"Well, greed?"

"Think again," Mrs. Tucci tsk-tsked. "Why was he so upset when your Papa died?"

"Because he owed him money."

"But what motivates a man's desire for money?"

"Power. Station. Reputation."

"Ah, now we're getting somewhere. Does your working for him make him a richer man?"

"Well, actually, no. He'd be making the same amount of money regardless of my efforts. He's just getting free labor."

"When your father lost his business, it not only squandered the investment, it hurt something else, didn't it?"

"Their relationship. His trust in Papa and his pride."

"Precisely."

"So if I can somehow use this opportunity as a way to feed his pride, perhaps I might have some leverage. Perhaps I won't have to work quite so hard to convince him to let me go because I want him to, but because he will get something out of it."

"Yes," Mrs. Tucci's eyes gleamed with pride. "Pull, don't push."

Jo clapped her hands. "What if we offer him a line on the San Francisco street maps? Say we put a note on the front of every map that says 'Compliments of Giuseppe's Produce,' with the address. Like a sponsorship."

"Now you've got him! Hook, line, sinker. All that remains is to cut off his head and make him into a stew." Both women roared with laughter.

"I'll figure out a way to tell him. I'll do it. I don't intend to run away like my mother did."

Mrs. Tucci's laughter ceased, and she again reached for her, this time caressing her cheek. "Dear, your mother did the best she could under the circumstances. One day you'll understand this better. But for now, just know that you've got so much of your father in you . . . always daydreaming bigger than your britches. He would be proud of you, you know."

Jo felt a smile take over her face that caused her eyes to squint. She didn't remember the last time she had smiled this big. Papa always told her it made her eyes sparkle like moons.

Mrs. Tucci removed the map from the desk before handing it to her. "For your collection, dear."

Jo rechecked the clock. 5:49. It would be dark soon and she had to be up early in the morning. She would need to help her uncle put the cart out and sell as much produce as she could before escaping back to Mrs. Tucci's—hopefully with good news.

She dragged her feet as she scooped up her coat and bookbag from under a few books on the floor, carefully folded up her new map, and put it inside.

"There's some dinner on the stove if you want some before you leave. Goodnight, Josephine. Let me know tomorrow if you are able to take my offer."

Jo nodded as she said goodbye and scooted out the door and across the hall to the kitchen.

The salty smell of fresh seafood warmed her from the inside out. She could tell right away it was Mrs. Tucci's glorious cioppino. Mrs. Tucci always had some kind of old country-inspired brew simmering on low heat. Those smells sent her back to a time when Mrs. Tucci would have her, Papa, Mama, and baby Peter over for supper on nights his restaurant was so busy they ran out of food to feed themselves. But that was before those nights at the restaurant got so slow they could no longer stand the smell of brine. Before their doors closed for the last time and the place was boarded up.

She grabbed the ladle, dangling on a hook next to the stove, and plopped it into the oversized pot, sending red broth shooting into the air in every direction. One of the liquid projectiles landed on her blouse. Sure to stain, she grabbed a cloth from the counter and began to dab at the spot.

Papa's voice echoed in her mind. "Looks like you earned yourself *una medaglia*," he would have said, as though stains were medals, earned by waging war in the kitchen and worn with pride and honor. Every time he said this, it would end in her giggling at him slurping up his spaghetti as loud as he could muster, while Mama scolded both of them for playing with their food.

Jo poured herself a bowl of the hearty soup. She sat at the table, careful not to drip on the yellow floral tablecloth as she delivered soup to her mouth, one spoonful at a time. When the chunks of fish, scallops, crab, and tomatoes were gone, she set the spoon aside and drank the rest of the vibrant broth directly from the bowl. She was glad Mrs. Tucci wasn't looming over her shoulder lecturing her on table manners.

She savored the peace and quiet for as long as she could but quaked at the thought of what she had to do next: walk into that house that was not her home and convince Uncle Giuseppe to let her leave.

Chapter Two

Market Street, Tuesday, April 17, 1906, 6:32 p.m.

tto gripped the slender white handrail secured against the glass to help reinforce his stance at the front of the cable car. The ride was bumpy, and progress was slow. A slot embedded in Market Street is what held the mechanism that pulled the car down its tracks. Horse-drawn carts and the occasional automobile darted back and forth across the cable car's path, taunting the vehicle as it dragged along, bouncing with meticulous rhythm.

The broad thoroughfare divided the city into two discernible worlds: Otto's to the north was filled with tailored suits, rifle competitions, and ritzy operas. To the south, the city's underbelly. "South of the Slot," it was called. The gritty, crime-ridden streets were home to riffraff and working-class men. Otto was secretly fascinated by the unobstructed lifestyles of those who resided there. It must be nice, he thought, to be able to live your life doing honest work without high society breathing down your neck. It was one of the reasons he decided he had to leave.

What may have been hypnotic to the other passengers was

slightly irritating to Otto. He didn't have the patience for this mode of travel. Even children were running along faster than this bum of a cable car.

"Hey, skyscraper, watch it," a stout older gentleman next to him complained as he pushed Otto's elbow away from his chest. Otto accidentally banged into a woman holding a small child who sat on the outward-facing bench next to him.

"Sorry, ma'am," he said, smiling at the toddler, whom he guessed was close to his younger sister's age. The little guy took this as an open invitation to make faces at Otto for the whole rest of the journey. Otto returned the gestures in kind.

The inside of the cable car was so crowded that men lining the street-facing edge hung one foot off the side, their arms clutched to the outside poles. The pleasant weather had brought people out of their homes and offices to take in some of the rare uninterrupted sunshine that made the bayside city sparkle. For a moment, he regretted not having his father's automobile, but the feeling quickly dissipated. He couldn't have taken it; he was leaving. For good this time.

Otto filled his lungs with a deep breath, the mixed smell of opportunity and horse manure drumming against his nostrils. The streets were alive with activity, people jetting every which way. The men dressed in suits and the women in gowns with stunning hats; each made a bigger statement than the last. Crowds of pedestrians gathered at street corners, waiting for their turn to gamble at whether or not they could make it across the thoroughfare unscathed.

There were just so many *people*—walking, driving, and riding on horseback and bicycles. The clopping rhythm of horse-drawn carriages argued with the putter of the new-fangled horseless variety. There seemed no discernible pattern to their movement; except for the cable car, whose bell chimed in tune with it all as it continued down its predictable path.

Otto studied one of his favorite buildings as he rolled past it: a gorgeous grey and white Queen Anne Victorian with Gothic Revival touches in the intricate details. The anatomy of buildings enchanted him. Every outward-facing surface was an opportunity for expression. He could stare at rounded cutaway bay windows and multi-textured facades for hours at a time and still find fresh nuances.

He adored their craftsmanship but was dazzled by their multi-toned coloring. The master painter could turn those meticulously carved posts of tight-grained, old-growth redwoods and Douglas Firs into a conversation. A carefully selected color palette and skilled brushstrokes made each building a work of art. One could paint a house a set of colors, say golden yellow with black trim, and repaint it with light greens, purples, and creamy whites with fine hints of gold on the hand-whittled flourishes and have a completely different building. It's what inspired him to become a painter and why he planned to go to New York. And maybe even Paris to study under the greats.

As the cable car chugged past 3rd Street, the passengers started to chatter as they pointed upward. The San Francisco Call building was magnificent. Standing at twenty-one stories high, it was the tallest building in the city. In fact, the tallest west of the Mississippi.

Otto imagined life in another city like New York, where buildings grew taller daily, and nobody knew him or his family's reputation. The thought of his father's name not preceding him both scared and exhilarated him. San Francisco was very much a can-do city, and while he was fond of it, the expectation of taking over Pop's business was more than he could bear. He refused to accept that he would be trapped in a lifelong commitment just because he was the son of August Frei, builder of the finest billiards and pool tables in the western United States. Not that he had anything against his father, but he couldn't bear the pressure living up to being even half the businessman and craftsman he was.

Otto's attention pulled ahead of the traveling car. With its majestic clock tower, the Ferry Building grew larger, standing proud and tall against the blue sky above the bay. The sun was beginning to set, and puffy pink stripes appeared behind the prominent landmark.

As the cable car dragged into the turntable before the great arched doorways, the conductor shouted the end of the line. Wheels screeched as the vehicle came to a jerky halt. The cramped crowd dismounted, forcibly dragging Otto with them. He looked back, and the car had already rotated 180 degrees to begin its journey back whence it came.

Otto turned back around and stood in front of the great gateway to the city, fists on his hips in silent celebration for making it this far. The transportation hub was bustling. People were milling about in every direction, daring the cable cars to chase after them. He gripped his parcel that held all the possessions he would be bringing with him to his new life. He shoved it under his arm and began to walk.

He took a pensive breath as he thought about his ferry journey, scheduled to depart to Oakland, where he would catch a train tomorrow morning. Despite being this close to the bay, the air was oddly warm this evening. Even the wind seemed confused, blowing in from the east. Unusual, he thought, then defiance and rebellion consumed him once again.

Otto walked west on Market Street and turned left when he saw the sign for Steuart. He heard this was where he could find a bed for the evening and a drink before an early morning departure. Passing several storefronts, he spotted a series of saloons attached to boarding houses.

All sorts of cagey characters gathered out front. Sailors and wayward travelers leaned against posts and facades, staring shifty-eyed at passers-by. The lowlife made Otto slightly uncomfortable. No doubt he was out of his element.

He read "Alice's Rooming House" on a hand-painted shingle that swung from hooks on the roofline of one of the establishments. He recognized the name from his father's ledger. "Rooms for Let" was painted on a wooden sign in the dust-encrusted window. The hint of familiarity drew him nearer, and he entered the accompanying saloon.

Otto looked around the room. The dank stench of whisky and piss hung in the air like a thick fog on the Golden Gate. His nose couldn't help but scrunch up noticeably. Saloon patrons eyed him up and down. He didn't like this feeling of being silently measured for the kind of man he was. He knew he had to get used to it, though. He was about to be out of his element and in an environment where first impressions would either put wind in his sails or sink him. Even though it made him uncomfortable, he had made his decision, and there was no turning back.

Otto approached the bar at the back of the saloon. He noticed one of his father's hand-crafted billiards tables sitting in a dark corner.

"Do a smile?" the burly bartender asked as he stared at him with his right eye, his left tightly shut as he stroked the curl of his wax-fused mustache.

"Pardon?" asked Otto.

The barkeep seemed to move in slow motion as he stopped fondling his facial hair and put both hands firmly on the bar in front of him. He was a mountain of a man, and anyone could tell he relished intimidating young men like Otto. He leaned in, uncomfortably close.

"Have a drink?"

"Oh, yes, please, sir." Otto took a seat at the bar and rubbed his cleanly-shaven chin. "Whisky, please. And a room for the night."

"I ain't no sir," he scowled. He turned to shout to the other end of the bar. "Oi! Alice! *Pizen* and a bed for the *li'le* gentleman *o're* here."

A woman of about sixty, sure-footed and all smiles, approached from the far end of the bar. "Well, I'll be jiggered," Alice's voice was raspy and booming. "If it ain't August Frei's boy!"

Otto was surprised she recognized him. He didn't recall ever meeting her before.

The woman grabbed a small shot glass and a bottle of Hotaling Whisky, whose distillery was located over on Jackson Street. "I'd know that mug anywhere. You look just like your father, boy. It's the eyes, blue as the bay and sharp as tacks. Couldn't deny it if you tried." She poured the shot sloppily, letting it spill over the edge before pushing it toward him.

"Thank you, ma'am. But I'd prefer it if you didn't tell my father I was here." Otto tossed some coins on the bar top.

"I see," she paused as she reached for the coins, "trying to make a run for it, are we? Make a go of it on your own? You're your own man and all that. I'm all too familiar with the plight of lost young souls. Oh, and there's no place for formality here. Call me Alice."

For a moment, Otto pondered why Alice was so taken by his plight. Until, that is, he took a swig and immediately allowed the feeling of lightness to replace his blooming curiosity. He welcomed the familiar tingle that came with the first shot.

"Well, Alice, you see right through me," he started. He might as well tell her what he set out to do. What did it matter? He would be long gone by this time tomorrow. "The world had a plan for me, but I'll tell you what, I've got one or two of my own. Plans that is."

Alice's eyes widened, and she leaned forward. "Oh, do tell, deary."

More whisky flowed into his glass. "My father, the brilliant and infallible August Frei, expects me to follow in his footsteps," he swept his full shot glass above his head, spilling precious drops. He winced at the splash of whiskey upon the bar, gulped it down, and smacked his lips. It warmed him from the inside out. "He expects me to carry on his *legacy*."

"And what legacy might that be?"

"The most gifted and meticulous craftsman to society's most

well-to-do elite."

Alice nodded, filling his glass again. "Now that be a tall order to fill."

"No one in this town seems to care about what *I* want. What *my* plans are. You think I want to be building damn pool tables for the rest of my life?" Otto immediately regretted saying that. He didn't mind the building so much as he knew he'd never be good enough. When comparing his craftsmanship to his father's, he always fell short. His father had constructed Otto's destiny for him, but Otto decided to create his own.

"And what do ya strive to be, then?"

"A painter," he swallowed his whiskey and coughed.

"Well, that's a fine plan."

"Thank you, Alice," Otto hooted in astonishment. This was the first time someone hadn't laughed at him when sharing his desires. Instead, she seemed to take him seriously.

Another pour. He stopped and stared at the glass. He shouldn't. Okay, he thought, just one more. He took a swig, and it was gone.

"And what of everyone else? What do these horrible folks expect outta ya?"

Alice poured him another. He pushed it back, but she cocked her head and waited.

"Everyone in this whole damn city keeps expecting me to measure up to what they want. I'll show them. Tomorrow I'll be gone, and what will they say then?"

"Oh now, who expects so much of you then?"

"Cecil Miller, for one," Otto groaned, sweating under his collar. He took off his jacket and emptied his glass into his gullet again. He hated that he was getting all riled up. Somehow this unknown woman had gotten in his head. He tried to catch his breath.

"A friend'a yours?"

"If you could even call it that," Otto seethed. He knew he should stop talking, but his tongue moved quicker than his mind could muffle. "Maybe a friendship of convenience. Cecil lives next door. His father imports rugs, the really fancy ones from the Orient. He and Pop were business associates. 'What's a hand-crafted billiards table without a fine rug to set it upon?' they would always say."

Alice nodded. She was just a blur now. She resembled some of the post-impressionistic paintings Otto wanted to one day learn to emulate—streaks and swirls of blues, browns, and yellows that only start to look like something if you take a step backward.

"Me and Cecil, our friendship isn't so, eh, symbiotic. He's always trying to one-up me and gives me hell if I fall short. I'd be lying if I said he weren't a factor in my deciding to leave town."

"And why is that, deary?"

"We had what I *thought* was a friendly game of Five-card draw the other night. Then Cecil, the cheating bastard, obliterated me! I'd seen the corner of the damn ace up his sleeve! I swear, the cheater had some kind of mirror set up over my shoulder or something. He kept calling my bluff. But it was what he said after flipping over a full house, aces high, that was the last straw. 'Why do you even try, Frei? You're a disgrace. Might as well call you Never Try Frei.' I tell ya, Alice, what I wouldn't give to pop him with an uppercut that sent him into next Tuesday."

Otto pivoted on his bar stool to swing punches at invisible targets in the air to demonstrate while he watched Alice's husky friend nod in her direction. He pulled a small, unmarked wooden box out from behind the bar and handed it to her.

"Now, now, boy. Calm your nerves," she said.

Only then did Otto realize just how tense he was, and he made an effort to drop his shoulders. Alice handed him a hand-rolled cigar. "On the house." She passed him a match.

"Really? Thanks, ma'am! Oh, sorry. I mean Alice." He blinked his eyes slowly for a moment to put the stogie into focus. Just what he needed. A puff or two would do him some good. He sniffed—musty with hints of rich sweetness, like taking a walk through the botanical gardens. He lit it up and got a whiff of burning maple syrup. It was a familiar smell, but he couldn't place it. He shrugged and drew in a long, smooth mouthful of smoke. He rolled it around on his tongue before letting it out slowly. It tasted both sweet and bitter. Like flowers dipped in vinegar. He swallowed his fifth glass of whisky. Was it his fifth or his sixth?

Before he could even put the glass down, his head spun. It must have been the alcohol, but it felt different somehow. Perhaps it was the cigar that he just realized smelled like walking through Chinatown late at night. A warm pressure toward the back of his head appeared and expanded slowly downward into the rest of his body. He lost his balance on his stool and fell to the floor, but he didn't hear a sound.

Was he on the floor? He didn't care. He felt good. Really good. The air around him became warmer. It was as if he were lying on the crest of a grassy hill in Alamo Square, staring up at the clouds floating by. He was so happy to be there in his city.

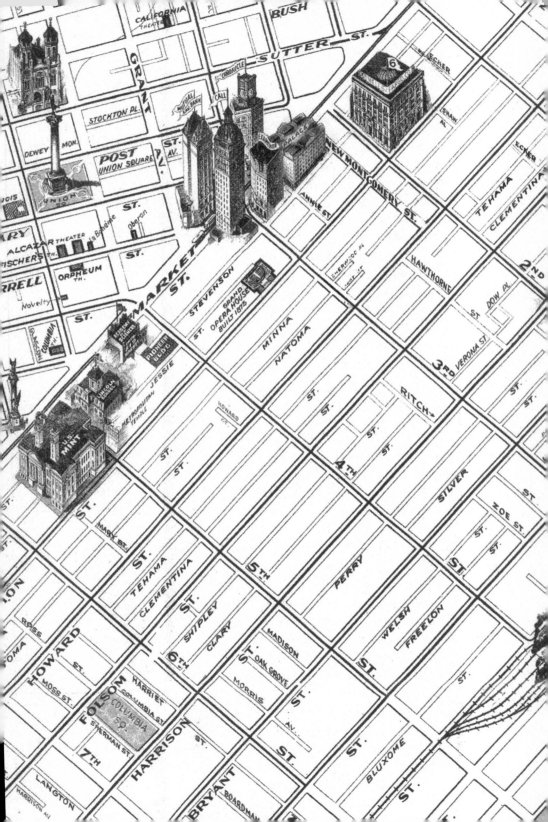

Chapter Three

Jo raced down the wooden stairway to the shop floor; she licked the bits of soup from around her lips. She wove around piles of print materials and huge machinery to make her way to the exit. "Not so fast, little lady," a gruff voice scratched from behind a printing press.

"Oh, hey Fitz, I didn't see you there. Working late?" Jo asked.

"You know the Missus. Can't keep up with the demand, so I do my part."

Ever since Mrs. Tucci's husband passed away, Fitz always found one excuse or another to stay late and help. In reality, Jo knew he couldn't bear to leave Mrs. Tucci alone in that big, empty building drowning in memories. She suspected, however, that Fitz was the one who needed the company even more. He was an Irishman, probably in his late fifties, but smoked like a chimney, so he looked to be in his seventies. He never married and didn't have family nearby, so Mrs. Tucci had adopted him the way she had Jo. Together they were an odd patchwork family, but it worked.

"Get some rest, Fitz," Jo leaned over the press to kiss him on the cheek.

"Aw shucks, Miss Josephine. Have a good night, now."

The sun sank below the fogless skyline, and the city began a vibrant degeneration into twilight. It was unseasonably warm but windy. Tonight, on her walk home, Jo didn't even need her coat.

She looked across the street at the restaurant on the corner. The place that used to be Papa's oyster house now sat empty. Jo noticed the sign advertising the building for lease had been taken down and wondered what would soon claim the space that was once everything Papa had dreamt it would be.

Jo pushed the painful memories from her mind and focused on her journey home. She should hurry to talk to her uncle before he went to bed. She would have to convince him to let her leave. A part of her hoped he would already be asleep. He usually retired before dark because he had to be up before sunrise. Jo usually slept in until the last possible moment.

While Jo contemplated what she would say to him, she tested her knowledge of the meandering city streets, envisioning the grid as it appeared on the map's page. She hung a left on Minna at New Montgomery past the stained-glass factory that sent shards of colors dancing across the sidewalk during the brightest parts of the day.

She crept past humming machine shops fully wired with electricity, workers probably staying late to finish orders. She passed hotels and restaurants whose savory smells of onion, garlic, and spices wafted through open doorways, trying to seduce her to come inside and indulge. Tenants hung out second-story windows keeping an eye on their children who dodged horse-drawn carriages on chaotic streets.

Jo rounded the corner of Bryant to 6th and slowed as if a dog grabbed the back of her dress. She was almost to her aunt and uncle's house and would rather not have anyone notice her late arrival.

Emi Nakamura, a girl of ten, stood at the base of the front steps of a narrow, rickety house. It featured faded blue shutters and stood next door to Jo's destination, a place she refused to call home. Jo silently welcomed the additional obstacle which would delay the inevitable stalemate. Emi wore a pristine white dress lined with lace. A small brown toque was pinned attentively to the top of her head. It was trimmed with a double twist of brown silk and punctuated on the side by a white quill.

Emi balanced on an apple crate with one foot, the other dangling off the edge, swinging her arms like mill wheels in the strong breeze. She sang aloud the lyrics to a popular tune.

In the shade of the old apple tree
Where the love in your eyes I could see
And the voice that I heard
Like the song of a bird
Seemed to whisper sweet music to me

When she noticed Jo, Emi kicked off the crate and sprang into a run toward her. "JoJo!"

Jo's little friend threw herself into her arms, but Jo reciprocated half-heartedly. She adored Emi, but she didn't exactly share her enthusiasm for all things pretty and proper.

"JoJo," Emi panted, "Mama says if I learn how to walk like a lady, she'll get me a new hat! With black straw and horsehair, chiffon trimmed with pretty, pretty lace and purple flowers!" She was almost out of breath by the time she finished. "The purple flowers look just like wisteria, JoJo, you should see it! They look just like the real thing! The side is full of them, like a waterfall. Isn't that wonderful?" Emi liked to go on about the next thing her Mama would buy her so that she could fit in at school.

"That's great, Emi." Jo placed her hands on her hips. "But do you really need another hat? You've got two already."

Emi stared up at her friend. Her eyes grew wide. "What do you mean? Of course, I need it! All my friends from school have at least two for each season, and that doesn't even count all the ones they wear year-round. Mama says that since my name means "beautiful painting" in Japanese, I deserve everything the other girls have and more. She says I have a real shot at being a sophisticated lady if I can just keep working on my etiquette."

Etiquette. When Emi spoke that word, she over-enunciated the 't' sounds, so they smacked like sticky toffee inside her mouth. Of course, Jo could understand why she was so caught up in making an impression. She was the only Asian girl in her entire school, and her mother wanted to ensure she fit in with all the other students. If she didn't, Emi said, she might be asked to leave.

Jo didn't know if this was true, but the whole idea of Emi needing to change herself so that others wouldn't feel uncomfortable made Jo's skin crawl. She hated that girls, herself included, were expected to wear certain things or walk a certain way to be considered worthy of being a part of civilized society. Jo often felt this kind of pressure from Aunt Rosalina and Uncle Giuseppe, and she hated it. Not only did Jo despise their coercion, but she repelled it with the entirety of her being.

"Emi, you shouldn't worry about wearing costumes to get people to like you. You're smart and pretty without all that extra, well, *fluff*. It's silly."

Emi's rosy bottom lip pushed outward and quivered.

"Emi, come inside!" an impatient voice with a thick Japanese accent echoed inside Emi's house. Mrs. Nakamura's head popped out of the door. "Bed. Now, Emi."

Emi pivoted; she painted a reverent grin across her face. "Coming, Mama!" Mrs. Nakamura nodded and withdrew inside, seemingly satisfied with her daughter's obedience.

Emi's attention refocused on Jo and her smile instantly turned bitter. "That's an eighteen-carat lie!" she huffed. "What would you know? You don't even want people to like you! I'll bet you only have one hat—and, and—" She took a breath, "Your dress is ugly! Just look at that stain! Your Mama would be ashamed!" Emi began to sob as she ran back into her house, slamming the front door.

Mrs. Nakamura reopened the door behind Emi; her expression shot daggers at Jo.

Jo shook her head and turned away. While she understood Emi's defensiveness, what business did she have bringing her mother into this? Jo didn't care what her mother thought. Mama had lost her right to tell her what to do as soon as she left. Emi would get over it. Tomorrow morning Jo would see her playing with her Teddy bear out on the front steps, and she'd forget the whole thing even happened.

Jo climbed up the steps to her aunt and uncle's house. As she opened the front door, she turned around and looked across the street. *Her old house.* It was her private ritual, the remembrance of another time so far away. Jo made sure she felt no eyes on her before reaching into her pocket to grab her pearl so tightly she could feel her pulse. She missed her father something fierce.

The day Papa gave it to her had been a warm evening, much like this one. She was twelve, and he had come home late from closing up the oyster house, as usual, only this time he strutted in, smiling big as life. He unfolded a scrap from a torn rag one careful corner at a time and presented a perfectly formed pearl. Jo had never seen one before. They were so rare. And there one sat humbly in Papa's large, cupped palm.

He pushed his hand toward her, looking at her gleefully, waiting for her to take it. She could hardly believe that he was trusting her with this treasure.

Papa's voice echoed, thick with Italian inflection, "What makes a pearl so special isn't how beautiful it is, *Passerotta*, but all it had to go through before it got plucked from the sea. Do you know what makes a pearl, Josephina?"

Jo shook her head.

"Each one starts as a speck of dust under the flesh. The creature protects itself by covering it with ahh—a *fluido*, a concoction of its own making. Remember the pearl, Passerotta. Remember that the things most beautiful and *prezioso* in the world had to work hard to get that way."

There was a thud and a shuffle as Aunt Rosalina's cat, Tilly, scurried down the steps and made her way to the door to greet Jo. She chattered as she made figure eights around Jo's ankles.

"Hush, Tilly," Jo whispered as she scooped up the tabby and squeezed her. "They'll hear us!" This scrappy, stringy thing was the only living creature Jo could truly be herself around. She knew Aunt Rosalina resented her because Tilly always snuck out of her room at night to join Jo upstairs. That shared aversion of her aunt only made her love the cat even more. Jo wasn't ready to ask—no, *negotiate* her plans to leave. She had no idea what she would say, but Jo feared what she might need to do to convince her aunt and uncle. It wouldn't hurt to delay the confrontation until morning.

Jo was tired of hearing that if she didn't get her head out of the clouds, she would end up a failure like Papa. They had even pulled her out of school to work longer hours at the fruit stand when she was fourteen. "Schooling is a waste of a perfectly good pair of working hands," Uncle Giuseppe would say.

She crept up two flights of dimly lit stairs, Tilly following closely, carefully skipping the steps that she knew sent loud creaks echoing through the house. Three steps from the top, the cat scooted under Jo's foot and forced it to land on a loose board. She cringed and hoped no one heard the wood's attempt to alert the house.

Jo stepped into her room on the third floor, though it felt more like an attic. It wasn't insulated, and there were spots where she could see through the cracks between the boards. Jo opened the window so the last bit of daylight could creep in and looked at the oil lamp that rested atop the dresser. She would need to light it soon, but not quite yet.

Once again, Jo's attention turned to the unseasonably warm weather. Tonight she wouldn't need to sleep in several layers of clothes for extra warmth. After Jo closed the door behind her, she sat on her rickety bed where she unlaced her boots, pulling the laces out of the top hooks until they slid off her feet with ease.

Tilly hopped onto the bed and danced around, turning Jo's dirty stockings into a nest. She purred as she pushed her head up into Jo's hand. "You have to promise to keep a secret," Jo told her feline confidant as she dug through her pack and removed the newest map to add to her collection. Her gaze shifted between her two hands—one held her window into Paris and the other Papa's pearl.

"Sometimes, I think of what it would be like to get out of here and see the world. No more produce cart, no more print shop, no more San Francisco. *This* could be my ticket, Tilly." She held up the precious gem and let the cat sniff. "I could leave tonight before they even know what happened. I could sail to Paris and climb to the top of the Eiffel Tower. I could go to New York to see the Statue of Liberty or even Milan to see the World's Fair."

As Jo stared at pictorial illustrations of the Louvre and the Eiffel Tower, a hundred times larger than scale, a silent sadness overcame her. She would probably never get to see the places on her maps. Her whole body went limp as she leaned back against the bed frame. She was old enough to realize the difference between imagination and delusion. "Oh, Tilly, who am I kidding? I can't negotiate. I can't convince Uncle Giuseppe of anything. I thought maybe it wouldn't come to this. But I fear that it will. It breaks my heart, but I might need to give up my pearl to have my freedom." Jo gulped and instantly regretted what she had just said aloud. She wished she could take them back and prayed no evil spirits had heard her.

Jo got up and placed the pearl inside its home, a chipped teacup on the top of her dresser. Within her reflection in the dresser's dirty hand mirror, she eyed her plain gray gown that hung across her shoulders. After removing her simple straw hat, Jo studied its wide, flimsy brim with the dirty white ribbon. She thought back to what Emi had said and scoffed. "Maybe it is pathetic and two seasons out of date, but what does it matter? I'm not trying to impress anyone. Except you, Tilly." She walked back over to the bed and gave her furry companion a scratch under the chin.

Heavy footsteps creaked up the stairs. There was a rap on the door, and it opened without waiting for Jo's response. A towering Uncle Giuseppe appeared, and a slighter Aunt Rosalina trailed behind him. *The pearl!* If Uncle Giuseppe spotted it, he would take it. Then she would surely lose every ounce of leverage she had in the argument. He didn't even know it existed, and that's the way she wanted it. Jo lobbed her hat on top of the teacup. She cursed under her breath for waiting so long to place her hat at its post. She wasn't ready. *What were they doing here? They never came up here this time of night.*

The pair stormed into the room, sending handheld lamplight bouncing off the walls. "Where is she?" Aunt Rosalina screeched. "What did you do with my baby?" She focused on the cat lying in a pile of dirty stockings on the bed. "It's okay, baby, mommy's here. You're safe now; you don't have to sleep up here in this drafty attic."

Tilly's eyes locked on the woman in her laced nightgown as she approached the bed, the cat's pupils enlarging and muscles tensing with each aggressive advance. Aunt Rosalina reached out to scoop up the cat. "Mommy knows how much you hate being around dirty, cruel children."

Aunt Rosalina rarely spoke directly to Jo. When she talked about her, it was in front of her but directed toward the cat or her husband. She liked clarifying her distaste for Jo's presence and even her general existence. The moment her bony fingers touched Tilly, the cat wound up as tightly as a spring. Aunt Rosalina screeched as the cat flew out the window and thudded onto the second-story rooftop below. Aunt Rosalina folded her arms in protest and retreated from the room without another word.

Uncle Giuseppe stared at Jo like a statue. He still hadn't said anything. She hated when he did this—like he expected her to read his mind. Or maybe he liked to pause for dramatic effect. Her gaze darted to the dresser to see if her treasure was concealed, and it was. She let out a breath she didn't realize she had been holding in. His gaze didn't follow hers, so maybe he hadn't noticed her suspicious efforts to hide something.

"Gee, Uncle Giuseppe, what is it already?" His extended silence gave her a sense of unbridled anxiety.

He looked over at the rolled-up map, then back at her. "Over at that printing place again, Josephine?" He was a man of few words who left so much meaning open to interpretation.

"Yes, sir."

A long pause ensued.

Jo shifted her weight to the other leg and waited. Even though he was her father's younger brother, he acted like an older man. She stood in excruciating silence for his next words.

"I don't want you going back over there," he said.

"What? Why?" Jo felt her lips quiver and her posture stiffened.

"Nothing but childish whimsy. You're a young woman now." He entered the room but looked away from her, seeming uncomfortable when admitting that she was becoming a woman. "Besides, you know we need you up and alert early in the morning. This behavior is unacceptable."

"But Mrs. Tucci says . . ."

"I don't care what Mrs. Tucci says. That woman is full of hot air. No respectable woman her age . . ." He gritted his teeth.

She knew already what he and other people thought of Mrs. Tucci. A woman who put her career before raising a family was irresponsible and improper.

"Child . . ." Another of his long pauses. This time with a begrudging sigh. Funny, his calling her child when the exact point he was trying to make was that she wasn't one anymore.

"If it weren't for your obligations," he continued, "I do not know what I would do with you." That's what he so often called her indentured servitude. *Obligations.*

"In fact, if you can't commit to spending all your time working for us here, it's high time you find yourself a proper husband to take you off my hands. And you'll never meet a suitor as long as you continue going to that damned print shop." His nose scrunched up like a dried-out prune. "Flights of fancy. Pointless nonsense. A *working* girl. Pah!"

Jo could lie down and die. This was the most she had heard Uncle Giuseppe speak in some time. His words made her heart sink, not because she cared what he thought, but because it was far from what Papa always taught her. The last thing she wanted to do was get married. Especially since the only reason Uncle Giuseppe wanted it was to get some coin in the form of a dowry. And get her out of his hair. She remembered her mission—use his pride against him. Get him to want her role as Mrs. Tucci's apprentice just as much as she did. "Uncle Giuseppe, I understand you're upset. But there's real opportunity in the map business. Not just for me but for all of us. If you'd like, I could—"

Uncle Giuseppe belly-laughed. "Young lady, what do you know of business opportunities? If you're anything like your father, I want no part of whatever you're fixed on selling."

Jo stepped back, and her arms fell to her sides in resignation. Her plan had failed. There was now only one way out of this. The pearl.

Uncle Giuseppe sauntered over to the dresser and fixed his gaze on her hat. "If you ever hope to make a favorable impression, you'll have to do better than this old thing." He picked up the hat and dusted it off. The cup that held her pearl sat exposed. *Please don't look down.* "You'll need some new dresses too. We'll have your aunt see to that."

He tossed it back onto the bare dresser, and his eyes followed, then widened. "What's this now?"

Jo let loose a wail as she lunged toward her pearl. "No, don't!" She grabbed it, sending the teacup careening to the ground. It smashed into a hundred pieces as Jo planted her bare feet squarely on the floor and held the pearl in a fist behind her back.

"Give it here, girl," he grabbed her arm, spun her around, and forced open her fingers; the pearl plunged to the floor.

Jo looked in horror as her most cherished possession bounced across the floor, and she dove to the ground in pursuit of the pearl.

Uncle Giuseppe's eyes ballooned with surprise as he watched. "Now that's the ticket! From one of your old man's oysters? You devious little thing, how did you manage to hide this from me all this time?"

She bit her lip, stood up, and tried to keep from screaming. "I'm leaving to work as Mrs. Tucci's apprentice. And one day, I'll take over the shop."

The rafters shook in response to Uncle Giuseppe's boisterous laughter. "Oh, you naive little girl. What of your obligations?"

This was the question she had feared the most. Jo forced herself to swallow her diffidence. She held out her open hand, the pearl resting comfortably in its folds.

"Hmm," he reached out to grab it from Jo's open hand, but she clasped it again and pulled it to her chest.

"As far as my obligations," she tried to say through welling tears so he would take her seriously. "I believe you'll find that this pearl is more than sufficient to cover the balance of Papa's debts. Mrs. Tucci has a room all ready for me. I can leave in the morning." This was a sacrifice; Jo attempted to remind herself that she had to take the opportunity for the future she deserved. She hoped that wherever

Papa was, he would forgive her.

Uncle Giuseppe grunted and gave Jo a slight nod to indicate his acceptance. "Let's see it, then."

Jo moved her closed fist closer to him and peeled back her fingers, exposing the precious bargaining chip.

He snatched it from her. He held it between two fingers, up to one open eye, and inspected it like a professional jeweler. "Well, it's not the finest quality, but this little gem is decent enough to fetch a few dollars."

"Enough to satisfy my obligations?"

"More than enough, I'd say."

"So, I'm free to go, then?"

"Not so fast. Unfortunately, that won't be possible. We agreed to a four-year term of repayment. I'm afraid it's beyond my control. You see, child, this pearl was never yours to begin with. It's an asset of the business and, therefore, rightfully mine."

"If you won't accept it as repayment, give it back," Jo pleaded. "It's not fair. It's the only thing I have left from Papa."

Uncle Giuseppe stepped across the hall into his private office. He put the pearl into his secretary's desk drawer, locking it with a small key he always kept in his shirt pocket. He closed the door behind him, giving her a smug look of satisfaction as though he finally had the last laugh regarding the rivalry with his late brother. "Be ready to shuffle first thing in the morning. The Gravenstein apples will go like hotcakes. And then we'll see to your impending engagement."

And with that, he slammed Jo's door shut, and the whole house shook. She heard a key clang inside the lock on her bedroom door. *He locked me inside! He's out of his mind.* She had to do something. She absolutely must get her pearl back. She sat on her bed and pressed her palms against her eyes to hold back tears. Mrs. Tucci's favorite word danced in her head. *Perspective.* She tried to figure out what possible change of view would get her out of this mess, but she couldn't. She was trapped.

Jo knelt on the floor and reached for her map that had floated underneath the bed. Something pierced the skin on her palm, and she recoiled in pain. Blood trickled down her arm. She brought it close to investigate. A shard of the cup's glass had made its way into her hand. She removed it carefully with her fingers and used her now bloodied and crumpled map to sweep the rest of the glass into a pile in the corner. She went to the window and called for Tilly. She didn't come. Not even the cat wanted her now.

Jo inspected her soiled map. Now that it was dark, she got up and fetched her gaslamp and a match from a box inside her top drawer. She took both to the floor and set them next to her map. Next, she removed the soot-scorched globe from the lamp, struck the match, and lit the wick. But instead of replacing the globe, she turned up the gas, sending flames higher and higher until they nearly licked her bedpost.

"It only takes one spark to ignite," a dark voice inside her head cooed.

She didn't have a death wish exactly, but she had become painfully aware of the fragility of life. Ever since her father's accident, mortality had fascinated her. One day Jo had found "The Imp of the Perverse," a short story by Edgar Allan Poe, in Mrs. Tucci's book collection, and she must have read it a dozen times. Poe described a person's urge to do the exact wrong thing purely because it *could* be done. Jo called it "The Pull."

She watched the open flame as it fluttered wildly with the cadence of her breath. The sweet smell of kerosene glided around her shoulders and lulled her into a trance. She watched the map's curled-up edges bounce uncomfortably close to the unprotected flame.

"Just one kiss of flame to paper, and the fire will catch."

Jo shook her head until common sense regained control. Of course, she didn't want that to happen, not really. And she certainly didn't want to die, but Uncle Giuseppe had made her so angry she couldn't help but feel The Pull. She hurriedly placed the globe back onto the lamp and pushed back against the feeling, forcing herself to refocus. Papa always told her, "Never act when you're angry." By the morning, she would have a plan. She would find a way to get free and get her pearl back; nothing would stop her. She would spend tonight plotting, planning, and thinking through every scenario.

She studied the misprint some more and ran through the steps that would be needed to correct the machines. The running of Mrs. Tucci's shop was the one skill she knew. She was more confident than ever that she could not give up. She would go over there tomorrow and take that apprenticeship. If her uncle insisted on keeping her prisoner, he would have to go over there and drag her back himself.

She clambered into bed, closed her eyes, and hoped sleep would soon overtake her.

Chapter Four

tto awoke groggily. A sharp pain jabbed the side of his head. A sliver of light from the rising crescent moon crept in through a small window high on the wall across from him. His eyes adjusted to the ambient light, and he found himself lying on a putrid mattress on the floor. He sat up, holding his head to keep his brains from spilling out his ears. The air was cool and damp. He opened his mouth and smacked his lips. He was parched, still half-rats drunk, and his insides felt like somebody had chewed them into dishcloths. He felt around for his belongings, but his hands sensed only the dampness of the mattress fabric.

A low, scratchy voice hurled at him unexpectedly. "Better a *gonger* than a goner!"

"What? Who's there?" Otto turned sharply in the direction of the voice.

"Gonger! You know? Opium addict. They really got you good. I watched you up there. Didn't even see it coming, did ya?"

"See what coming? What happened? Where am I?" Otto panicked

as the memory of Alice rushed back. The cigar. Maybe it had been laced with opium. He wondered if she knew he was coming. Someone who knew the identity of his father might have made an elaborate plan to capture Otto and hold him for ransom, knowing full well that his father would concede.

"Well, I bet you dollars to doughnuts we're in the same boat. Which is funny, you see, because odds are that's just where we'll be." The stranger's inflections were curiously playful for their circumstances. There wasn't a trace of panic in his tone, like he had been in this situation before. "Ya see, my friend, if my suspicions are correct, in just about half an hour when the sun comes up, we'll be taken to a ship bound for China or India or the North Pole for all we know and be forced to join their crew. Name's Bernard, by the way." Chain links rattled as Bernard's shadowy figure took a bow.

"We're getting shanghaied? You mean I'm not getting kidnapped?" Otto shouted toward his enshadowed companion. "You're out of your gourd!" He couldn't believe he preferred kidnapping over the dismal reality of his fate. At least then, he would be safe at home in a few days.

"Nah, kidnapping requires way too much planning and has a hefty lot of loose ends. The beauty of crimpin' is there's no one to go lookin'. Nobody asking questions."

While growing up, Otto had heard stories about sailors crimped ages ago from brothels and dance halls on the Barbary Coast. Many were dropped through trap doors or lured by women, never to be seen again. But this couldn't be happening to him, not here, not to someone of his stature and his family's reputation.

"You're nothing but a low-class know-nothing trying to pull one over on me. There's no way this is happening. Not by a long shot." Otto thought Bernard must be messing with him.

"Now, now, no sense in kickin' a lung out o'er it. I ain't tryin' to make the fur fly. An' didn't yer dear old pappy teach you not to slander a poor, defenseless old man to his face?" Bernard held up his arms and wobbled them against the weight of the handcuffs to exaggerate his fragility. Otto still couldn't see his face. "Anyway, our girl Alice up there must get paid a pretty penny for her part in the grift. Hash dispensaries like hers are prime pickins for would-be sailors and men at the end of their respective ropes. That's nothing but a good sense partnership for a crimp."

Otto considered the logic for a moment. It did make perfect sense. He had told Alice he was leaving and didn't want anyone to know where he was going. She must have seen that as an open door. Easy money. "But how do they get away with it? It must be illegal, like kidnapping?"

"Now that's the funny thing. Once a fella's name is on the ship's contract, it's *illegal* for him to step foot off the ship before voyage's end. Talk about a kick to the kite, ey friend?"

Otto couldn't breathe. He needed a drink of water. And he needed to find a way out of this basement. *Now.* He looked nervously around the room. Barrels were stacked to his right; behind them sat a shovel.

"It's time you get down to brass tacks, friend. That crimp will be here soon to knock us into cocked hats. Once we're on that boat, it's lights out. Alice got the drop on us."

Otto pondered the situation. *This was crazy.* At the very least, this fellow Bernard certainly acted like he wasn't quite all there. Then Otto realized that Bernard had said something about watching him upstairs as it all went down. "Well, if you know so much about this business," Otto said, "how did you get in this mess, same as me?"

His comrade crept out of the shadows, the pre-dawn light illuminating his face with each step. Bernard was a slender man with a sunken face that was more spindly grey beard than skin. There was an uncompromising evil behind his gaze. Otto leaned forward and got ready to push himself to his feet.

"Because, *friend*, I'm here to make sure you don't, shall we say, latch onto the idea that you can escape." Bernard laughed uncontrollably as he dropped his arms and the cuffs slid effortlessly off his hands, hitting the floor with a *clang*.

"You! You're behind this. You're mad!" shouted Otto. Bernard was only down here to toy with him, like a cat with a mouse. Otto jumped to his feet but stumbled, still feeling the stomach-churning effects of the whisky and drugged cigar. He checked his pockets for his belongings. "And you stole my billfold. And my pocket watch!"

Before Otto could pull his hands back out of his pockets, Bernard lurched toward him, securing a grip on Otto's neck with his icy cadaverous fingers, pinning him to the ground. Otto felt Bernard's weight shift to his left as his other hand reached for something on the floor. Otto leaned into Bernard's reach, throwing off his center of gravity, and tore at the assailant's fingers around his throat. Still, he barely managed to loosen one of them. Bernard cackled with hubris as he captured his prize. His right arm shot up, clutching a brick. He held it for an extended moment, seemingly for dramatic effect, before swinging it toward the side of Otto's head.

Otto let go of the hand around his throat to block the masonry-turned-weapon, causing it to strike Bernard's upper arm right above his elbow. Bernard lost his balance from the blow and tumbled onto his back. Otto coughed from the release of pressure around his neck as he rolled to his right, grabbed the shovel, and gripped the shaft.

Bernard scrambled to his hands and knees. Then, with one swift movement, Otto whirled the shovel around his head, and the brunt of the blade landed sharply on the back of Bernard's head. He dropped to the floor, blood pooling underneath his skull.

Otto panted, attempted to catch his breath, and wondered what had happened. He looked at his lifeless attacker on the basement floor. Though defensive, the gravity of his actions struck him harder than the brick would have. He stumbled backward in disbelief at what he had just done. Was the man dead? Did he kill him? Otto inched closer, shovel in hand, and prodded at Bernard. He didn't move.

Otto shook his head. *No.* He would feel guilty later. For now, his survival was all that mattered. He refused to let Bernard or anyone else take him, force him into a crew, and lose years of his life in servitude to the sea. He ran to the door and pulled, but it didn't budge. He scrambled across the room to the high window, but it was just out of reach. He looked for something to climb on to get to it.

But then Otto heard a rumble in the distance, like thunder, and the window, walls, and all the barrels began to shudder.

Chapter Five

I t rolled in from the southwest like a stampede of wild horses. Striking with such intensity and purpose, it was as if the earth were a beast caged for an eternity and had just broken free. It was barbarous and blood-thirsty, and had no remorse to speak of.

Jo's bed jolted and tossed her into the air like a rag doll. She awoke believing she was dreaming of being on a ship in a storm. The walls around her rattled, expelling dust from the cracks, and caused everything contained within them to shake. She reached her arms out to steady herself but lost her balance, bouncing in her bed like a fish in a frying pan. She coughed as the force pitched her side to side and slammed her to the floor. This is no dream. *This is an earthquake—the end of days. Surely it will be lights out at any moment.*

A momentary lull allowed Jo to pull up to her knees. Still, her debilitating horror became a morbid fascination as she moved toward the open window, catapulting herself over splintered furniture. She clutched the windowsill with rigid fingers and took a deep breath of dust-free air. *Perhaps the shaking is winding down or . . .*

Then, as if the creature had also drawn a great breath, the second wind of the quake struck with a more brutal and violent vengeance. Jo listened as the rattling of dishes, cracking of timber, and smashing of glass harmonized in wild cacophony until it surged into an opera of utter cataclysm.

Peering out the window, Jo could see the green light of dawn illuminating a staggering scene. She watched in horror as the entire row of wooden buildings across the street swung sideways, houses folding like a deck of cards.

Her house. The one she shared with Papa, Mama, and baby Peter—gone. In an instant.

It would only be a matter of time before her uncle's house toppled. Instinct told her the street would be the safest place to be. She looked down. Maybe she should jump out the window. Before she could convince her arms to latch onto the frame and pull herself up, another massive jolt released a plume of dust that mushroomed upward, causing her to retreat into the room.

Jo coughed as she headed for the door, staggering on the uneven floorboards and stepping on a piece of broken glass from the teacup. She threw herself onto the bed and did her best to remove the glass. Blood covered her foot, but Jo fought against her shaking and slid into her boots without bothering to lace them. Then, about to head back toward the window, Jo remembered something. *Her pearl. She had to get it.*

She grabbed hold of her doorknob, and it didn't budge. She forgot her uncle had locked it. She threw herself against the door once, twice, three times. She took three steps back and screamed as she ran and struck the door a fourth time, breaking through the wood and falling to the floor. The door to the office was closed. She grabbed ahold of the knob to lift herself off the ground. She twisted and pushed, but it didn't open. It wasn't the lock. The frame had warped so badly that the door wouldn't budge. Jo fought to free it, but then . . .

With a howl and a whirl, the quake reached its poignant climax. A violent twist, and the floor from underneath Jo's feet dropped once, then twice. *Crack!* Still clutching the door handle, Jo felt a sudden push as debris piled on top of her and forced her to the ground. The darkness took hold, and all went silent.

Chapter Six

Steuart and Mission, 5:12 a.m.

t struck like a cannonball to Otto's gut and knocked him onto the hard cobblestone floor. He bounced back and forth as if he were in an automobile with a missing wheel. He couldn't believe what was happening. Maybe he had fallen back asleep and succumbed to a second bout of effects from the opiates. At first, it hadn't seemed real, but he shouted into the empty air when it didn't stop. "Earthquake!" he gasped.

Bernard did not move.

Otto heard a chorus of shattering glass from the saloon above, like a dozen belligerent drunks heaving an arsenal of bottles and jiggers. The rack holding the whisky barrels cracked under the pressure of the massive jolting. Managing to gain his footing, Otto dodged a barrel rolling swiftly toward him and heard it crash violently into the door. When he turned around, the liquor erupted from the cask, spilling out like a flash flood and permeating the basement with the rich bouquet of vanilla and molasses.

The force of the collision had splintered the door. Otto was free, so he bolted for the exit. But something caught his leg and forced him to turn around. Bernard was awake and clutched Otto's ankle. The quaking slowed, and Otto shook his leg, breaking free from Bernard's grasp. The earth churned with a low rumble. Otto looked down at the crimp and saw raw, unfiltered fear in his bulging, unblinking eyes. He was helpless, and he knew it.

"Bastard," Otto mumbled as he scooped Bernard up and sup-ported his weight with his right arm. He couldn't just leave him.

The monstrous locomotive-like tremor returned with vindictive fury as Otto pulled Bernard through the broken door and up the stairs. He dragged him through a minefield of broken glass, splintered furniture, and disintegrated plaster. When Otto made it out of the building, he dropped Bernard on the street and didn't look back. As the quake gathered steam, Otto sprinted back toward the ferry terminal, where he aimed to get a better view. He dodged falling bricks that rained from above. Chunks of tall structures broke off and crashed into the tops of shorter neighboring buildings, tearing through their roofs like parchment paper.

Otto surged toward Market Street, stopped in the center of the wide thoroughfare, and stared in awe. Ahead, the streets pulsed like waves on the bay in a winter storm. Cobblestones popped and danced like corn kernels on a hot stove. The tallest buildings rocked east to west, reminding him of trees bending in a squall.

Just when it seemed like it would never end, there was a sudden twist and hard stop, the disaster's last-ditch effort to take the city down. With the earthquake's dying breath, all the remaining window frames retched, and their respective panes cried out in a colossal eruption of glass.

Then it was still. A great silence fell upon the city. For a moment, not a weep, nor cry, nor whisper could be heard.

Otto had passed the point of being afraid. Instead, he was focused. He spun in a slow circle, taking in the scene around him. The once mighty monuments of Market Street were now piles of crumbled ruins. Few buildings still stood, and the defiant ones that did looked as if they were only held together by spit and prayers. This was not the same city as yesterday. *Nothing would be the same again.*

Chapter Seven

moke. Jo sniffed, then coughed. Did Aunt Rosalina burn breakfast? She opened her eyes. At least she thought she did. Why was it so dark? And why did her head hurt? The morning's devastating memories flooded back. She remembered the roof collapsing on top of her and realized she had been buried.

She couldn't see her hand in front of her face. Her left hip dug into the floorboards below her. She had enough clearance to feel around with her right hand and assess the situation. She pushed up on every inch of debris she could reach, but nothing shifted. After further inspection, neither would the rubble to her front and back. She slammed and tugged every which way. It was as solid as a fortress. She was trapped.

She screamed in desperation, clawing at the boards while the air grew thinner. Jo took a series of sharp, rushed breaths but couldn't seem to regain composure. She mustered up all the strength she could to scream for help, but dust seeped into her lungs and choked out any chance of a cry. She coughed forcibly and wondered if she was about to meet her everlasting end.

Papa. Maybe she would see him again very soon. The thought was oddly welcoming.

"Don't move. It's easy. It will all be over soon," The Pull beckoned her again. Her limbs went limp with resignation. She thought of her pearl, most certainly lost forever in the wreckage. If only she had the smooth comfort of it now against her fingertips. Jo heard a muffled yowl from an indecipherable distance.

"Tilly! Is that you?"

There was no answer.

"Tilly, girl! Come here," she called and held her breath so she could listen for her feline companion.

A more distinctive mew came from above Jo's head, followed by a soft scratching. Tilly must not have made it back inside after evading capture from Aunt Rosalina. Her survival instincts were impressive for such a common housecat. She remembered something Papa once told her.

Every creature is born of survivors. Never underestimate their strength.

Every animal on earth had a lineage that withstood extinction against all odds, people included. The men and women in her family had survived. She should be no different.

The Pull sang to her. It tried to lull her into soft submission, but Jo closed her eyes and imagined holding her pearl between her fingers. *Around and around.* She could almost feel the bead against her skin. When her breathing became sharp and focused, she pushed against the debris on top, looking for any point of weakness.

"I swear, I will not allow this to become my grave." Jo grunted, pulling at the rubble. "I will not die here; I refuse! I'm coming, Tilly."

She had no idea how, but she would escape. Had Uncle Giuseppe and Aunt Rosalina made it out alive? Since the house had folded in on itself, anyone on the lower floors would have been crushed. And Emi. Jo recalled the last words she said to her the night before.

She now regretted upsetting sweet, precious Emi. She must be so scared—that is, if she were still alive.

She thought of Mrs. Tucci and Fitz and even her mother. Either the destruction was limited to her neighborhood's precarious structures, or no city was left. There was no way of knowing. Mrs. Tucci's lesson was engraved permanently into her mind. She closed her eyes and whispered. "With perspective comes opportunity by design."

Mrs. Tucci first told her those words when Papa was still alive. She was waiting for him to close the restaurant by doing a crossword puzzle on Mrs. Tucci's shop floor. She was stuck on seven across when she crumpled up the newspaper and threw it into the bin. A calm Mrs. Tucci retrieved the puzzle and sat her down. "Remember to have perspective, little lamb. When you have perspective, you know your place in the world. It can reveal the smallest detail or simplify the most complex problem."

There must be a way out of the rubble that was not obvious. "Perspective," she said. Something she hadn't tried. She pictured herself taking three steps back from a map on the desk, watching as her perspective flew back from the earth. She slowed her breathing and angled her head to imitate the change in her mind's eye. What if she first had to go down first in order to go up?

"That's it, Tilly! I must dig down!" she exclaimed to her feline guardian angel.

It was worth a try. Jo reached behind her head and grabbed a fractured beam. She carefully maneuvered her fingers around what she thought was an exposed nail and grabbed hold. The beam shifted. "That's it! Tilly, I've got it!"

Tilly meowed from above Jo's head.

Jo dislodged the beam and placed it off to her side. With that piece removed, it opened up a gap wide enough where she pried loose several more pieces of wreckage from over the back of her head. Then she inched her body forward.

All her limbs appeared to be in working order, and miraculously, she could feel her boots around her ankles, despite only having an inch of wiggle room in each direction. She shimmied clockwise until she made it onto her elbows, fighting the panic in the enclosed space. She continued to pull at the pieces of wood and shrapnel—until she saw daylight.

Jo hoisted herself out of the wreckage until she sat on top of the pile of timber and dust that had moments ago been her house. As she gasped for a pocket of fresh air, she was greeted by a ramshackle feline. Tilly stepped into Jo's lap, giving a generous push of her head into Jo's hand.

"Sweet girl, I'm so glad you're okay," Jo closed her eyes and rubbed her face against Tilly's fur.

Plumes of smoke and ash billowed into the skies to the north. Jo had emerged into the middle of an urban firestorm. She stared at the fiery skyline. "No, this can't be real."

It was like a scene out of Revelations. To the north, Jo counted eight individual shafts of smoke that conjoined above the tallest buildings. Their ominous layer blanketed the city at an alarming rate.

"No, no no!" Jo climbed to her feet and looked down at where she was standing. Her aunt and uncle were down there, somewhere. "Aunt Rosalina! Uncle Giuseppe!" Jo shouted in between coughing fits. She listened, and she heard nothing.

She scoured the wreckage looking and listening for any sign of life—still, nothing.

She climbed down the precarious heap. Then she saw it—*a man's arm.* And then a woman's leg, with the bottom of a nightgown. Both were buried in the pile of timbers that was her house. No, *their* house. She scrambled to get to them, clambering over broken wood and glass. She reached out to touch the man's arm. *It was cold.* Her arm shot back and her whole body trembled. She had never touched a dead body before. Summoning her bravery, she reached back toward the appendage. The skin's chill permeated her fingers and traveled down her spine. She felt the leg—*the same icy stillness. Dead.*

While she never was fond of her aunt and uncle and resented her life under their charge, she never wished them any actual harm. Not like this. *This* was surely a fate worse than anyone deserved. And her pearl was gone. Most certainly never to be seen again. It was the loss of her pearl, not the deaths of her aunt and uncle, that brought a tear to her eye. "I'm sorry, Papa," she said. It was as if she lost him all over again.

Sixth Street and the surrounding avenues had disintegrated into mounds of matchsticks. The houses were toddler's blocks wiped out in a fit of infantile rage. Jo squinted as dust-covered figures drifted across the panorama like ghosts in a graveyard. As she walked, she heard the moans of the hurt and dying. One of them, higher in pitch, stood out amongst the rest. Jo bounded through the cluttered street toward the mound of Emi's house. "Emi! Emi, is that you? Where are you?" Jo shouted, then silenced so she could hear. "Why isn't anyone else here to help?" she asked.

"Help. Over here." The voice was soft but clear.

Jo pounced on the source of the cries and dug frantically. She didn't have to go far before finding a pair of tiny arms near the edge of the debris that had been Emi's house. Emi whimpered as Jo pulled her up. From her position in the heap, she must have been close to the front door when the house came down.

"Emi, are you okay? Can you walk? Where's your Mama?"

Emi wiped tears that continued to flow down her cheeks. "Mama," she gasped. She spoke carefully, apparently trying to control her crying. "Mama pushed me out the door. She went back upstairs for my father. She, she . . ." Emi stopped for a moment and gulped a mouthful of air. "I couldn't hear them. I lost them."

Without saying a word, Jo pulled Emi close. She wanted to tell her there was nothing to worry about. Everything would be okay. She wished she could believe it herself, but the world was different now. *No guarantees*. Even promises made with the truest of intentions were only dreams and wishes. Jo held Emi out at arm's length. "We'll go get help; that's what we'll do. Can you walk?"

Emi nodded. She was wearing her coat and boots. It seemed as though, until her dying breath, her Mama had ensured Emi didn't leave the house unprepared.

Jo grabbed Emi by the hand to lead her up what remained of Sixth Street. Emi pulled back. "Wait!" she yelled, threw herself upon the pile, and started to dig. "My hat!"

"Emi. Em, stop. We have to go. Look, even Tilly is ready to go," Jo pointed to the cat with her left hand as she grasped Emi's hand with her right. "We'll get you another hat. The black one with the wisteria, just like you wanted."

"Ah-ha!" Emi sniffled and dragged out her dusty, flattened hat underneath some splintered lumber. She brushed it off, forced some shape back into it, and fitted it on her head.

Chapter Eight

crowd was already gathering in front of the Ferry Building, attempting to evacuate. Otto classified it as a scene of organized chaos. For the most part, folks were stunned silent. Men and women tried hard to hold their composure while commenting about the extraordinary tragedy that had just befallen their home.

People rumbled, asking if the crowd had seen so-and-so or whether what's-his-name was safe. Some asked pointed questions about what had happened; many had no preconception of an earthquake, let alone what kind of damage it could do. The disaster could not possibly harm a civilization as sophisticated and progressive as San Francisco. It wasn't called The Paris of the West for nothing.

Otto thought of his family in Western Addition. He wondered how his own house had fared. If the damage was even half as bad as it was out here, he should check on them, even if it meant facing some uncomfortable questions from his parents.

After studying architecture in school for a semester, Otto knew the critical role a building's foundation played in withstanding earthquakes. Here in the financial district, the ground was mostly mud and clay. When constructing most of the older buildings, no one had taken precautions. As Otto looked at the aftermath, that fact was evident. Most of Western Addition, however, was built on solid bedrock. Based on what little he knew about construction, he held onto hope that his family's home was without significant damage. So, he clung to his original plan to leave town without overwhelming guilt.

Otto observed several shafts of smoke south of the slot. Wooden boarding houses, apartments, warehouses, and other establishments had no chance if the fires spread. If he was going to make it out of the city, now was his chance before the city erupted into mayhem. It was only a matter of time. The Ferry Building looked to be mostly undamaged. Some pieces of decorative spires lay in the street, but the foundation seemed secure. A commotion ensued in the foyer of the transportation hub, where Otto suspected the ticketing counter was located.

This was it. What a spectacular farewell the city had given him. He persuaded himself to believe this was the city telling him to leave and never return, that there was nothing left for him here—the ultimate validation of his plight. But a seed of doubt began to feel like a pit in his belly.

Yes, the house was probably fine, but what about Pop's business? His father's manufacturing shop was on the corner of Golden Gate and Market Street. He wondered what would happen if there was significant damage. And if the shop had survived unscathed, would there even be any customers left?

He imagined his family waking up in a start and calling for him, only to receive no answer. They probably started out fearing the worst of him. When they found that he was not in his bed and saw the note he had left them explaining his absence, would they even try to look for him? The thought of Ma thinking he was dead made him sick in his stomach.

When he reached the counter, there was no teller on site. A few frantic men pushed their way to the front, demanding that a ferry take them as far away as quickly as possible. Their assertive cries fell on an empty post.

A door opened from the back, and a man who seemed in charge approached the waiting crowd. People rushed the counter, repeating their inquiries. "The ferries will begin to run in due time," he spoke to everyone. "All telegraph and telephone lines are down. We've lost communications with Oakland and Alameda stations, and we do not know if they are operational."

The news threw the crowd into a frenzy. Otto had never seen such unbridled fear in a swarm of people. They all spoke about the world coming to an end. Panic filled the air from all sides. It created a vacuum in the space and made him gasp for air. He was closed in and felt anxious, close to near madness. After he pushed through the bodies, he inhaled again. He couldn't handle being around so many people, especially ones as desperate as these.

He realized that his motivation had shifted entirely though he still wanted to get out of the city. It was not a matter of escape to make his own choices but raw survival. He wanted to get to his family, but Pop's automobile was his only chance to flee San Francisco. A sense of liberation would come with being able to travel freely beyond the city limits, away from the hysteria and horrific destruction. Surely soon, there would be nothing left.

The tracks from the cable car were twisted and mangled, and brick and mortar filled the streets. Some parts of the road had sunk another four or five feet into the ground. The land had pushed upward in other areas, cracking the pavement and exposing the city's underbelly. Since the cable cars were not running, Otto wanted to find someone with a vehicle. He would even settle for a buggy with horses—something to get him across town in a hurry.

"Hey, you! Hold on there!" he shouted at a passing driver of a two-horse-drawn cart packed with several of the man's personal belongings—a trunk, blankets, crates full of odds and ends, and a dog. The young man stopped. He studied Otto a moment, looking him up and down. "Where ya headed?" asked the driver.

"Western Addition. Mind if I hitch a ride?"

"Well, now, that all depends," he said snootily. "Got twenty berries?"

"Twenty dollars! Are you mad? This is a crisis."

"Hey, now, that's a fair price. Why I just heard someone up Market getting twenty-five. And this here is a high-demand location if you ask me." He pointed to hundreds of individuals preparing for a mass exodus.

Otto put his hands in his pockets—empty. "You swindler!" He snarled.

"Suit yourself, cheapskate." The driver grumbled under his breath as he rolled away.

This earthquake was already bringing out the worst in people. He had seen an ugly, selfish, and greedy side of humanity. He didn't like it one bit.

Chapter Nine

Jo knew the closest firehouse, Engine 6, was a few blocks north on 6th Street past Shipley, just before Folsom. She clutched Emi's hand tightly as they walked. There was a sudden rumble under their feet. When she was certain it was another tremor, a string of four horses rushed by with fear in their eyes. They must have come from the firehouse. Jo instinctively jerked Emi's arm to pull her out of the way just in time.

With Tilly trailing behind them, the girls quickened their pace until they reached Engine 6. People milled around—tenants from neighboring houses, some half-dressed, others with nothing but bedsheets wrapped around them, pleaded with the single on-site firefighter. The fireman raised his voice, addressing the congregation. "Attention, ladies and gentlemen. The horses got spooked and ran off. Half our men are 'round the corner up on Folsom battling a blaze, but the hydrant ain't working. The other half put axe to timber and are pulling folks out as we speak."

The crowd erupted. "No horses? How are you supposed to fight fires with no horses?" a woman shrilled, pointing to the lonely engine with unattended equipment.

"Forty souls trapped in Corona house," one man cried, pointing across the street. "We need men!"

Jo's panicked gaze skipped from face to face—a realization hit the crowd in unison: it would be up to them to step up and help, not the firemen who were spread so thin. If they relied on the firefighters for saving, there would be no survivors left. The crowd split into small groups to assist one another's rescue efforts.

Jo looked up 6th and saw what looked to be the Brunswick Hotel. The building lay several blocks in the distance, entirely engulfed in a torrent of red fire. The flames jumped the street and made their way east toward the city center. Her view of the blaze became obstructed when puffs of new smoke began to rise from the rubble of the bakery on the next block. Before long, that fire would spread, too. The firefighters were too preoccupied either digging through rubble or tending to the fire up Folsom to notice.

A fire hose lay flaccid and abandoned while attached to a hydrant in front of the firehouse. Its coils and runs marked the company's path while attempting to use it.

"The earthquake must have cracked the water lines," Jo said to Emi. "This is not good. Not at all."

"You mean there's no water? How are they going to put the fires out?"

"I don't know." Jo fought the helpless terror rising from her gut. "There has to be a way."

She noticed a lone firefighter staring in her direction. Normally, girls like Jo went unnoticed, so when someone was drawn to her, the feeling didn't sit right, and she resorted to thinking she was in the way. But the expression on his face appeared helpless and sad—he was the one asking for help. When she didn't divert her gaze, he walked over to her. The name on his jacket read "Perkins."

"My friend's parents. They're buried a couple of blocks that way."

Jo pointed behind her. "Can you please help us?"

"Can you hear them? Are they responsive?"

"No." That was the only reply she could muster.

Jo saw Emi's eyes well up with tears.

"Sorry, kid. We can only try to save the ones we know can be saved."

Emi lunged at the fireman. "No! You have to help! They are in there—I know they are! I can't believe you wouldn't care! Why don't you?"

She beat on him like a drum with both fists. Instead of pushing her away, he took her in his arms and pulled her close.

"I'm sorry, little one. I'm so sorry," he cried.

His eyes filled with tears. Jo saw that Emi had a way of bringing emotions out in people. She had a natural brightness that not even a stranger could bear to see extinguished. Something about her round cheeks and big eyes that sparkled like they were made of starlight. She stopped fighting and fell into him. The two held each other for a time. Jo couldn't tell which of them needed it more.

"What about the fires?" Jo asked. "Is there any way to put them out?"

"We're trying everything. I'm afraid we're fighting an uphill battle here."

Jo remembered seeing an obscure city map showing all the underground cisterns while she was at the shop a couple of years back. The shop designed it and printed a couple of test copies, but the funding never came through for the run, and it got scrapped. She remembered it like it was yesterday—the carefully laid-out lines of the streets, bedazzled with blue jewels of giant underground water wells.

She wracked her brain to focus on her neighborhood. *There's one right here!* "What about the cisterns?" she pointed. "There's supposed to be one just there at the intersection of Howard!"

"Empty. Cracked and drained," Perkins deflated like a balloon.

Another firefighter came running up to his comrade. He was out of breath, and his sweat was dark and full of soot.

"We found water! Eastward on the Folsom salt-water system. We think we can rig the hose to tap right into the pipe."

Perkins jumped up and sprang into action. "Don't hold up a corner, kid! Help me with that hose!" Jo realized he was talking to her, and she gathered up armfuls of loose slack as he twisted the end attached to the dry spigot.

Handing the hose off to Perkins, the two firefighters darted toward the Folsom fire and disappeared into the smoke.

Even if there was the hope of extinguishing the Folsom Street fire, the firefighters from all the city stations couldn't keep up with so many fires. Most of the buildings south of the slot were made of wood rather than brick, and they nestled between the city's hills. Folks would have to escape toward the eastern coastline or find higher ground toward North Beach, the Western Addition, or Rincon Hill if they were lucky. That's if fires didn't start in those areas. There was no way of knowing with no water. It was only a matter of time before they all burned.

A woman screamed, and Jo turned toward her home to see a new fire growing right at the corner of Clara Street. There was no going back. The Sixth Street inferno to the north inched nearer. Jo stopped her fear from overtaking her and determined how to safely navigate the streets to get to Mrs. Tucci's shop at Minna and Second.

Once again, Jo reached for Emi's hand. "Listen, Em, we have to get to Mrs. Tucci. I can't very well leave you here by yourself. Plus, someone needs to look after Tilly. Do you understand?"

Emi nodded.

"It will get warm, but you have to keep moving. You have to trust me. You got it?"

Emi did not make eye contact. "Yeah, JoJo, I got it." She squeezed

Jo's hand. "I trust you."

Jo didn't know what caused her sudden stroke of confidence. As the saying goes, she was going through Hades with her hat off. Whether she was brave or foolish, all she knew was that they couldn't stay put. Shipley Street was their only option. The way looked clear, but she could see no people from where they were standing. It was a gamble, but one she was willing to take.

Emi scooped the cat up in her arms. Tilly wasn't one to concede to being held, but she didn't make a peep. The poor thing must be terrified. They trekked up Shipley, weaving in and out of the rubble until they reached 5th Street. They arrived at the back of the Folsom fire, the air hot and thick. Jo could hardly see her hand in front of her face, let alone street signs.

"JoJo, which way do we go?" Emi coughed. "I can't see a thing!"

"Don't worry. I know the way," Jo reassured her.

If they were to continue forward, they would reach a dead end, so they took a right-hand turn away from the fire and then veered left onto what had to be Clara Street. They started to see people again, which was a good sign, but soon they passed collapsed buildings, a now-familiar scene.

Human cries came from all angles. Men and women called out for loved ones, children begged for help, and disembodied voices pleaded from indistinguishable points under the rubble. A frantic woman stood in the middle of the narrow street. Her hair was a mess, and she was barefoot. She pleaded for help, directing her cries to no one in particular. An automobile acting as an ambulance sped by, filled with the injured.

A woman's terrified voice sprang up from the pile of sticks at her feet. "Help me! For God's sake, help me!"

Jo looked down at Emi, who stopped in her tracks. "We have to help her!" Emi said.

Jo looked around a moment and assessed the situation. So many people needed help. But if they stopped, it would put them in more danger, and Jo couldn't live with herself if anything happened to Emi.

"We have to keep going."

"But they need help!" Emi screamed.

"I'm sorry, Emi, the fires are coming. I can't risk anything happening to you." Unrelenting guilt filled Jo—she couldn't be sure how she would live with herself after this, but she would worry about that later. She pursed her lips and dragged Emi forward.

"Let's go." While continuing to feel her way northeast, Jo became disoriented. The usually recognizable landmarks had disintegrated or shriveled, so they were undecipherable. She had hoped to take 4th Street all the way to Minna, but the looming hysteria in that direction was so overwhelming that they had to continue up Folsom.

They made it as far as 2nd Street before they could cut over safely. Only five blocks to go. As they approached the intersection at the base of Rincon Hill, they could see people gathered in the park. This might be one of the neighborhood's main evacuation points. Maybe Jo might find Mrs. Tucci here somewhere.

"Wait right here. Don't you move for an instant!" Jo left Emi's side and pushed her way through the crowd, searching for anything remotely familiar in a sea of dirt-caked faces.

She wove left and right through the crowds who hadn't had time to gather more than the clothes on their back, pet cats, bird cages, hat boxes, and bedding. She recognized no one.

The crowd's chatter reflected horror and confusion, but some words resembled acceptance mixed with optimism. Jo thought it odd, but then her thoughts returned to her matters.

"Josephine? Is that you?" a raspy male voice probed the horde of newly homeless.

Fitz. Jo prayed it meant that he was not alone. She leaned far to either side, looking for Mrs. Tucci, but she saw no one by his side. He hobbled over to her; his left leg appeared to be hurt and dragged awkwardly behind the rest of him.

"Fitz, are you all right?" She hugged him, then took a better look at him. He had an open wound on his leg, and a dress shirt-turned-tourniquet was tied right above it. "You don't look so good."

"Never mind me." He brushed off her question. "Mrs. Tucci's hurt. I came here to get help. Thank God I found you. Quick, follow me. She keeps asking for you."

This couldn't be real. Jo half expected this was just another one of Fitz's pranks. "Pistol pockets!" Mrs. Tucci would say, and they would all swear like sailors, Mrs. Tucci the worst of all. Then she and Fitz would burst into uncontrollable laughter as Mrs. Tucci threatened to kick him in his keister.

The rest of the journey toward the shop was as hard as wading through water. Slowly in single file, Fitz led the way, Jo followed, and Emi brought up the rear with a tight grip on Tilly. It took a moment before Jo realized where they were. The landscape looked completely different than the night before. Her old friend Mrs. Tucci lay on the ground surrounded by broken glass just outside the shop.

A warm glow from a nearby fire illuminated everything, but Jo paid no attention. All she saw were Mrs. Tucci's eyes. They were closed. Her face was swollen, and her wavy hair hung loosely around her shoulders. Jo fixated on her hair. She had never seen it in any other configuration but swooped and twirled into a perfect sculpture with one silver wisp that always hung to each side of her face, and never without a hat to top it. Mrs. Tucci looked vulnerable and weak—*unnatural.* Her body lay limp, and she bled from several places on her stomach and chest. A large shard of plate glass protruded from her middle, and her chest rose and fell with an irregular, labored rhythm.

After seeming to sense Jo's presence, Mrs. Tucci smacked her dry lips as if getting ready to speak. Jo took a step forward. Part of her wanted to throw herself on top of the woman and beg her not to leave her behind. She wanted to grip her hands in hers and reassure her that she would be all right, just as Mrs. Tucci had done for her countless times before. But all she could do was stand there in stunned silence.

"You're a good girl, Josephine." Her voice sounded small. A hint of a smirk appeared on her face. Her eyes opened, and she seemed to focus on a point just past Jo's face. "The light in my life. The daughter I never had. You truly have no idea how much you mean to me."

Jo's innards wailed. This was so out of character. Mrs. Tucci usually spoke in riddles or mysterious ways to make Jo think about a deeper meaning, often inspiring her to draw her own conclusions. She was seldom direct.

"There's always a deeper truth to a thing," she would say frequently. "Sometimes, you can't see what something's made of until you look away."

She wondered what could be the deeper truth in what was happening around her. The greatest city in the West was falling, and soon there would be nothing left but dust.

Mrs. Tucci had always been the one who backed Jo. She helped her with her homework and gave her advice about friends. She supported her when her mother did not and when her father could not. But they never spoke candidly that they adored one another so completely.

And now she was dying. Jo's head knew it, but her heart wouldn't accept it. *Don't you leave me, Mrs. Tucci. You can't. Everyone leaves me. Without you, I'll have no one left. I can't go on alone.* But she just stood there. How do you put into words a lifetime's worth of unspoken love and adoration? Her face scrunched up, trying to hold back any tears. She hated to cry and refused to let out the hurt for people to see. Better to remain invisible.

"You're going to have to go on without me, lamb." Mrs. Tucci's words were heavy on her tongue and hung in the air like the echo of a train whistle. "You're lost, child," she said.

"I'm not lost. I'm right here with you. Exactly where I need to be."

"It's not where you are but where you're going. Where you're meant to be. You can't see where you are headed because you can't see the full picture—the entire map. You are in your own way. When you fight who you are, what you can be, you lose perspective."

Mrs. Tucci coughed hoarsely, wincing from the pain.

Jo threw herself to her side and grasped her hand. Even though it was familiar for Mrs. Tucci to speak in a roundabout way, Jo wondered if delirium had set in. Nothing she was saying made sense. Jo had always been certain that she was meant to be here in the shop, with Mrs. Tucci, learning the craft and taking over the shop one day.

"Stop. Mrs. Tucci, please. I don't understand. Don't! I need you! What do I do?"

Jo aimed her question at Fitz. "What do we do? What can we do?" Her voice shook in desperation.

Fitz opened his mouth, but no words came out. Instead, he put his hand to his forehead, turned away, and began to weep.

Mrs. Tucci's breathing was shallow. "There's something I want you to have," she murmured, barely audibly, "You'll find it in the letters."

"Which letters? What do you mean? I don't understand."

But she didn't answer. Her chest no longer rose with inflated breath. She was gone.

"No!" Jo cried, throwing herself into Fitz's bony arms. He patted her head with one hand as he wiped his own tears with the other.

She looked up at him. "What did she mean? What did she want me to have? What letters?"

Fitz shrugged. "Haven't the foggiest. Maybe the blocks for the letterpress that we use to spell things out? But don't you even dare think about going in that building, Miss Josephine. It's crumbling worse than the boss lady's pie crusts. And the fire looks like it's spreading closer."

She must have meant the box of old letters from the hand press she kept in her office. She wracked her brain to think of what Mrs. Tucci might have stashed in there for her. Maybe keys to the shop? The deed to the building?

"Fitz!" Jo exclaimed, kissing him on the cheek. "You are brilliant."

And then Jo ran into the shop.

Chapter Ten

Otto turned away from the Ferry Building and didn't look back. He followed Market Street inland for what seemed like an hour, even though he had only trekked four blocks. He felt disoriented despite knowing full well where he was. Most citizens had evacuated their buildings in the metropolis and flocked to the great thoroughfare to witness for themselves the quake's level of damage.

He had traveled this same route twelve hours before, but this was not the same great city it had been. Dust and smoke filled the air. Shattered panes from numerous windows littered the street. His beloved architectural masterpieces that once stood with pride were now sad and shriveled. Some looked as if their pillars and arches had broken along with their wills to live. Other buildings had rolled over onto their sides like submissive hounds. And some looked like a hatchet had sliced the front of it clean off, collapsed into the basement, and left the occupants to wonder how they would survive a fall from a third-story jump.

People everywhere carried all their belongings out into the

streets. They took to the sea and the seven hills. Men dragged trunks and chairs, while women brought clothing, blankets, birdcages, and ironing boards.

As Otto approached the intersection of Fremont Street, he saw firefighters attending a blaze in the Mack & Co Drugstore. Curiosity got the better of him, and he approached the scene to witness the attempt to save the building. The closer he got, the more bizarre the scene. The firefighters gathered around, watching the building burn rather than trying to put it out.

Otto neared a bystander. "Where's the engine?"

"Pipes are no good. Gas lines broke too. That's what sparked this one, they say. I suspect it's the same all over."

No water—the whole damn city was starting to burn. Otto took in the scene around him. He couldn't see much past the rooflines, but it was enough to tell that the fire that burned before him was only one small tree in a forest full of flames. Each fed a substantial cloud of darkness that hung over the city like a black curtain. An automobile sped by in a hurry toward Mission Street. Otto chased after the car to see where it was headed.

The man he talked to yelled after him, "Taking 'em to Harbor Emergency Hospital."

No sooner had Otto's curiosity pulled him away from the burning building than there was an explosion inside the drug store. The force of it blew him onto his hands and knees. From the ground, he turned to find the gentleman who had spoken to him was missing. He did not know whether flames engulfed him or if he was on the other side.

The explosion caused sparks to fly and catch hold of the paper box factory across the street. Otto froze a moment. He didn't come down to this part of the city often, and if he wandered too far from Market, he was afraid he'd get lost. He was fairly sure that at least Mission Street ran parallel to it for a while, so he'd stick to that until it started to turn too far southward.

As soon as Otto rounded the corner, he entered an awful scene. A warehouse that had made up the entire block on the left had collapsed and crushed about two dozen cattle. The wreckage formed a knotted conglomeration of horns and brick. He found the conditions hard to digest. For some reason, witnessing innocent livestock dead was more upsetting than imagining how dead people must look. He wasn't sure since he hadn't seen any yet. Then again, he hadn't gotten close enough to the buildings to see the dead. Now that he had taken to narrower streets, he wouldn't be able to avoid it. He felt the burn of bile in the back of his throat and vomited up what was left of the whiskey.

The wreckage blocked Mission Street, and Otto climbed over some pieces to pass it. Cow shit smell mixed with the smoke from the surrounding fires. An unhinged broken sign read Studebaker's Wagon Warehouse. Next to it, several cattle were piled on one another like prime cuts of steak. The steer at the top had a gunshot wound to the head. *Right between the eyes.* A mercy killing. Rifle, from the looks of it. The one underneath had released its bowels out of fear. Two who were crippled by falling cornices had also been shot. The poor creatures' tongues were hanging out of their mouths, and the animals resembled spifflicated buffoons.

Otto realized he was correct in his prediction that the scene had changed drastically now that he was not on the main thoroughfare. The injured lined up, waiting for volunteer ambulances to come and pick them up. Furniture lay stacked outside buildings. Even a piano sat unattended.

He couldn't help but be immersed in the plight of what it meant to be a San Franciscan on this morning. Now that he was south of Market and had entered the one-horse district, he could not ignore the reality of the tragedy. *How many had lost their homes? Lost their lives? What would it take to recover when you have nothing left?*

"Help! Someone, please help me!" a frantic voice hollered from the middle of the intersection ahead.

Looking forlorn, a young girl stood in the middle of the street with a cat under her arm. Passers-by seemed to glance at her and then carry on with their business. She was Asian, which might explain their reluctance. Always considering himself a good mixer, Otto approached the girl.

"What's wrong, Miss?"

"My friend. She's hurt. I don't know that for sure, but she might be. She ran into a building that just caught fire, and she hasn't come out."

"So, you need someone to go in after her? Why can't you do it yourself?"

"Some of the stairs have collapsed, and I can't reach her."

She held the feline close to her chest and rubbed her cheek against its fur.

"What makes you think a stranger would risk their life for a kid? Especially one stupid enough to run into a burning building?"

"You don't understand, Mister. She must be trapped." The girl's face grew as red and plump as a tomato as her eyes welled up with tears. She gripped her hands together in prayer as best she could around the animal in her arms. He guessed her to be about ten or eleven. "Please. My Mama and Papa are dead, and she's all I have. I need her to be okay."

Her brown eyes pleaded with him. She was genuine and endearing. He looked down at her hands clasped in the air, oscillating back and forth in front of her chest as best she could while holding the cat. Something about the look in her eyes made him feel like he was her only hope.

Dammit. "Fine. Show me the way," Otto muttered begrudgingly. The girl cast him a wide smile.

After grabbing his hand, she exclaimed, "Follow me," and

dragged him a block down 2nd and around the corner at Minna. A man sat on the north side of the half-decimated narrow street near the bloodied body of a deceased woman. He was covered in dirt and soot and nursed what looked to be an injured left knee. His leg was wrapped with torn fabric ripped from his shirt and fashioned it into a tourniquet.

"Did you find someone? Good girl, Emi," the man said with a thick Irish accent, visibly relieved. The grimy gentleman reached out his hand to Otto in greeting. He had a soft smile, and laugh lines embraced his eyes. Under normal circumstances, he was the kind of fellow Otto would want to kick back a pint with and hear a tall tale or two.

"Name's Fitz. Leg's busted, or else I'd go up myself. The girl is stubborn as all hell. My employer is—sorry, *was*—a mentor of sorts to her." Fitz's voice cracked at the use of the past tense. Otto could tell it took a conscious effort. He nodded at the body. "The girl looked up to her something fierce. Once she passed, it's like the girl had a fire under her boots and took off into the shop."

"Easy enough. I'll get her back for you."

"What's your name, son?"

"I'm Otto."

Emi and Fitz gave Otto willful looks, both apparently aware that he may not return with good news—*if he returned at all.*

Otto nodded and disappeared into the creaking, dying structure. Following no discernible pattern, he dodged machinery scattered about and grew frustrated that there was no clear path to the stairs. At the back of the shop on the stairwell, he realized he didn't even know the girl's name. He had forgotten to ask, and Emi and Fitz had been too flustered to include that bit of information.

He made it only four steps before needing to use the flimsy railing as an aid in spelunking his way to the next solid step. About four steps were obliterated, leaving a splintered mess. *No wonder they needed help.* There was no way either of them would have been able to make it; Fitz had his lame knee, and Emi was too short to reach it with her little legs.

Safely on the second floor, Otto searched the rooms one by one. "Kid? Hey, kid? Girl!" he shouted.

The building shifted audibly, and smoke permeated the walls and rolled in visible spirals across the floor. Otto wondered what the hell he was doing. *This wasn't safe.* He needed to find this kid and get out of there as soon as possible. He formulated a plan in his mind. He would run through the rest of the floor, and if he couldn't find her, he would get out before it was too late.

"Kid! What the hell? Where are you?" His head peered into what looked like a stock room. He watched a girl yank a drawer out of the wall shelving and dump its contents on the ground.

"I'm no kid," she spat at him without eye contact. She dove into the spilled contents and sifted through them.

Otto stormed into the cluttered room. Shelves encumbered with a mixture of books and loose documents lined the walls. The shelves appeared to do their best to support the load of publications, but gave up somewhere near the floor where contents were strewn like flowers over a grave.

A desk sat rigidly at the center of the room. Papers covered it, too. Maps, in fact. From appearances, some maps had been previously rolled up since heavy objects stood on the four corners to flatten them.

"What are you doing?" he asked the girl.

"I need to find something."

"Come on, kid. We gotta go. This building is going to go any minute."

"Help me." She turned and looked at him for the first time with pleading doe eyes, maybe confused and almost belligerent. She was no little girl. This was a young woman. And the sight of her took his breath away.

"Help you what? What are you looking for?"

"Letters."

"What letters?"

"I don't know—I'll know when I find them."

As if Satan himself was listening, the back wall split open, and the next door's building chimney broke through, throwing smoldering ash everywhere and blowing a pile of maps to the floor. One of them began to smoke, and the girl ran to grab it, bringing it back to the desk. She smoothed it out and stared at it.

"Hey, kid, this is nuts. This building is about to go."

She stood there in silent defiance, her eyes becoming glassy and distant. Her fingers gripped the map in front of her, and she crumpled the edges of the print until it was almost unrecognizable. Otto moved closer, trying to glimpse what she examined. It was a map of the city of Chicago.

"Cubs are gonna sweep it again this year," he said.

The girl squinted at him. "Huh?"

"Chance. Three-Finger," he stammered. She must know what he was talking about. "Three-Finger Brown? Ah, hell, kid. Don't you know a thing about baseball?"

"I'm no kid! And do I look like I give a hell about baseball? Who are you anyway?" she demanded. "What are you doing here?"

"I'm here to rescue you, princess."

An ear-splitting *snap* pierced the air from above as the ceiling struggled in futility to hold itself together.

Chapter Eleven

The strange man walked around the desk and knelt next to Jo, babbling about being her knight in shining armor. She couldn't decide if he was arrogant or just an idiot. Either way, her blood boiled.

Her head spun when she thought too hard about what had just happened. Mrs. Tucci lay lifeless outside, her beloved mentor and friend who was fine half a day before. Her aunt and uncle were buried and, by now, probably burned up. Her house was gone. The last remaining reminder of her father was gone. The only thing she had left of the life she knew was this place, her hideout among the maps, and she was about to lose that too. She would cling to it like a hornet to a piece of meat.

Jo heard the stranger cough, and she looked in his direction.

"Who are you? What are you doing here?"

"I'm here to res-cue you," the blonde-haired young man enunciated. "Come on, kid; it doesn't look like your legs are broken. Let's go. You got a death wish or something?"

How easily she could just sit down and wait. *"Stay put."* And what would happen if she did?

"The Pull . . ." she mumbled, and she didn't move. The Pull chuckled at the stranger's question in a morphed imitation of Jo's voice. This young man looked a year or two older and had no idea how much The Pull drowned him out. The Pull knew her. He did not. From the look of him, he wasn't even from her world. His finely-tailored clothing, though dusty, meant he hailed from the well-to-do side of town. The way he stood led her to believe he'd probably never put in a hard day's work in his life. *Spoiled. Entitled. Expecting her to follow his orders.* A resentful fire grew in her belly.

"Rescue me? Rescue me?" Jo's voice escalated an octave. "I'm perfectly capable of *res-cu-ing* myself. I don't need some high-brow pinhead coming in here and doing it for me."

He stiffened and stood up straight, clearly taken aback. "Oh, really? Listen, little girl, the roof of this place just lit up. This old piece of bread will be toast soon, so if you're going to rescue yourself, you'd better do it now, or else you'll be burnt up right along with these silly maps of yours."

"Maps? Silly? Who do you think you are coming in here and—" Timbers blew apart above them as a strong wind began to whistle through the cracks in the ceiling and walls. Jo felt herself flinch. The shrill sound reminded her of Uncle Giuseppe's house right before it collapsed.

Jo didn't feel like there was much of a reason to try to save herself. The Pull had never before had such agency over her. *"You have nothing left,"* it sang to her. *"There is no reason to continue living. It's easy, just don't get up."* She didn't budge. Whether out of fear or submission, she did not know.

The stranger's voice replaced that of The Pull. "If you want to live, you've got to run, and you've got to run *now*." He turned away and began to leave the room.

"I . . . can't," was all Jo could muster in a reply. She wanted to say so much more. But how could she articulate that she felt hopeless in a way that did not make her appear weak?

She wondered if this was The Pull acting under extreme conditions or if she had a death wish. Was she that self-centered and stupid to ignore that she still had two friends waiting for her outside? Not to mention a mother out there somewhere?

Under normal circumstances, any trial such as this would leave Jo at Mrs. Tucci's doorstep, where she would provide her with advice over a steaming bowl of pasta. But she wasn't here anymore, and she never would be again, so Jo imagined what Mrs. Tucci would say to her in this situation.

For some reason, the phrase *it's always darkest before the dawn* came to mind. Mrs. Tucci would always say that whenever Jo had a particularly bad day.

"It looks like Fitz was right," said the stranger. "You are bullheaded. Stay here for all I care. You can't save a person who doesn't want to be saved."

The accusation sent shockwaves through her system. She let her anger from the insult grow larger and overpower The Pull. With the stranger's every step, Jo's uncertainty peeled away. If she didn't make a move now, she might not make it out at all. The whistling wind became a frighteningly loud wail, and the smell of smoke from a hungry blaze grew stronger. Jo bit down on her bottom lip so tightly it hurt.

"Wait!" Jo screamed at the young man as he disappeared around the corner. She was a fool for coming inside after Mrs. Tucci died. She had come in trying to find whatever answers Mrs. Tucci had promised her with her dying breath, to hold onto whatever was left of her broken past. But she wound up nearly succumbing to the darkness inside her.

She refused to be held back again. She hoisted herself to her feet. But the stranger was gone, and she was alone again. The weight of that sudden isolation was more than she could bear. He had vanished. Jo looked around her in a panic, but she couldn't leave. *Not yet.* There were so many precious documents to gather. So many memories, irreplaceable artifacts of her life. She couldn't just leave them here. She didn't even know where to begin.

Jo scrambled to grab whatever precious maps she could—New York City at the turn of the century, Chicago, New Orleans, and her city of San Francisco. She stuffed them down her nightgown and prepared to run. And then she spotted it, there on the floor. The falling chimney must have knocked them loose—a pile of letters addressed to Mrs. Tucci in her mother's handwriting. The one on top was written in Mrs. Tucci's handwriting, *For Josephine.*

Jo lunged forward to retrieve the stack of letters but only made it a few steps before the ceiling gave an unforgiving groan and split open above her head. "Damn," she whispered, crouched down, squeezed her eyes shut, and threw her arms above her head in desperate defense. She hit the floor with the force of the entirety of the third-floor bedroom. *Her bedroom.* Or at least the one that would have been hers, starting today. It was hot, and the back of her head felt warmer than the rest of her.

Before she could even begin to assess her situation, she felt someone yanking her out by her left arm. When she opened her eyes, she saw his face in front of hers. Blurry at first, she had to blink a few times before believing it. The stranger had come back for her.

His blue eyes were piercing and steady. They held her attention firmly while the rest of the room spun beyond recognition. He was handsome. She hadn't noticed before. "Don't worry, kiddo. I got you." He held her by the forearm. His confidence only amplified her dizziness.

The air was so thick and granular that she could chew it. She gasped for breath, which only dried her tongue out like sandpaper. It burned and shriveled. "Water. I need water," she wheezed.

It was hard to gain her footing, but before she could think about where to place her feet to hold her weight, his right arm reached around her waist as his left scooped up her legs. Her head whirled with a mixture of pain and a sensation of relinquishing all her control.

He fled with her in his arms out the door and down the hallway to the landing. The second floor behind them started to cave in—a plume of solid smoke and debris barreling through to the floor below. Flames whipped around the corners of all the doorways in the hallway. They both looked down at the six-foot gap halfway down the staircase. He took a few cautious steps down the stairwell and paused.

"What? No, you can't possibly," Jo barked.

"Hold on!" He shouted, and she threw her right arm around his neck to anchor herself. She had no control over what was about to happen, and she felt him hurry down one, two, three steps, then kick off the fourth. They hung in the curdled air for what seemed longer than it should have been, falling forward. He landed sharply, twisting his body so his back hit hard against the wall, absorbing most of the impact and sparing her legs. He stumbled but caught his footing. Without a break in his step, he ran until they cleared the shop's threshold.

Emi was in Jo's face before she knew it. She spoke so quickly that Jo barely made out her words above her and her rescuer's coughing. "JoJo, you're okay! Oh, Otter, you got her! Just in time, too. I was sure you weren't going to make it."

"Otter? Your name is Otter?" Jo giggled as he set her down on the ground carefully.

"Ott—," Otter spoke, but Jo coughed over him and didn't hear what he said.

Emi threw her arms around her neck and squeezed as Tilly bonked her head against her hand, begging to be petted.

"Are you all right, Josephine?" Fitz asked.

"She had a blow to the head. She's not bleeding; she should be all right," replied Otter.

Jo wondered when he even had time to assess her injuries. She reached around to the back of her head, which felt hot. She might be bleeding, but she had to see it to believe it. She looked at her hand to inspect the evidence. No blood, but there was a bump beginning to grow. It hurt, and her vision was a little hazy.

"The letters!" She shot to her feet and, coughing, slapped both hands against her chest repeatedly, but she did not feel the rigid lumpiness of folded papers. They were gone. Grief rose in her belly like mercury in a thermometer.

Fitz stared nervously in the opposite direction, and Jo realized this was because she grabbed at her chest in front of everyone. "Emi," said Fitz, still facing away from her. "Go find them some water."

Emi obeyed and ran up the road toward the park, handing Tilly to Fitz.

Otter smiled proudly. "Looking for this?" He drew out a single crumpled envelope from his back pocket with *For Josephine* written in careful handwriting. Jo hollered and yanked it out of his grasp, opened it, and pulled out the note. As soon as she unfolded it, a thin, grey paper, a part of a newspaper, fell to the ground. She picked it up carefully and read the headline.

ENDS HIS LIFE IN A STARTLING MANNER.

Victor Moreci Kills Himself While in Bed With His Wife and Baby.

Jo stopped and let out a short and sharp wail which surprised even her. She dropped to the ground to hide her discovery.

"What?" Otter screamed.

"No," she said almost inaudibly. "It can't be . . . "

Victor Moreci, an Italian aged 36 years, living at 439 Sixth Street, committed suicide at an early hour this morning by blowing out his brains.

"Papa, no . . . " Jo said, tears building in her eyes. "This can't be real."

The suicide was 36 years of age. Moreci conducted an oyster house at

NOTHING LEFT BUT DUST

Minna and Second Street at one time. Unable to find employment, he became despondent, and last night he killed himself with a pistol while lying in bed with his wife and child tucked in at the foot.

Jo's chest tightened, and the destruction around her spun until it became a nebulous, shadowy amber. She heaved, reaching for anything that could steady her. Her hand found Otto's leg, and she clutched it.

"He . . . he . . . but I would have known." She couldn't formulate her thoughts well enough to say the words. *Papa killed himself?* That couldn't be right. Jo had been told it was an accident. Papa was cleaning his gun, and it went off, so she had never thought anything of it. She thought it odd that it happened in the bedroom but never doubted her mother's story. But there it was in black and white. The only reason she knew it involved a gun was that she had heard the shot.

"I *should* have known. How could I not?"

An explosion boomed inside the shop, blowing her forward and slamming her hands onto the pavement. Otter stood his ground, but Fitz stumbled back, dropping Tilly, who scampered out of sight. A wall of solid flame illuminated Mrs. Tucci's still and lifeless body. Jo wiped stinging gravel off her palms, gripped the last remaining piece of her—the envelope with her handwriting—and held it to her chest. She knew that she possessed the last item belonging to Mrs. Tucci, but that was not the sole reason behind the tears. It was simply a reminder, a catalyst to her feeling the extent of what she had just lost.

"Tilly!" she called hoarsely. "Time to go!"

The winds picked up and carried glowing embers. A few caught in their hair and immediately went out. Jo held the envelope, and her fingers traced the letters in the name *Vittoria Tucci*. It killed her that they had to leave her behind. *It wasn't right.* A woman like her deserved a proper burial. She clipped the unread letter back in the envelope, folded it in half, and stashed it in her boot.

"We have to get out of here. Now," Otter said loudly enough for everyone to hear. "Can you walk?" He shouted toward her.

Her sweet scraggly feline friend came bounding back to her and swirled around her ankles. The fur's comforting touch gave Jo the needed pause to stop crying and test her steps. She faltered a bit, and before she knew it, Otter once again wrapped his arm around her waist, supporting her weight.

"We should go back to the camp at Folsom," Fitz directed. "It's the safest place right now while we get our bearings. And until these nasty fires burn themselves out."

Jo nodded.

Emi returned with an open can of creamed corn. "This is all they had," she said and handed Jo the can that was full of water. Emi grabbed Jo's hand. "I'm sorry your friend died."

"Thanks," Jo said and drank the water. She handed the can to Otter.

"You know, you can be a real bonehead sometimes," Emi said. Jo knew it was true, and she couldn't help but smile. The girl was starting to sound like her.

"Thanks for calling me out, Em. I was a nut back there. I won't do it again—I promise." She kissed Emi's forehead. Jo turned to look back at what they were leaving behind. The embers had reached Papa's old oyster house now, and the restaurant that had replaced it was now aflame. The heat of the fires warped the air into a dream-like scene. Her whole life as she had known it was not just gone, but with the discovery of that article, she questioned if it was ever real to begin with. She had so many questions.

Jo hung back from the group when they cleared the path of danger, allowing space between them. She slid out the rumpled envelope from her boot and removed the letter. She unfolded it carefully. Short—just one page. She recognized her mother's handwriting. The note read *May 14, 1905*. Almost a year ago. How long had she and Mrs. Tucci been writing to one another? She scoffed. Both of them had been communicating without her knowledge; they kept things from her. She read the letter, hearing Mama's voice.

Vittoria,

I thought about what you said, but I do not think Josephine is ready to know the truth. Not yet. Maybe never. Please respect my wishes on this matter.

Alma

Jo grew red hot with anger at the betrayal and deception. They must have been talking about the contents of that newspaper clipping. The fact that Papa killed himself. That it was, in fact, no accident. Why wouldn't she have told her? *What really happened that night?* Mama and Mrs. Tucci had both lied. And they had been in touch behind her back for at least a year.

Mama had told Mrs. Tucci not to do something, and she obeyed. The idea made Jo question everything Mrs. Tucci had ever told her. Mrs. Tucci felt she had to keep this from her; that fact made Jo's stomach churn even more. She questioned everything Mrs. Tucci had ever taught and promised her. And if they could keep a secret this big, what else could they have hidden?

Jo shrank into a crouch, replaying what had happened after the night Papa died. She began to piece the memories together, images she had pushed down and tried to forget. The police had come to see them day after day afterward. Mama told her to stay in her room when the reporters came "just to check in." Their home editions of the *San Francisco Chronicle* went missing or stolen for about two weeks. Mama kept her home from school. Then when she went back, the kids chanted, "Josephine, Josephine doom and gloom, Daddy went batty, and his brains went *kaboom!*"

How had she forgotten that? How had she not put it together? She was upset at herself for being so stupid. *So naïve.*

"What is it? What happened?" Otter asked.

An audience hovered above her, their faces coming into focus, and Emi's eyes appeared worried and concerned. Jo wouldn't make Emi worry anymore—the girl had been through enough. So she said, "Nothing, Otter. My ankle hurts. I think I may have sprained it."

Fitz hobbled toward her, but Otter took one look at Fitz's leg and waved him off.

"Here," Otter slipped his arm under Jo's and grinned. "And I told you the name's O—"

Jo sighed frustratingly. "Fine!" She didn't want to be babied, but she would tolerate it for Emi's protection. Even though her ankle felt fine, she hobbled along. But all she could think was one single word.

Suicide.

The word sounded funny in her head.

Papa killed himself.

Papa KILLED himself.

What could have made him want to do such a thing? She had to know more. She needed answers.

Chapter Twelve

The base of Rincon Hill was not the safe haven Otto expected. Home to a collection of mansions, the entire hilltop was ablaze. Men scrambled back and forth in their attempts to rescue women and children and bring them to the open space at the base of the hill.

Otto was in a fog, strangely oblivious to the horror. Instead, he fixated on Jo's weight against him. With his arm fitting perfectly around her waist, Otto couldn't believe how much he was drawn to her. Though he didn't even know this girl, he wondered why she had made such a strong impression.

Jo was not prim and proper like other girls his age. Instead, she was feisty, ornery, and forthright. She fascinated him, and he searched for something to say. For once, everything he thought was not quite good enough. He decided to start with an easy question. "Where's your family?" he asked.

She pulled away, and the instant anguish on her face answered the question.

"I meant to say that the Irishman and the Chinese girl are not your kin, so what's the story?"

"She's Japanese," Jo said.

"Huh?"

"She's not Chinese, she's Japanese."

"Oh. You must forgive me; I don't spend much time south of the slot."

Jo stopped in her tracks. She seemed to look right through him. "I can't," she whispered. Fitz and Emi were ahead of them and didn't notice that she had stopped.

"What do you mean you can't? You can't what?"

She seemed to ignore him, and he felt invisible. Fitz must have sensed they were no longer behind, and he turned around to check. "What's the matter?" he asked.

"I have to go find my mother," she said. "We're going the wrong way."

Fitz looked down at Emi and seemed sad. He grabbed her hand tightly and looked back at Jo.

"I've got Emi," he said. "She'll be safe. You do what you need to do."

Otto studied Jo as her teeth bit down on the right side of her bottom lip. She turned to the side and stared off into the distance. He wondered what was running through her head. He thought he remembered her saying that she didn't have any family left, but she just said something about her mother. No, it wasn't something she said, but it was the look she had given him. It didn't quite add up.

Without saying anything, she looked at Emi and opened her arms.

Emi took her cue and ran to Jo.

"Listen, Emi," said Jo. "Go with Fitz. He'll look after you until I get back."

Tears began to well in her eyes. "Do you have to go, JoJo?"

Jo nodded as she kissed Emi's forehead. "And I'm trusting you to take care of Tilly. She needs you. I'll see you soon, Em."

"It sounds like they are relocating everyone over to Golden Gate Park," said Fitz.

"Then it's a plan. I'll find you in the park." Jo paused. "Meet me tomorrow morning in front of the Conservatory at about eight o'clock. I'll be there, I promise."

"Okay," Emi paused thoughtfully. "But please, please be careful."

"Aren't I always?" Jo said with a playful smile. She hugged both Fitz and Emi and turned to leave.

Fitz called out to her, "Jo, wait. Otto's going with you."

Jo stopped walking and turned to face Fitz, nose wrinkled. "Who?"

Fitz turned to Otto and spoke in a low but firm voice, "You stay with her. She's hurt. She needs help getting around. And make sure she doesn't do anything else careless, would you?" He sounded like an overprotective father.

Otto nodded—the message was received loud and clear.

"Oh, *Otto!*" Jo exclaimed. "I like Otter much better. It suits you." She smirked, and Otto felt his cheeks flush. They watched the horizon where Emi and Fitz disappeared into the hazy streets. Once they were no longer visible, Jo took off down Howard Street.

Otto chased after her, reached out, and grabbed her arm. "What happened? Your ankle. You're supposed to be hurt."

"Looks like I'm all better."

"Huh, how 'bout that. Well, wait up. Where are you going?"

"Why are you following me? I'm just a dumb girl from south of the slot, remember?" she said.

"Jo, stop. I'm supposed to look out for you. I promised Fitz."

Jo kept walking.

"Listen, dammit—" he started, but she interrupted.

"No, you listen," she said firmly. "I've gotten along just fine until now, going unnoticed by folks like you. I don't have to explain myself to anyone, least of all you. You wouldn't understand."

"Hey. Slow down! Do you even know where you're going?"

Jo relaxed her arms and spun around. "Of course, I know where I'm going. I know these streets better than anyone."

"Is that so? Then what is your mother's address?"

Jo huffed. "Well, I don't know exactly, but she's somewhere in North Beach."

North Beach was a primarily Italian neighborhood, though peppered with Germans, Russians, and Eastern Europeans. Located at the city's northeast corner, it sat just beyond Broadway. Most men were in the fishing trade, so docks, wharves, and warehouses lined the nearby waterfront. She would have to pass through the Barbary Coast, an area housing some of the most questionable and despicable characters San Francisco's darkest corners had to offer.

Otto grabbed the envelope out of Jo's hand.

"Hey! What do you think you're doing?"

"Do you want my help?"

"No. I want my letter back."

"I'll give you your letter if you let me help you."

"You scoundrel, that's not fair."

Otto held up the envelope with one hand and pointed at the return address with the other. "Oh, look. What do we have here?"

"Hey! Give that back!" Jo lunged for his hand, but he moved it higher, taunting her.

"See, kiddo? You need me," he flashed her his most charming grin possible, making sure to flutter his eyelashes in a way none of the ladies could ever resist. "Besides, nobody should be traveling alone in these conditions. You know, just in case."

After giving him a long hard look, she said, "Fine. Just give me the address. And try to keep up."

Otto lowered his arm and let Jo snatch the letter away.

"Green Street. Got it. This way." Jo tucked the envelope with the letter inside into her boot then took off, Otto following at a quickened pace to keep up. As they made the sharp turn up New Montgomery Street toward Market, the ground beneath them started to shake.

The city around them rattled yet again, and Otto stood astonished. The powerful aftershock sent Jo tripping into him. She grasped his arm and held her breath, waiting for the trembling to be over. While not nearly as violent as the one from earlier, the temblor finished off some structures that had struggled to hold on the last few hours.

When the shaking subsided, Jo let go of Otto. She seemed embarrassed and took three large paces backward to put space between them.

A woman with tousled hair came shooting out of a building that had received a fresh dose of damage. She paced back and forth. "Oh!" she cried. "My husband is dead, my son is dead, and a woman is dead." The poor woman repeated herself several times over. The woman's cries were haunting.

Jo gave Otto an apologetic look.

"Let's keep going."

"Don't you think we should help her?" Otto knew he couldn't possibly stop to assist everyone, but he wanted to help since he was close enough to see the woman.

"Out of all the people that need a hand, what sense does it make to dig out the dead?" she asked.

At first, he was upset that she could be insensitive, but he knew she was right. So he turned away from the despondent woman.

As they walked in silence, he studied Jo: this girl who was not a girl but a young woman. She wore nightclothes. Her dirty white gown fell below her knees and billowed slightly in the firestorm-fueled breeze. She wore plain brown boots with thick rubber-soled heels and no stockings.

Her long hair was the color of dark chocolate which made waves down her back and curled up slightly at the ends, right at her shoulder blades. It fell effortlessly around her face—he was tempted to reach out and touch it. She had full lips, and her hazel eyes were rich and expressive. Her skin looked as sweet and smooth as honey. He tried to be discreet about his discovery of her, but surely she must have noticed him staring.

She turned away suddenly, glanced at him out of the corner of her eye, and cocked her head. "Why are you looking at me like that?"

"Like what?" he asked.

"Like you've never seen a poor Italian girl before. It's making me uncomfortable."

"No, it's not that."

"Then what is it?"

Otto tried to find an excuse for his staring. "It's your dress—it's just awfully—well—dirty."

"It's my nightgown, you idiot!" Jo turned away, seeming humiliated, and folded her arms.

"Well, it looks like you climbed out of a grave."

"Maybe that's because I did," she said. "The house collapsed."

"With you inside it? You're kidding. Those piles of matchsticks you people call houses were just an accident waiting to happen anyway. One spark and poof, that's it."

"*You people*? You know Otter, you're a real highbrow know-it-all."

"I mean the people that have to live in those places. Working people. I didn't mean anything by it. And my name is Otto."

She smirked, and her expression softened a bit. "How does it feel to have a taste of your own medicine?"

He shifted the conversation back to her escape. "How did you get out?"

"I almost didn't. I almost didn't want to."

"You got a death wish or something, kiddo? That's twice now that you've almost chosen to face the final music. You don't seem the type."

"What do you mean the *type?*"

"You seem too smart to be a fatalist, is all."

"Well, I'm not."

"I saw you with your books and stuff. No young lady in her right mind would dare joke about spending the last moments on earth surrounded by anything not embellished with lace or feathers. You've got a curious mind but a flair for the dramatic."

"You think you have me all figured out, do you? You and your rum-dum postulations."

"Well, what made you change your mind?"

"Pardon?"

"Something must have happened to make you choose to live. What was it?"

"That's a very personal question. You wouldn't understand, anyhow."

"I bet I could rustle up enough smarts to follow. Try me."

Jo paused for a moment, appearing to gauge whether he was sincere. Then she said, "When I was buried, it was tough to find hope, I mean the hope of escape or even hope that if I did escape, was it worth it? But I thought of something my Papa taught me. He always told me I was strong and that strength can come out of the most horrific and unexpected situations."

He relaxed his face and quieted his voice to communicate his genuine concern. "It sounds like your father was a smart man. Was he a fisherman?"

"He had an oyster house. Why?"

"No reason. All those old-time fisherfolk seem to have a lot of wisdom. It's almost like the best notions are farmed from the sea like, well, oysters."

Jo grinned.

Her smile melted him like a block of ice. "So, what about the second time? After I found you?"

"The woman you saw lying there—she was my friend. My mentor Mrs. Tucci. She has been my compass since my father died and my mother left. Without her, I felt lost. At that moment, I didn't know what else to do."

"So, you tried to hold on to what you had left?"

"Yeah, and I guess, for a moment, I thought I would find comfort in burying my head in my maps like I normally do. What a fool I am."

"Not at all. I get it, actually."

"You do?"

"Why, sure. Just the other day, my father gave me an ultimatum. Take over his business or go to school to be a doctor."

"What does he do?"

"Doesn't matter. The point is, rather than choosing either option, I ran to the comforting ear at the bottom of a bottle."

"Ah, I see. So you're a rum hound."

Otto winced. "Oh, that's not all. I up and decided to skip town on the next ferry."

"You didn't! Where were you going to go?"

"I don't know. I think New York first. Then London. Or maybe Paris?"

Jo laughed loudly. Her smile wasn't as charming when she was laughing at him. "You were going to run away, but you aren't even sure where? To do what?"

"I sort of always wanted to be a painter."

Jo lost all the control she had left. She snorted as tears leaked out and made her eyes shine. She stopped walking and pushed him playfully. "You must be joking! You were going to leave San Francisco, a city full of wonder and dreams and every possibility imaginable to humankind, and go to *maybe* Paris and *maybe* be a painter? That city would have chewed you up and spit you out. You'd better be damn sure of what you want before going somewhere like Paris."

"Hey, don't make fun of my dream." Otto started to feel a little hurt.

"That's no dream. That's panic, pure and simple. You were afraid."

"Well, that's sort of my point. So are you."

She stopped laughing then and pouted. "I guess you're right. I am a bit frightened. I take that back—I'm absolutely petrified."

The two walked in silence for a few minutes while they digested the reality of the fear inside them. They were near Market Street.

Jo said, "So, were you actually going to do it? Leave, I mean."

"That's what I was on my way to do. I left the house last night and was going to catch a wink at a boarding house before grabbing the first ferry. Only I got snagged by a crimper and was locked in a basement about to get Shanghaied. If it weren't for the quake, I'd have been halfway to China by now."

Jo once again broke into laughter, and this time Otto joined her.

"Sounds hard to believe, ey?" he said.

"A tale too tall to be anything but true."

Chapter Thirteen

New Montgomery and Market Street, 9:41 a.m.

Jo grimaced as her stomach growled. She hadn't realized before how hungry she was. She clutched her belly as the pangs worsened.

"What's wrong?" Otto asked. She could tell he was trying to get a read on her.

"Nothing. Just a little hungry," she said. She wondered where they might get a bite to eat. They stood in front of the court at the iconic Palace Hotel. The Palace dwarfed its neighboring structures, residential and commercial alike. She counted seven stories of gilded splendor.

"I bet you they've got something to eat here," Otto hooted. "Come on, let's go."

Jo's feet were anchored firmly on the ground. She had come this way before with Papa, but she had never dared to go inside. She felt like she was unworthy to even gaze through its windows. This was *The* Palace Hotel. Quite possibly the world's most beautiful resort, which hosted the likes of royalty. People still spoke about when former President Ulysses S. Grant stayed there for an entire week. Simply due to her social class, she was by no means qualified to even step into the lobby, let alone be a patron at such an establishment.

A combination of wealthy out-of-towners and well-to-do San Franciscans alike swarmed around them.

"Well, I thought he just put Olive Fernstead's performance to shame," one primly-dressed woman with Gibson Girl hair remarked.

"Oh indeed, he did. Enrico Caruso's variation of 'Carmen' was truly breathtaking. He's a magician," another woman replied, dressed in a long, black silk taffeta dress and a spotless silk-braided white coat.

Jo slowed her stride and studied her dusty nightgown.

"He evacuated the Palace early, did you hear?" the first woman said.

"Yes, I did! And a dragsman almost got away with his valises!"

"Scroungy thief. Where does he think he is, the Barbary Coast?"

The two women snickered, either unaware or unconcerned with the horror and chaos that was unfolding around them. Jo stopped walking.

"What's wrong?" Otto asked Jo. "I thought you said you were hungry."

"Are you kidding? I can't go in there."

"Why not?"

Jo grew frustrated. *Was he really that dense?* She posed, holding the corner of her nightgown in two fingers, contrasting her filthy garbs with the grandiose monument that towered over her. "Because I look like something the cat dragged in!"

"Nonsense. The trick to fitting in at a place like this is acting like you're meant to be there. Waltz in like the Mayor himself called for you." His eyes darted around suspiciously. He lowered his voice and shrank his posture. "And I tell you what. If anyone so much as looks at you sideways, I'll tell them to shut their chimney!"

Jo turned away and laughed. He seemed to take that as a signal of agreement because he grabbed her by the hand, yanking her toward the hotel's grand entrance on New Montgomery. They passed under an enclosed bridge that joined the Palace with the Grand Hotel across the street.

"The Bridge of Sighs," said Otto.

"What's it for?"

"Well, it's said that they built the bridge for wealthy businessmen who live in the Palace during the week. They have their mistresses stay in the Grand; that way, they can get to them without anyone seeing."

Jo wondered how Otto came to know that bit of information. As soon as they entered the grand doorway, her thoughts were swept away by the sight of an immense open atrium crowned with a glass ceiling and elegant lower lounge. Magnificent tall doorways with ornate sculpted arches and white columns bordered the room. Above were five floors of guest accommodations and a sixth, which looked to be a conservatory. The top floor was wrapped with open balconies, each laced with white railings and flanked by pillars.

"There must be hundreds of rooms in this place," she sighed.

"Seven hundred and fifty-five, to be precise," Otto exclaimed.

"Wow," was all she could manage. She drank in the beauty and splendor of the luxurious hotel. "How do you know that?" she asked.

"Architecture is a hobby of mine. This place has always fascinated me," he continued. "Nearly a hundred thousand square feet, which doesn't even include the basement. The first-floor ceiling is twenty-seven feet high; the rest are sixteen feet. The foundation wall is twelve feet thick and made of stone, iron, brick, and marble."

Something about Otto was different. He looked up at the glass ceiling with a twinkle in his eye. "Architecturally speaking, it is so simple. That's what gives the building its strength. It's a triplicate, you see. This atrium is a quadrangle flanked with lesser parallel courts."

She had no idea what he was talking about, but it sounded impressive. He turned to put his hand on one of the walls, "All the outer and inner partition walls are brick. They're two feet thick!

Reinforced with iron rods and bolts. Think of it like a wrought-iron skeleton."

His enthusiasm was infectious. Jo looked around at this modern-day wonder and saw more than just the fancy exterior, but its rich history and voluptuous engineering. The passion in his voice almost made it feel like The Palace had a soul.

He said, "This is probably one of the safest buildings to be in during an earthquake. And everyone knows it's fireproof."

Jo's heart sank as she remembered why she was there in the first place. "How can it be fireproof?"

"There are seven water tanks on the roof with a hundred and thirty thousand gallons of water, a cistern in the basement right under our feet with another six hundred and thirty thousand gallons, and a private artesian well and pumping station. It's fully wired from head to toe with electric, too. There are electric fire-detection devices, as well as call buttons, in every single room."

Otto pointed as he continued. "The devices trigger the sprinkler system. And see those panels over there? Fire alarms. If anyone smells a whiff of smoke, they can set it off."

An adjacent couple complained while Jo eavesdropped. They had to walk up four flights of stairs to get to their room—something about the rising rooms not being operational.

"And the elevators! I forgot to mention those. There are five of them. They operate on hydraulics," Otto said. They stepped down a hallway that ran alongside the lounge. Jo slid her fingers across the wood-paneled door to the rising room. A sign hung on it that read 'Out of order'. "And that's redwood from a giant Sequoia. Except it appears they are not in operation at the moment. Strictly a precaution, I'm sure."

"What does 'hydraulics' mean? How do you know all this?"

"Oh, it's a machine that uses oil for lubrication. So much better than the old steam-powered ones." He led her over to the Grand

Court, where they waited for a hotel servant.

A spindly black man dressed in a uniform rushed over. "Can I help you?"

"Yes, two for breakfast, please."

"Rolls and coffee for everyone in need today, on the house." He bowed and motioned toward a table. "If you please, sir."

Jo devoured two and a half rolls and half a cup of coffee before taking a full breath. By the fourth roll, she broke pieces off, dipped them in her coffee, and put them in her mouth at a slower speed. It was only then that she noticed Otto staring.

"Well, little lady, don't slow down on my account." Otto canted his head, teasing her.

Her cheeks heated.

"Really. No need to get all shy around me." He drew back so that she could take another breath.

She assessed the situation. *Well, all right. She wouldn't stop eating if Otto didn't want her to step on eggshells.* She shoveled more bread into her mouth, swallowed, and spoke. "So, your family. They rich?" She tested her boundaries.

Otto flew back in his chair, and his jaw dropped to the floorboards. "Zowie, Sheba! You certainly know how to render a fellow tongue-tied!"

He cocked his head slightly, leaned forward to rest his elbows on the table, and gawked at her. His blonde hair bounced defiantly above his brow.

"Hey, you done? Come with me." He took her hand and hauled her away from the table without letting her reply.

"Where are we going? Let go of me!" she barked. She was only half serious about him letting go.

"Hang on a minute, and I'll show you," he winked.

She grew flustered and stumbled, surprised by her reaction. *This was the first time a boy had distracted her.*

He led her out of the lounge in the atrium and let go of her hand. Her fingers tingled where he had gripped her. She rubbed them with her other hand. After winding around a couple of corners, they entered the gentlemen's parlor. Elaborate paintings circled the room, and billiards tables filled a bar at the back. "What could you possibly have to show me in here?" Jo asked.

Otto walked over to a pool table. "You asked about my family. This is what my father does."

"He runs the pool hall?"

"No." Otto pointed to the gold-plated emblem on the tabletop between two pockets. Jo inched closer and leaned over. The embossed lettering read:

August Frei Company
10 Golden Gate Ave
San Francisco

Jo asked, "Is that . . . ?"

Otto nodded, "My Pop." Jo took a step back. The walnut table had massive and meticulously crafted legs which supported a smooth, felt-covered top lined with carved, rope-like moldings. Each decorative panel had mahogany inlays, and fine leather, hand-woven netting delicately capped each pocket.

"It's exquisite," Jo cooed.

"I know," he grumbled.

"What's the problem?"

"My father moved here from Germany ages ago with nothing. He built this business with his bare hands. He's made many sacrifices to ensure his name is synonymous with the *epitome of high class*. His reputation is impeccable." Otto paced around to the other side of the table, letting his fingers trace the lines of the carved ropes. "His tables are the most sought-after in the whole of the Pacific. The Palace Hotel wouldn't settle for anything less." He dropped his shoulders and tapped his feet furiously.

"*The family business comes first,* he always says. Sometimes even before his own children," Otto's hands curled into tight fists. "It's not fair. I could live ten lifetimes and never be able to do what he does."

"He means to turn it over to you?" Jo asked.

"He never even asked me if it was what I wanted." His eyes smoldered, and he turned away.

Jo traced her fingers along Otto's path on the table. She stood next to him and spoke softly to bring down his temper; Mrs. Tucci had used that tactic with her many times. "There's this story my Papa used to tell me . . ."

He continued to look away, but his shoulders relaxed.

"There was a man and his young son," she continued. "They were walking through the woods one day. They came upon a stone. 'Do you think I can throw that stone?' asked the boy. 'I'm sure you can, little one,' said his father. And so the boy lifted the stone and threw it, and he smiled."

Otto opened his mouth to interrupt her, but his lips tightened, and he let her talk.

"They continued to walk, and they came upon a tree. 'Do you think I can climb that tree?' asked the boy. 'I'm sure you can, little one,' said his father. And the boy reached up and pulled himself up the tree, and he smiled.

"Then they came upon a big branch that blocked their path. 'Do you think I can move this branch?' asked the boy. 'I'm sure you can if you use all your strength, little one,' said his father. The boy grabbed the branch. He pushed and pulled, and it did not budge. He grew angry with his father and said, 'You said I could lift it if I used all my strength, but I'm not strong enough!' His father replied, 'But you haven't used all your strength. You did not ask me for help.' Then the boy asked his father to help him, and they moved the branch together, and they smiled."

Otto stood in silence and stared into the distance. Jo waited a moment before she spoke again. "Do you think your father expects you to do it alone? I bet all you need to do is ask for his help, and he'll teach you everything he knows."

"A question," Otto exclaimed, then thrust a finger into the air, signaling her to wait a moment. He ran across the room and disappeared behind a pool table. "Aha!" he clapped in victory and rose from the floor with a pool cue.

"Yes?"

He set up his shot, leaning over behind the white cue ball and closing one eye. "What's The Pull?"

Jo's whole body clenched. Good thing or she would have dived behind one of the tables herself and never gotten up. How did he know about that?

"You mentioned it when I found you. When you were scared stiff."

"Oh . . ." She had said it out loud but never explained it before. She tried to think of a good example. "It's . . . well, you know that feeling you get when walking along the beach, and you think to yourself, 'I could just walk into the water right now, right this second, and drown.'"

He looked up at her without blinking, "There's a name for that?"

"It's that feeling you get when you know you could end it all, and it would be so easy. It's not that you want to or anything, just that you could. It's about knowing you have the choice."

He took the shot, missing all the balls entirely. "That sounds crazy." He grabbed the cue ball from the table and rolled it forcefully toward a group of balls at the other end, making a loud crack. He stormed toward the bar and hopped on top of it, spinning his legs around and jumped off. He crouched down behind the bar and vanished.

Jo folded her arms in disappointment as she followed him and stood at the front of the bar. She felt like he hadn't heard a single thing she said. *He's so stubborn.* She should leave. If all he's going to do is call her crazy, what use is he to her? She can find Mama on her own. North Beach isn't that big.

But maybe he was right: she was crazy for thinking about The Pull that way. Maybe that's what Papa felt the night he killed himself. Perhaps he listened too closely to The Pull, and it got in his head, making him crazy and taking charge of his fingers.

Otto popped his head up from behind the bar wearing a brown bowler hat and holding a bottle of whiskey in one hand and a pair of tumblers in the other. "What'll ya have, kiddo? We're celebrating."

"The city is crumbling around us. What could we possibly have to celebrate?" Jo gasped. "Also, where on earth did you find that hat?"

"Well, firstly, I found it down here, and it suits me, don't you think?" Otto pointed at the floor and winked. "Secondly . . ." he said as he set the glasses on the counter and poured two generous servings of whiskey. He swallowed the whole gulp while he set the bottle down with one hand. Jo cleared her throat. *He must be trying to impress her.*

"And another thing," she added. "You keep calling me kiddo—but I'm not much younger than you."

"Secondly, kiddo," he smacked his lips, leaned across the bar, and pinched her on the arm.

"Ow!" Jo clenched her teeth. She couldn't believe his audacity.

"We're both still alive, aren't we?" He flashed her that frustratingly handsome half-smile again.

"What is wrong with you?"

"See?" Otto exclaimed as his face lit up with excitement. "Still alive. No earthquake, fire, or Pull could take us down. Test me too. Go on."

Otto held out his arm for Jo to pinch. Jo then shifted her gaze to his face. His smirk hinted at sincerity but was shrouded in bravado. She couldn't tell if he was always this arrogant and foolish or if the quake had somehow knocked a screw loose. She was half-insulted, half-intrigued.

Before she knew it, she reached over her head with an open palm. She slapped him clean across his face so hard it echoed off the few bottles that were left on the shelves.

He retracted his outstretched arm and held his cheek, mouth agape in surprise.

Satisfied, Jo grabbed the full glass of whiskey and swallowed her double shot in one go. But the liquid stung her tongue and dribbled down her chin instead of punctuating her brazen blow. Her eyes began to water as she wheezed.

Otto's astonishment from the slap was replaced with visible delight, and he doubled over with hearty laughter.

Her amusement percolated into humiliation; not just from the regurgitation of the whisky, but because of how stupid he must think her. After sharing such heartfelt stories, he only used them to get a rile out of her. That was the last time she would open up to him. From now on, nothing would distract her from reaching her destination.

"Thanks, Otter, you're such a big help," she snapped and stormed out. Heads of the rich tourists who had seen Enrico Caruso's performance the night before now drew their entertainment from watching a filthy homeless girl march down the hallway in her underwear.

"Jo, wait," Otto pleaded.

She ignored him and exited the Palace Hotel from the busy front entrance and reemerged in the smoldering city. The purpose of her journey rushed to the forefront of her mind. Urgency fueled her steps as she sighed and then proceeded toward North Beach.

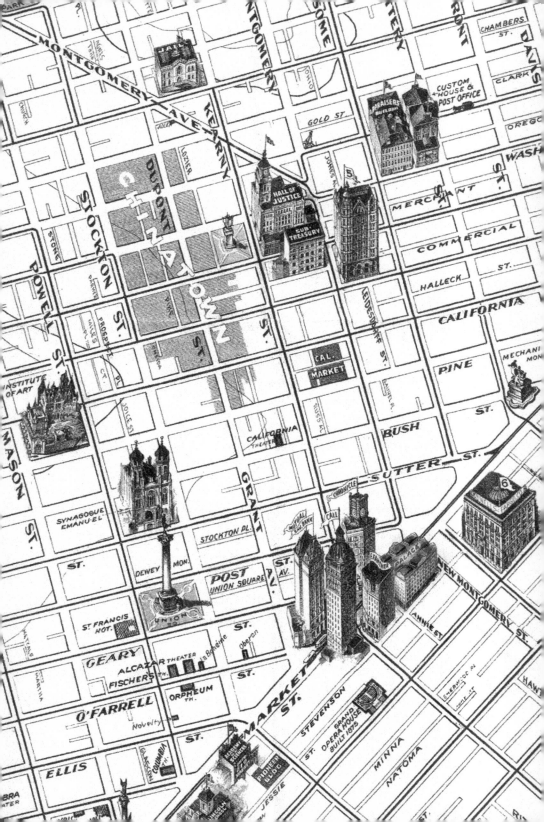

Chapter Fourteen

New Montgomery and Market Street, 11:30 a.m.

"here are you going?" Otto shouted. He scrambled over the bar and chased after Jo, whose determined pace made him question his tactics. Usually, after one bold stunt, women fell all over him. But Jo was different. She was hard-headed and had a mind of her own—he found this strangely refreshing. He was determined to get to the bottom of how this girl ticked. Exhilarated by this unfamiliar challenge, Otto couldn't help but grin as he opened the door leading to the street.

He had nearly forgotten the scale of devastation in the city outside the protective walls of The Palace Hotel. It reminded him of all the planning and dreaming he had done the previous night. When he had planned on leaving, he had made assumptions: he could come back any time he wanted; he could always come back if it didn't work out, and everything would be waiting for him, unchanged. That was no longer the case. He looked up Market Street, which now resembled a war zone. *At least the Call building still stood.*

Otto watched Jo sprint across Market Street, and he quickened his step. He caught up with her as she maneuvered around the massive piles of fallen masonry. He looked at the back of her, grateful for the earthquake, the event that led him to her. "Hey. I'm sorry for what I did back there."

Rather than stopping to look at him, she continued to head north on Montgomery. They passed what remained of the Occidental Hotel and the California Safe Deposit Bank, both completely leveled. Outside the bank, a crowd of men hollered, demanding their money.

Father. Otto pondered the extent of his small fortune lost inside the crushed walls of financial institutions throughout the city. The path led toward another giant plume of smoke. "Hey, kiddo, maybe we should go around."

"This is the fastest way," Jo said. Around them, the piles of debris grew higher, and the smoky air thickened until he couldn't see any more signs of life. They had no way forward without going over the mountains of debris.

"Jo, really. Isn't there another way to get around this?"

She stopped in her tracks, throwing her fists to her sides like a prizefighter in the ring. "No one asked you to follow me. Bug off if you're scared!" Jo flipped her hair and spun around to continue climbing the mounds of bricks, but she put all her weight on the brick near the top, and it slipped under her foot. She fell along with it, spinning sideways down the pile in his direction.

He ran to her. Her thigh had a large gash, and blood ran down her knee and into her boot.

"Dammit!" She screamed at her leg, bearing her teeth.

"Does it hurt?" he pinched his temple on both sides and side-stepped back and forth. *He didn't know what to do.*

"Of course, it hurts, you nitwit." She tried to stand, but she winced.

"Oh, stop it. You're stubborn as a mule," Otto approached her and softly placed his hand on her shoulder. "You're hurt. Stay still.

You need help." He knelt and scooped her up, just as he had done in the shop.

She squirmed and struggled as she groaned something inde-cipherable.

"I think the words you're looking for are 'thank you,'" Otto said. "I think I saw a pharmacy a few blocks back. Let's get you patched up." Jo's body settled against him; she must have surrendered to his idea of helping her.

"Yeah, yeah . . ." she mumbled into his ear.

"What's that? I didn't quite hear you," he teased.

"Gosh, do you need me to write you a letter?"

"You know, you should learn to take your own advice."

Jo breathed sharply through her teeth.

Otto couldn't tell if her reaction was because of the pain or if she was losing patience with him again. "What . . . do you mean?" she asked.

"Your story about the little boy using all his strength. You were lucky I was there."

"Oh . . ." she said. "Well, no need to gloat about it."

"Wasn't trying to." *That wasn't entirely true.* "I mean, I'm just glad I was there."

They backtracked their way to California Street, where the crowds thronged again. Caked in layers of dust, people paraded through the streets. Otto could remember seeing a drugstore somewhere, but he couldn't find it in the rubble.

He peered over the heads of the crowd as he moved west, listen-ing to the mumbling herd. *Evacuation.* People moaned while dragging their belongings in trunks behind them. Jo and Otto navigated the crowds of the homeless like two salmon swimming upstream.

The road ahead shot up into one of San Francisco's famous hills. Otto's pace slowed as he climbed. The echo of dozens of trunks scraping against the pavement got louder with every elevated step.

"Otter, stop spinning," Jo said, barely audible above the racket.

"I'm not," Otto looked down at her. Her leg was terrible, and she was losing a lot of blood. He had to get her some bandages right away.

"Hang on, kiddo. Let's get out of here. Stay with me," Otto cut through the mass of people, using his right shoulder as a knife. They emerged on Stockton Street, where he could breathe again—finally. Otto spied a pharmacy on the corner. He set Jo against a fence in a yard across the street. Her eyes were closed; she groaned and half-opened them.

"You all right?"

She mumbled something incoherent but didn't open her eyes.

"Kid? Jo? Come on. Wake up." Otto shook her shoulders gently. *No response.* If she didn't wake up, he would not, under any circumstances, let anything more happen to her. He was responsible for her, and she had just begun to trust him.

Otto looked at the pharmacy. Someone had smashed the windows, and a young man in a soldier's uniform guarded the front door. He ran across and approached the guard, who seemed very young to be a soldier, no older than sixteen by the look of his pale, oily skin. He held a bayonet-tipped Springfield rifle.

"I need bandages and alcohol. My friend is hurt," Otto said.

The soldier swung the rifle around and pointed it at Otto's face. His weapon shook frantically in the air like a branch in a strong wind. The boy tried to blink away beads of sweat that dripped from his brow to no avail. "Don't come any closer," he spat. "The mayor's issued a shoot-to-kill order for looters and banned the consumption of spirits. Don't you dare test me."

Otto spoke slowly and calmly. "The alcohol's not for drinking. You see that girl?" He pointed at Jo, who was propped against the nearby fence, eyes closed and bloodied. "She's hurt. All I need is a way to clean her up and wrap up her leg to stop the bleeding. Let me in, please."

The soldier looked in Jo's direction, wiped his brow with his sleeve, then placed his hand on the gun's shaft.

"Not one more step." He cocked the gun.

"And just waddaya plan on doing with that there firearm, son?" An eerily familiar voice came slinking from around the corner. *Bernard.* He crept toward them, pointing his bony finger at the boy.

The soldier's eyes grew wide as he swung the rifle around and aimed it at Bernard. "No closer! I swear I'll shoot!"

"Now, you're going to do nothing of the kind—here's why. My friend here, he strikes you as someone rash and foolish, does he not?"

The boy blinked and looked over at Otto, then swung the rifle and pointed it back toward his original target. He nodded at Bernard, seeming to agree with the strange tooth-gapped fellow who had asked him the question.

Otto watched Bernard as he inched forward, cocked his head toward the blocked doorway, and winked. Bernard said, "But let me tell you, he's as crafty and wily as ever. Why, just a few hours ago, he bested six men. Killed two of 'em with his bare hands!"

Otto went along with the ruse. He held his hands forward and stepped sideways, pretending to grab the larger man by his shoulders and yank him to the ground.

The boy shook uncontrollably. Otto flinched. Fear was the friend of an itchy trigger finger.

Bernard leaped forward, grabbing the gun's barrel and pulling it downward. The weapon discharged, sending a shot ricocheting off the ground next to Otto's feet.

Otto jumped and used the momentum to spin around and run toward the doorway.

Bernard rolled on top of the gun and took down the soldier who still clutched the trigger. Otto heard the two wrestling on the ground. He waded through cluttered aisles and searched through picked-over shelves before finding rubbing alcohol and bandages. When Otto exited the store, Bernard lay on his belly with a toothy grin, panting heavily and clutching the rifle. The soldier was nowhere in sight.

"Fool of a boy done scampered into the loony parade. You tryin' to get yourself shot, boy?"

Otto didn't know what to say. He couldn't figure out Bernard's motivation, so he dismissed him and rushed to Jo's side, bandages and rubbing alcohol in hand. Her eyes were closed, and when he touched her forehead with the back of his hand, she didn't respond. His fingers quivered as he cleaned her wound and wrapped the bandage tightly around her upper thigh. "Come on, Jo. Wake up. Please," Otto pleaded.

He sensed Bernard moseying closer. He strolled into his field of vision, swinging the rifle like a cane. "Well, well, well . . . what do we have here? Kitty's caught himself a little bird. What's wrong, little bird, can't fly?" Bernard poked at the boot on Jo's injured leg with the rifle like a child jabbing a dead frog. It was the one that held the letter from her mother. Bernard moved the tip of the barrel from the sole of her boot up to the exposed corner of the envelope and slowly used it to pull down on the sides. He cocked his head to try and see what it was he discovered.

Frenzy boiled up inside Otto like a bull in a rage. He waved his arms in Bernard's direction and stormed to his feet. "What did you do, follow me? You crazy old man."

Bernard sashayed around, positioning himself on the other side of Jo. "Sonny, when you plucked my old bones from what would have most assuredly become my grave, I was in your debt." He gave Otto a bow. "And with the amount of common sense you showed last night on that bar stool, I knew it was only a matter of time before it needed repayment."

"I didn't need your help! The last thing I need is a lunatic following me around who's trying to sell me to the highest bidder, not twelve hours ago. Get out of here. Don't let me regret saving your life."

Bernard swayed, gave the rifle another twirl, and swaggered the rest of the way 'round Jo's motionless body. He slipped in uncomfortably close to Otto. So close that he felt Bernard's damp breath on his neck. It made his whiskers stand on end.

Otto felt something cold against his throat. When he swallowed, he realized Bernard held a blade tightly against his Adam's apple. Bernard grabbed his left wrist and pulled it down, locking him into submission. Despite his slight frame, he had bested Otto by technique alone. "Yer going to want to rethink yourself before you go and make idle threats to a scoundrel the likes of me. Men tenfold braver than ye wouldn't dare take a gander at the demons that lurk in these undercurrents." He drew himself in closer still.

"But if you'd like an inkling," he scowled as the jagged blade cut closer, "I'd be happy to oblige."

Chapter Fifteen

Stockton and California Street, 12:05 p.m.

Jo was floating outside her body. She was aware of everything happening to Otto and knew he was in danger. But no matter how hard she tried, she could not get her muscles to comply with her demands. She had been turned to stone. Open your eyes. Focus and open your eyes. The muddy darkness flooded with blurry light. Jo blinked twice before the washed-out colors converged and sharpened to form recognizable shapes.

Otto stood over her; somebody pressed a knife to his throat. The spindly man wielding the weapon wore dust-encrusted rags and looked like he had crawled out of a grave. A sinister smile played a starring role on his otherwise flaccid face and pulled the corners of his eyes into clusters of wrinkled skin.

"Do what you want to me, just don't touch her," Otto said to the stranger, his voice quivering.

"Oh, really?" The wriggly stranger's tone mimicked surprise and intrigue. "You don't really seem to be the one in the position of making demands." The knife pushed deeper against Otto's jugular.

Jo was surprised at the next impulse that came over her. She felt protective of Otto. Even though he was a pompous, entitled jerk who didn't quite know how to talk to girls, it didn't mean she wanted him to die. She realized she enjoyed being around him. She had to try to save him.

"Do it, Bernard." Otto gritted his teeth.

Jo's leg throbbed, but despair rushed over her like a storm surge. Otto knew the man's name. But what had he done to make this Bernard fellow want to kill him? Her dismay stemmed from something deep, perhaps Otto's easy willingness to give in to peril. He seemed willing to surrender himself to his fate—for her. As far as Jo was concerned, the man did not have a good reason to kill him.

Bernard pulled Otto's wrist in one slippery motion, spinning him around in a circle. Otto fell backward, and Bernard snapped forward toward Jo. He knelt next to her and pressed the blade's tip against her side. She screamed. His eyes rose to meet hers, and he appeared stunned when she looked back at him. "Well now, good morning, princess," Bernard said.

Jo pushed with every ounce of will; her right arm shot up like a whip and thrust Bernard away, causing him to roll backward and kick up an outrageous amount of dust. Her body was shocked into action. Using her palms, she propelled back while making mental checks that she controlled all her limbs.

Otto used this opportunity to lunge for the firearm, but his fingertips slipped on the barrel, allowing Bernard to scoop it up.

Bernard's guttural laughter swelled into hysteria as he rolled up from the ground and stood, his rifle in hand. He waved it in Otto's direction. "I propose," he whistled, "a little pow-wow. A consultation of sorts. Be it that my line of work has all but vanished as a result of . . . unforeseen geologic circumstances." Bernard twirled his fingers around his stringy beard. "I'll have to go back to good ole fashioned methods of kidnapping. We're going to pay that pappy of yours a little visit."

"Kidnapping!" Jo screamed. "What on earth is he talking about, Otter?"

Otto had mentioned almost being shanghaied, but she didn't believe him for a moment. He had just been trying to make her laugh or impress her.

Otto faced Bernard. "What *are* you talking about?" he asked, mirroring Jo's question. "You said that kidnapping was too messy. You'll never get away with it."

"There are people everywhere. There will be so many witnesses!" Jo added.

Bernard smacked his lips like he had just sucked a lemon. "These sheep care not of others' woes," he scoffed. "They're all just set out to save their own hides."

"You're wrong," Jo shouted. "People *will* notice, and they'll do something about it too. You're not going to get away with this."

"So sure about that, are ye, girlie?" Bernard danced backward, waving the rifle in the air where all passers-by could see it plainly. "Are ya willing to bet yer fella's life on it?"

Jo had believed her whole life that people were inherently good, that sometimes they acted selfishly but would never do something if they knew someone would get hurt. But so many things lately had made her question this—Papa killed himself, Mama left, Mrs. Tucci talked to Mama behind her back, and Uncle Giuseppe never cared about her at all. Maybe people weren't inherently good; maybe they only did good things when other people were looking. She had seen a lot of high society activity that led her to believe that most of what people did was for show.

Jo watched Bernard twirl the loaded gun, then looked to see if anyone was watching. A few people walking by carrying armloads of belongings glanced up a moment, then put their noses back down to their business. Jo shuffled her feet and rubbed the sweat from her eyes. *Maybe Bernard was right. Maybe people did only just care about themselves.* She felt a heaviness in her chest. Otto's family would surely pay the ransom for his life, but what about hers? *She was nothing, just some guinea from the wrong side of the tracks.*

"Not so sure, are ya, lass?" Bernard chortled. "Oh look, there be our ride."

The bell clanging on a fire engine reverberated off the damaged buildings and changed pitch as it sped toward them. Bernard cocked his head and grinned maniacally. She didn't like the look he got in his eye as he turned slowly toward Otto.

Bang!

The shot rang through the air like a crack of thunder. Bernard's skeleton recoiled and lost balance.

Jo watched Otto's stunned face as he looked down and reached over to check his right side. When he held up his hand, there was blood. *Lots of blood.* Otto stumbled sideways and fell.

Time seemed to move in slow motion as Jo scrambled to her feet and ran to Otto. She fell against his side. If only she could help, but she didn't know how. Her touch would only hurt him more. "Otto! How bad is it? I can't believe he shot you! Why would he do such a thing?"

Bernard picked himself up off the ground, looked over in Otto's direction, and nodded in satisfaction before turning around and heading back toward the crowd of people.

"How bad is it?" Jo asked softly, trying to remain calm.

"I don't know," he groaned. "Can you look for me? I'm worried that I'll lose my lunch."

Jo shushed him. "Let me see." She took his hand from over the wound and moved it away slowly. She lifted his shirt carefully with her other hand. Under normal circumstances, this interaction would have delighted or even aroused her.

Jo didn't know what she should look for once she found the wound. She didn't have much experience with blood. Once, Papa had cut his hand shucking an oyster and almost lost a finger. Luckily Mama had been there and knew what to do to stitch him back up. He never regained full movement of his fingers, but he used to say, "A downhill road follows the uphill road."

Papa always tried to convince her that life would get better no matter what. But in retrospect, maybe he was trying to talk himself into believing it. It hadn't made sense that a man that optimistic would give up on life so easily. He had lied to her throughout her entire life. Every little thing he taught her about how the world was beautiful and full of potential felt like a lie. Maybe he believed that the world was hard, cruel, and unforgiving and finally stopped trying to convince himself it was anything else.

Otto grimaced audibly, and Jo shook her head to refocus. His side wound appeared minor. She took some of the excess bandages off the ground and used them to soak up some of the blood. "I need to put pressure on the wound," she told him. She wasn't sure, but her instinct told her that Otto needed reassurance more than anything.

"A Springfield can hit a 27-inch bulls-eye at 500 yards," he said.

"What are you talking about?"

"The gun could have killed me. He missed on purpose. My father is a champion rifleman. I know a thing or two about firearms."

"You call this missing? This is not a miss. He shot you. Maybe he missed by accident. He doesn't look like he'd have the best aim."

"Are my new companions ready for their ride?" Bernard howled from the direction of the main boulevard; some volunteer firefighters in tow were carrying a stretcher.

So that's what all this is about—a free ride.

"I got us a one-way ticket to Hayes Valley."

Hayes Valley had only one hospital, as far as she knew. The Central Emergency Hospital was located in the basement of City Hall. It was attached to the prison and wasn't very big. She was concerned he wouldn't get medical attention as quickly as he needed it, but she didn't share this with him. She didn't want to give him more to worry about beyond his pain.

Bernard had uncertain motivations behind this most peculiar kidnapping, and she was petrified. He was unstable, and she did not know what to expect. Once Otto had a clean bill of health, they would figure out how to get out of this.

"You crazy bastard. You can't be serious. You shot me!" Otto seethed.

Bernard waved his hands in defense as he stumbled into the back of the cart. "Oh no, the poor young man is delirious. Went one step too far with a store clerk, he did. Pay no mind to his nonsensical ramblings."

"He shot him! Don't let him on this cart!" Jo shouted.

The men continued prepping the wagon for departure. "None of our business, Miss. We're just told to carry the hurt, and that's what we're doing."

Jo climbed into the open cart, took a seat beside Otto's stretcher, and glared at Bernard, who sat in the front, out of earshot. The cart jerked forward as the horses resumed their journey toward the hospital. They sat beside several other injured people with a myriad of different injuries. As they wobbled back and forth up the road, she thought about how she had been the one lying helpless moments before. She inspected the handiwork of the bandage on her leg. It was tight and clean.

"How are you feeling, kiddo?" Otto whispered, barely audible.

He looked at her with watery blue eyes that expressed both anguish and adoration. His gaze held fast as if he didn't dare look anywhere else, or he would lose all control.

Maybe people could be selfless and kind after all. "You're the one that gets shot, and you're worried about me?"

Otto attempted to squelch a laugh, resulting in a coughing fit that looked quite painful. Jo shushed him and inched forward to stroke his hair. She had only ever stroked her cat, never another person, and not nearly so tenderly.

With every repetition of her fingers sliding through his hair, she imagined what it would be like to kiss him. What was she doing? She hadn't known this person only hours ago, and he had proven to be everything that she wasn't. How could she be attracted to him? Yet, never in her life had she been drawn to someone so completely.

He had saved her life twice now. This fact stirred up a cocktail of emotions inside her.

"You shouldn't have come back for me."

"What was I going to do, just let you lie there and bleed to death?"

"I'm sure I would have been fine without your help."

"Oh, you're so sure? I don't think so, kiddo. You weren't looking so hot there for a minute."

"Yeah. I guess not."

Otto smacked his lips and looked away. "I . . . was pretty worried about you." He looked back at her as if he had just admitted a guilty pleasure and sought validation.

Jo swallowed at least some of her feelings and thought carefully about the following words before saying them. "Thank you," she said. The words tasted foreign.

"You're welcome. See? That wasn't so bad." He flashed her a sappy smile as the cart trod over a high pile of something in the road. The wheels spun feverishly and then hit the ground with a thud. Otto doubled over in pain, forcing the firefighter to pin him down and yell at him not to move.

Chapter Sixteen

Hayes and Larkin Street, 1:15 p.m.

tto's eyes were closed when the wagon came to an abrupt halt, jostling him into an uncomfortable position while leaning on his bad side. He cringed. When he opened his eyes again, he looked up to get his bearings. They were stopped in front of the Mechanics Pavilion on Hayes Street.

"We're in the wrong place. Isn't Central Emergency Hospital over there?" Jo asked. They both looked and were surprised at the level of devastation. City Hall, as they knew it, was gone.

"It was," said one of the firefighters. "All of City Hall was completely decimated. The hospital never stood a chance."

Otto wondered how the entirety of City Hall could have just vanished instantly. What about the people inside? He imagined what it must have been like to be asleep, wake up to the brick walls rumbling and crumbling around him, and be too sick or immobilized to run and save himself. The idea terrified him, and he did his best to push it from his mind.

"The whole of the Mechanics Pavilion has turned into a hospital ward," the firefighter added.

"Unbelievable," Otto said. The Mechanics Pavilion was the largest building in San Francisco. It was strange to think it would be transformed from the host of prize fights, concerts, and political rallies to being the only place big enough to house all the hurt people after the earthquake.

The Pavilion towered over the cart's bed and stretched an entire city block—the massive wooden structure burst with activity. People hummed like honey bees around the massive makeshift infirmary. Hospital bed frames without mattresses were strewn around the block as soldiers, sailors, and marines patrolled the streets.

The sight reminded him of the crowds that had turned up for the 1903 prizefight between heavyweight champ James Jeffries and Gentleman Jim. Jeffries had knocked Jim Corbett out in the tenth round with a blow to the stomach. It was a huge turnout. Over ten thousand people paid five dollars each to set foot in the building; twenty dollars or more for ringside seats where he and his father sat. He remembered wiping Gentleman Jim's sweat off his cheek when it landed after the final blow.

They unloaded Otto from the back of the wagon. One of the nearby soldiers looked at his side and followed him with a suspicious expression. He must have recognized a bullet wound and concluded that Otto was a criminal. Otto formulated a story in his mind, an entire explanation that would make him sound as innocent as possible. He tried to sit up to see, but the pain in his side came spilling back to the forefront of his attention.

"I'm here," he heard Jo say and felt her touch his arm. "Don't worry." She walked alongside him as he was carried toward the splintered main doors.

The locks looked like they had been busted open, similar to how his insides felt. Dreary speckled light trickled through broken windows—rows of injured divided the landscape into linear patterns like a graveyard. The air was putrid. At the far side of the auditorium, the dead were stacked like firewood.

They passed indiscernible collections of injured and dying. Some lay in cots, others in beds moved from a nearby hotel, and some on mattresses on the floor. Men and women were horribly mangled, many with bones protruding through their skin. Mothers rocked babies with charred flesh, and young, bloodied children cried for their parents. The grisly spectacle made him dizzy, so he locked his eyes on the ceiling.

The men dropped Otto onto the ground and hoisted him onto an empty cot. Several folks carried in more hotel beds. Nurses dressed in white ricocheted from bed to bed like pool balls. One of them looked up to see him getting situated and ran over to greet them.

Bernard leaped forward to intercept her before she reached them. "It seems my nephew here had a run-in with the wrong end of a barrel."

The nurse nearly ran into Bernard, staggering backward to catch her balance. "Excuse me, sir?"

"Just a graze, I assure you. A few stitches, and we'll be outta yer hair."

She looked him up and down slowly, looked over at Otto, down to Otto's wound, then back to Bernard. "Are you a medical professional?" she snapped.

"Well, I, uh . . ." Bernard bumbled and looked at the ceiling.

"Scoot," she shooed him. "Patients only in the infirmary. You may wait outside."

"Well, no, you see . . ." Bernard tripped on the leg of a neighboring cot as the nurse chased him away, flipping her skirt at him like a stray cat.

She chased him all the way out the side entrance, then closed the door after him.

Jo squeezed Otto's hand and leaned in so close he could feel her breath on his ear. "We have to do something!" she whispered. She looked about as concerned as Otto felt.

"What *can* we do?" He seethed. "I can't move, and you can barely walk. This loon is not going to let up."

"I'm fine now, really. Just a little dizzy."

"Well, if you say so," Otto shrugged.

The nurse reappeared. "I'll be right with you two," she said and pivoted her step about to scurry away.

"Do I have to leave too?" asked Jo.

"Oh no, sweetie," she smiled. "you sit tight."

The nurse scuttled away and tended to another patient.

"But yes, you're right," Otto admitted. "We have to do something. Bernard won't be happy when he discovers there's no money to be had."

"No money? What do you mean?" Jo stood straight as a board.

Otto thought about what to say. He didn't want to scare Jo, but their currently manageable situation was about to become dire. "My father keeps all his money in the bank. Did you notice that the banks, the ones not destroyed, are under heavy guard?"

Jo gasped. "Nobody can get their money out."

"Right, and once Bernard finds out my father can't get him the cash, who knows what he'll do next."

He watched reality set in on Jo's face. He wasn't about to let anything else happen to either of them. The destruction from the earthquake was enough. "We'll figure something out. Don't worry, kiddo." He noticed her shoulders drop and her features relax. His attempt to reassure Jo seemed to have worked.

"*Shhh*, she's coming back."

"Hello there, I'm Lucille. You can call me Lucy. Your *uncle* told me you had a little accide—"

"Nothing but a graze," Bernard bellowed as he flew into the scene from the opposite side of the Pavilion he had exited. Otto opened his mouth but had no chance to object to this man, who was not his uncle, being at his bedside. "See? I told you. Just a little stitch job, and he'll be right as rain."

"Where on earth did you . . .?" Lucy spun around, apparently searching the entrances to see how the old man had breached.

Bernard was trying to get them out of there as soon as possible. Otto knew their staying under the nurse's care long enough would give them a better chance at survival. He conjured up his inner stage actor and forced some tears. "I think the bullet's still in there; it hurts so much."

"Crocodile tears," Bernard barked over Lucy's shoulder, releasing a spray of spittle. "A flesh wound, nothing more."

"I'll be the judge of that." Lucy wiped spit off her cheek and assumed a defensive position between Bernard and Otto. "Sir, I'm going to ask that you please give us some room."

Bernard took a few steps back and crossed his arms proudly as if he had won.

Lucy peeled back the blood-soaked tailored shirt with careful movements. Otto shuddered when her fingers tugged at the skin around his wound; there was no need to fake that reaction. He felt light-headed as he attempted to focus all his energy on trying not to tip over when she poked at his side.

"Well, the good news is you'll be just fine."

"Is there bad news?" asked Jo.

"It's not quite as harmless as a graze. Son, the gunshot took out a piece of you, and good, but we can get you stitched up and give you something for the pain."

"How soon will we be on our way?" Bernard was getting antsy.

"Sir, I have nearly fifty patients I'm attending. In due time and not an instant sooner."

Bernard sneered at Lucy like she had spit in his eye.

Otto chuckled at the irony.

Bernard was displeased at the inconvenience of the situation.

To look at him, you could almost see the gears physically turning in his head to calculate what to do next.

"What about you, dear. Do you need anything?" Lucy crouched next to Jo.

Jo opened her mouth to speak, but Bernard, positioned over Lucy's shoulder, slid his thumb across his throat and then dramatically stuck his tongue out the side of his mouth. Jo closed her mouth again and swallowed a gulp of air before finally speaking. "Just some water, ma'am, if it's not too much trouble."

"I'm afraid that's in short supply today, dear, but I'll see what I can do." The nurse left to tend to other patients for several minutes and then returned with a suture kit and handed a small water cup to Jo.

She threaded a needle and then dipped it in a metal container full of alcohol to disinfect it. She cleaned Otto's wound, then, with a gimlet's precision, she pierced his skin with the needle.

She bandaged him up so tightly that it hurt more than the wound. She disappeared and then returned holding some medicine. "Something for the pain." She handed the bottle to him and pinned a tag to his shirt, indicating the completion of his treatment. "Now rest up. You're not in bad shape, so we'll likely soon need the bed for someone else."

His sense of urgency grew—he had to act before he was discharged. He threw looks in Jo's direction, trying to communicate anxiety while endeavoring to play it so Bernard would think it was a symptom of his pain.

Jo peeked out from behind her cup and gave him a slight nod that she understood his message. She dropped the cup, spilling the rest of her water on the floor.

"Fire!"

Heads turned, and patients sat up in bed, looking around in panic. Bernard shot them both glances like daggers.

Chapter Seventeen

o never imagined she would wish to be in another burning building. She knew that if Bernard succeeded in taking them back to Otto's father, Bernard would not have any reason to keep them alive. Also, he had proved he was willing to go to any length to capitalize on others' desperation.

The entire hospital room hummed with palpable tension. A man came running through the set of doors closest to them. He went to consult with the doctor she presumed to be in charge. Everyone heard what he said next.

"She's right! Hayes Valley is lit up. It's heading this way. We must evacuate!"

The word "evacuate" spread throughout the facility quicker than the blaze. The doctor in charge never announced the evacuation but whispered to nurses to keep everyone calm.

But people weren't calm. The ones that could move started to get up and run.

Bernard unsheathed his knife, stared at Otto, and gritted his teeth.

"Go!" Otto shouted to Jo.

Panic sent Jo's stomach surging toward her heart. No one in that building wanted to get out more than she did, but she didn't budge—because Otto didn't move. He was acting as if he wasn't coming with her. He must have expected her to save herself while he stayed behind. She wouldn't let that happen. *Why was he so stubborn?*

"Come on!" she yelled.

Bernard used her hesitation as an opportunity. He lunged toward Otto, knife first.

Jo jumped with full force into Otto, propelling him backward with the weight of her entire body. The hospital bed tipped over under their weight, Bernard's knife wedging between the mattress springs.

She was furious, not with Bernard but with Otto, and she could no longer hold her tongue. She shoved his shoulders to call his attention away from Bernard and onto her. "Otto, stop trying to sacrifice yourself for me. From here on out, no one gets left behind. Understand?"

Visions flashed before her of Papa's headstone, Mama's full trunk, and Mrs. Tucci's body.

Otto gulped and nodded vigorously, looking half-frightened at what might happen if he disagreed.

She got up and pulled him to his feet.

Bernard waved his knife in the air. "You think you can get away from me that easily?" People around them screamed at the unsheathed weapon.

Jo assessed the pathways to the exits as crowds, looking for more information about the fire situation's severity, blocked each way out. She grabbed Otto's hand and ran toward one of the doorways and hoped she would be able to get lost in the crowd. But the people were crammed in like sardines, and every time she pushed, Bernard closed in quicker.

She looked frantically around the stadium for somewhere to go.

The only clear route was the stairwell on the far wall. They sprinted in its direction and climbed several flights, ascending to the balcony three stories up.

Otto leaned over the side and caught his breath. He was clearly in pain. "He's coming."

Jo looked over the edge. Bernard looked like a drunk tripping side to side over patients lying in their beds, and more heads turned toward him with his every step.

"Quick, onto the roof," Otto insisted.

Jo ran the length of the building with Otto hobbling alongside. Roof access lay at two easternmost front corners. They climbed more stairs to get into the spire decorated on all four sides with Victorian-style round windows. Ordinarily, the light would enter from all angles, but no direct sunlight could sneak past the smut and smoke that saturated the air around the Pavilion. They exited through a door onto the roof, where a brightly painted railing lined the edge facing the street.

She took in the scene below. From this vantage point, they could see nearly the whole of San Francisco. She looked across the street to what was once the shining icon of the city, now a sad, crippled version of what was once familiar. Wagons gathered on the street in front of the concourse, assisting with evacuating the hundreds of people still alive inside.

"Once Bernard comes through, we'll sneak back inside and lock the door," Otto said.

"But he'll be trapped."

"That's the idea. It's him or us."

Him or us. That was an oddly comforting way to justify their choice to sacrifice a person's life to save themselves. *When, if ever, was it okay for a person to make that decision? To take a life?* Jo tried to imagine what Papa would do. She found it hard to focus under pressure.

The firestorm drew near the building's west side. Embers floated, landed on the roofline, and smoldered out. This prominent wooden structure would light up within minutes like a pile of kindling.

Heavy, blocky footsteps trounced up the stairwell. Jo threw herself against the exterior wall behind the open door beside Otto. Her breathing was heavy with the burden of her choice, and when her uncontrollable whines of panic escaped, she couldn't silence them. *Quiet!*

Otto pivoted and straddled her against the wall. He took her face in his hands and took slow and deliberate breaths, insisting she imitate his movements. She felt comfort in pressing her face into his hand as she concentrated on synchronizing their rhythm. His focused gaze was hypnotic.

Murder. Planned and premeditated. Not the overly dramatized bloody stab-someone-in-the-back murder in plays and books, but the deliberate choice that would directly result in someone losing their life. And yet, today, the world was different. Death surrounded them. The body would most certainly never be discovered. They weren't in any danger of being caught. But still, was it wrong?

Him or us.

"Ready?" Otto's low whisper made Jo wonder if he had spoken at all.

Him or us. It was easy now. She chose to live. She was ready.

Bernard stormed through the doorway, shouting. He tip-toed as if trying to be stealthy, but it wasn't close to working. Before she knew it, she pushed Otto toward the door. Bernard spun around like a top-heavy sailor holding an armful of rope. "There's nowhere to go!" he sputtered. Then he growled in a low, slow baritone. "You crafty cats, what are you doing?"

She thought about ignoring him, but she surprised herself by staring him right in the eye, stone-faced.

"No. You don't have the guts," Bernard snarled.

The door slammed, leaving Jo and Otto on the inside. They

barricaded the locking mechanism with a wooden plank. Bernard howled and pounded frantically from the other side. Neither of them turned to look as they walked away. *It was done.*

A strange calm came over Jo as she walked down the stairs. She floated past the chaos like a ghost. A flipped switch had shut off her feelings. She passed sick and dying people, but she felt nothing. If she let herself feel, it would all be too much.

When they were at least a block away from the Pavilion, she finally heard Otto's voice calling her name like she was coming up for air after a deep-sea dive. He sounded impatient and slightly concerned, making her wonder how long he had been trying to get her attention.

She spun around, and her eyes finally connected with his. He looked desperate and vulnerable. It was too much. She turned away from him again.

"Jo, answer me!"

"I'm fine."

"No, you're not. You're doing it again. You're shutting me out."

She knew he was right, but she couldn't help it. She couldn't face him right now. To admit to herself what had just happened.

"I . . . can't."

"Yes, you can. Just look at me."

She stood her ground and squeezed her eyes shut. Otto came up behind her and set his hands on her shoulders. He gently pushed her toward a clear corner of the curb away from foot traffic. She didn't fight him when he motioned for her to sit down.

"We did what we had to do back there, kiddo. You know that." He placed his hand on her back. When she did not object, he rubbed her gently to console her. She felt her muscles relax, the effect of his touch surprising her. "It was an impossible situation," he continued. "But you were so brave. You were amazing back there. You saved us, Jo."

A bit of an exaggeration. She was no hero.

"Just take a moment," he said. "Talk to me when you're ready."

"I killed him," she murmured.

"It's not that cut and dry, you know. Technically, the fire will kill him. And if you think about it, his decisions led him there. He got what he deserved."

"I know. Like you said, him or us."

"And you made the only decision you could under the circumstances. You know that, right? He was going to kill us, Jo. And he might have killed my family, too. He was the bad guy, and we needed to do it to survive. It was the only thing we could do."

Was it, though? Was it really? Maybe instead, she could have told someone, one of the nurses, perhaps. Maybe they could have done something to help. Jo didn't know what to believe, but she didn't want to keep talking about it. "I suppose so."

Otto shook his head. "We wouldn't be in this mess if it weren't for—"

"What?" Jo cocked her head in confusion. "If it weren't for what, Otto?"

"Nothing . . . never mind." He turned her chin with his finger so she looked at him. He stared so deeply into her eyes that she became self-conscious. She felt as if she should be crying; as if she owed Bernard that much, but she wasn't. She couldn't.

"Jo, you saved me. You saved us both. You survived."

Is that what she is? A survivor? She felt more like a victim forced by circumstance to take a man's life. But she tried to view it from the perspective of being a resilient fighter who chose life over death. She hadn't come from a long line of survivors. Her mother and father both took the easy way out—the whole concept of pushing forward when things got hard felt foreign. And besides, half the time, she needed Otto to step in and convince her to choose to live.

Jo wondered if she could trust Otto with her secret. If she were to ever hope to trust someone again, it might be him.

But then she thought about the story she told him, about the father and the son: the strength you have is not just yours but belongs to the people on your side—the people who love you.

"My Papa killed himself." She slammed her eyes shut in anticipation of the fallout. "I know. It's horrible. I understand if you don't want to be seen with me after this."

She felt his hand touch the top of hers and squeeze lightly. She peeked at his face out of one eye, expecting to see at least a look of pity, and waited for him to think of an excuse to leave.

Otto sat for a moment, looking out into space, sighed deeply, and cleared his throat.

Jo swallowed a big mouthful of ashy air and waited.

"You don't got a thing to worry about, kiddo. You can tell me anything."

Chapter Eighteen

tto's familiarity with the subject of suicide was limited. He was aware of the stigma, of course, but had no idea where it originated from or why. There were overly-graphic newspaper articles highlighting a variety of self-inflicted injuries in gruesome detail. Reporters, it seemed, took certain sick pleasures in describing the effects of self-inflicted fatal wounds.

When he was young, he remembered hearing stories about the neighbor on the corner killing himself by ingesting rat poison. Within just hours of his death, it was discovered that Mr. Becker, the butcher, was also found dead by the same means. Rumors quickly circulated about a love affair between the two men. Their families never recovered and had to leave the neighborhood.

"I was ten," Jo said. "He shot himself. I thought it was an accident. Until I read that letter. And saw the newspaper article."

Otto let the words sink in. He didn't quite know what to do with the information. He didn't want to say the wrong thing and upset Jo even more. He tried to imagine what it must be like to have a father kill himself when a person was that young. What could have gone so wrong that Jo's father thought suicide was the best action?

"You didn't know?" Otto thought that if he kept his questions brief and open-ended, that would allow her to drive the conversation. She did bring it up; she must want to talk about it. And selfishly, the more they talked about her father, the less likely it would be that she would press him to discuss what he almost let slip earlier—that if it weren't for Otto carrying that old bastard's bones out of the boarding house, they probably wouldn't be in this mess.

Jo appeared to ponder the topic for some time. She began several times before apparently changing her mind and biting her lip. "Killed himself in bed. Next to my Mama. And my little brother. Shot himself with a pistol."

Otto gasped audibly. The story itself was unbelievable, but as he looked at the beautiful, strong, and confident young woman, it was hard to imagine she had experienced something so tragic. "Why?" he asked.

"I don't know." She might have wanted to say more but gave up.

Seeking to comfort her, Otto steered the conversation in another direction. "What was he like?"

"I was born in New York. Papa's dream was to move to San Francisco and open up an oyster house. Back in the old country, my family were merchants. They weren't fishermen. But Papa heard there were a lot of opportunities here in oysters."

Otto knew this to be true. Oyster fishers went out daily on the bay and hauled in tons of high-demand shellfish.

"When he moved here with his brothers, he worked a bunch of odd jobs until he saved up some money to rent the space for the restaurant. My uncle loaned him the rest of the money to open it up." Jo took a breath, and a sad smile flickered across her lips. "You should have seen him; he was so proud. That little place sparkled, and I'll never forget it smelled like garlic and lemons. He put his whole heart into it."

Jo shifted, seeming uncomfortable. She looked down at her feet and forced out the rest of the words. "But then Papa found out the fishers, his suppliers, got mixed up in some bad business. Their boats got burned in the middle of the night, and then Papa's reputation went downhill for doing business with the wrong people. No one else would sell him oysters at a fair price. He lost the place."

"But it wasn't his fault! Didn't they know he had nothing to do with the fishermen who engaged in questionable business practices?" Otto asked.

"They knew or suspected, at least, so they didn't stop selling to him altogether. They wanted time for him to prove himself, but he didn't have the time. He was bankrupt within three months and never the same after that. When he couldn't find work, he couldn't support us. And he owed money to his family, so they never forgave him. So, I guess that's why he must have ended it— he thought we'd be better off."

Otto had a thousand questions, most of which were probably not appropriate. "What about your mother?"

"She left. She said she was doing it for me, but I didn't believe that for a second." Jo clenched her fists so that her nails dug into her palms.

"So why exactly are we going to find her?"

"I need answers."

A young woman in Salvation Army garb approached them. "We're beginning to transport less critical patients to Golden Gate Park. You look like you could still use some rest, son. Both of you do. Would you like a ride?"

Otto looked back toward the building. The quickly approaching firestorm turned the facade into a sharply contrasted silhouette against the glowing backdrop.

He rose to his feet slowly and nodded cordially to the woman.

"Come on, Jo." Otto reached out to touch her shoulder. "Let's go to the park."

When his fingers made contact, Jo pulled away slightly. He didn't know if she was drawing away emotionally or needed some space. After everything they had been through, he hoped no damage had been done. He tore off the medication tag identifying himself as a patient and slugged toward the waiting vehicle.

Chapter Nineteen

The wagon to Golden Gate Park meandered through the mangled city blocks of Hayes Valley and Lower Haight. Landmarks were unrecognizable if they stood at all, and a thick veil of ash shrouded everything in sight. Jo was rattled more from the retelling of her traumatic past than from the wagon traversing over the bumpy streets. Her upset was not with Otto's insistence on talking about Papa's death so much as her willingness to talk about it—to speak the words out loud.

It was the first time since it happened almost seven years ago that she shared it with another person. She never opened up to Mrs. Tucci about it, and Mrs. Tucci seemed to know that the subject was best left alone. So distracted, Jo lost track of the wagon's turning pattern amidst the havoc percolating at every corner. She was only vaguely aware of the roundabout trajectory they took, circumventing the fires toward the park that spanned from the middle of San Francisco all the way to the Pacific Ocean.

She decided that she was upset with herself for revealing so much to Otto. She had never felt so vulnerable. Now the reality of Papa's suicide was out in the open, and she couldn't just ignore it. So foolish. She let her guard down, and for what? A handsome young man who was kind. She felt weak. When she looked at him, he grinned in response.

Maybe if he learned too much more about her, he would see her true self—a broken, imperfect girl with a tragic past who only wanted to fade into the background. She couldn't let her guard down again. If she let him get too close, he would leave her, just as everyone else she cared about had. She was sure of it. It was too much to take. She'd be abandoned. Again. A feeling all too familiar. She became angry for allowing herself to grow attached to him.

The wagon jolted to a stop, and Jo dismounted. People greeted them. They spoke of a welcome supply of provisions back at camp. Jo realized how hungry she was and took them up on the offer. The pair ascended the path through the trees of the easternmost side of Golden Gate Park that reminded her of a forest.

Jo stayed a few steps ahead of Otto, choosing to ignore his existence. It felt unusual and foreign to have this much wildlife in the center of such a large city. It had an odd effect on her, taking the edge off her anger. Even though the air was smoky, the surprisingly dense plant life put a spark of freshness into the atmosphere that rejuvenated her.

She recalled times as a young girl when she had explored the park with Papa. He took her past the lily pond to the buffalo paddock to watch Sarah Bernhardt and Ben Harrison, the Park Commission's prized bison, graze in their urban oasis.

Then he would take her to the aviary. Jo loved how they could sit for hours on a green park bench inside a long hallway constructed of redwood beams and netting. They would watch hundreds of songbirds swoop, glide, and croon, feeling as though she and Papa were the ones in the birdcage.

"Listen to the sparrow sing, Bellisima! If you listen closely, you'll hear they don't all sing the same tune. How else would they shine brightly enough to fall in love? You are my little Passerotta."

Passerotta meant little sparrow. From then on, Papa liked to call her that. Though a term of endearment for a child learning to fly, the expression meant much more to Jo. She recalled Papa in the birdcage as he told her stories of how he met Mama. He saw her from a distance in the market when a flower fell out of her hair, and he picked it up, got down on one knee, and gave it back. She kissed his cheek, and they fell in love instantly. Every time Papa told the story, he would kiss Jo on the cheek and surprise her by putting a flower in her hair. Jo touched her hair, feeling for an invisible flower. Those were happy memories.

"Is that a smile?" Otto asked.

She had nearly forgotten he was there. "Perhaps . . ." she hummed. She wasn't as upset anymore, so she revisited her feelings for him. Never had anyone made her so frustrated, yet simultaneously, so captivated.

Jo was not prepared for what she would encounter as they exited the grove. Seas of people flowed through smatterings of makeshift tents and shacks as if an entirely new city had sprung up from the ashes. Survivors bantered, gossiped, laughed, and joked, not acting like people who had been displaced and rendered homeless just hours ago.

A young girl ran up to them, holding a couple of dented pewter mugs.

"Excuse me, Miss and Mister. Would you care for some stew?" The girl, about seven, was missing two of her front teeth and spoke with a lisp.

Jo took a mug and noticed a long line of folks waiting to receive food. Each person in the queue of hungry homeless clutched a different container: cracked cups, chipped plates, anything that would hold a meal. At the front of the line, a pair of middle-aged, motherly-looking types ladled indecipherable brown stew into each receptacle.

Jo and Otto joined the back of the line, which moved quickly. An aroma of sweet broth cut through the murky air as they made their way closer to the front. Jo saw a sign with big black handwritten letters that read Meals for Victims. She felt that she was not worthy of a free meal—so many others needed it more than she did.

"Here you go, dear. Plenty of fresh vegetables there will surely restore your strength." A woman with kind eyes scooped Jo's ration of stew and held it up. Jo did not lift her mug to receive it.

"Where did all this food come from?" Jo asked.

"Why, everyone." The gracious woman's wide arms motioned behind her where Jo could view the entire camp. "So many souls have cleared their cupboards of perishables to contribute to the meals. The benevolence of the many during times of great hardship never ceases to amaze me."

"Come on, sweetie, hold out your cup," the matron whistled. The ladle of stew dripped, but Jo didn't budge. "You okay, dear?" The woman's gaze seemed to show genuine concern, not only politeness. She shifted the ladle over to Otto's mug, which he accepted without hesitation.

Jo reflected for a moment and wondered if she was indeed okay. The gravity of the extraordinary situation settled in. She had lost everything. Every last thing she owned, though admittedly not very much. Every place she ever called home. She lost her family and her closest friend. It was all just . . . gone. She had no way to communicate the magnitude of her loss to this kind woman, so she just bit her lip, closed her eyes, nodded, and fought back the tears.

"Come on, Jo, aren't you gonna eat?" Otto grunted with a mouthful of potatoes. The woman got starry-eyed and ripped off her apron, tossing it toward her unprepared partner with nothing that resembled accuracy.

"Now, Gladys, don't go disappearing again. We have a lot of hungry mouths to feed!" said the woman left to pick up the fallen apron.

Gladys shot around the table and swept her arm around Jo's waist. "Hold your horses, Eloise," she huffed. "Now, child, I have just the thing." She led Jo deeper into the camp as Otto followed at a distance, shoving mouthfuls of stew down his gullet with his fingers. They wove around distinct piles of trunks overflowing with personal belongings until they came to a makeshift stove on an open flame with a saucepan resting on top.

Jo's mouth watered as Gladys peeked into the pan and took an exaggerated whiff, stirring the contents with a wooden spoon. Chocolate. She tasted the concoction and shook her head in disapproval before grabbing a metal whisk. "The trick is to use equal parts water and cream," she explained while violently whipping the mixture. "And just a dash of vanilla," she whispered.

Gladys grabbed the pan off the stove with one hand and stuck her pinky in it with the other. She took a look at the frothy consistency as it dripped down her finger, then stuck it in her mouth.

"There." She declared, grabbing a teacup from inside the box sitting on the stove.

"Would you like some?"

"No, thank you," Jo said impulsively. Aunt Rosalina had taught her that anyone who offered items of value to strangers did so out of polite societal obligation. Or because they wanted something. Either way, the only proper response was to decline.

Gladys held the cup out to Jo and insisted. "It's okay to say yes, dear. We would never get anywhere if we didn't let someone occasionally do us a kindness."

Jo reached out slowly to accept the cup.

"And one day," Gladys added, pulling the cup back a moment, "when you can do God's work, you'll hope for another unfortunate soul to accept your kindness, won't you?"

Jo nodded and took the cup. It was hot, and it burned her hands slightly. Jo had never had drinking chocolate before, but she had always wanted to try it. Before she could, a gruff uniformed man strutted up to them. The officer pointed at the fire with the end of his rifle and placed his finger uncomfortably close to the trigger.

Still a distance away, Otto backed away and waved for Jo to follow; she could tell he wasn't about to take any chances around another firearm.

"You have to put that out." The officer grunted, staring at Gladys without a hint of pleasantry.

"Sir, whatever do you mean?" Gladys asked.

"Don't be coy with me, ma'am. No open flames allowed on account of fire danger."

"Well, as you can see, kind sir, if you look around, there is no possible way these flames could catch on anything."

"Rules is rules, lady."

She looked him up and down, then reached into a bag by the fire and pulled out half a sandwich. "You look positively famished. You wouldn't be interested in this sandwich, would you?"

He shifted his weight uncomfortably. "Well, uh." His stomach growled, almost on command. "Just be careful, ma'am."

The soldier took the sandwich and went along his way. Gladys spun around with a satisfied look and shoved the drink back into Jo's face.

"Okay. Yes, thank you." Jo accepted the drink from Gladys. How could she refuse after the lengths Gladys had gone to keep her fire burning?

Jo took a sip. The luxurious liquid danced around Jo's tongue. The drink combined sweet and bitter perfectly, and the vanilla gave it a decadent aroma.

"You should invite your friend over," she nodded in Otto's

direction.

Jo called Otto over, and Gladys poured him his own cup.

"Normally, I wouldn't fix this in the middle of the day in April," said Gladys. "But I didn't want the cream to go to waste, and I find that nothing lifts the spirits quite like sweetened cocoa."

"Thank you," Jo said after a couple of deliberately slow swallows.

"It's the most delicious drinking chocolate I've ever had," exclaimed Otto.

Gladys was right. The chocolate lifted Jo's spirits, and for a moment, she ignored the layer of smoke hanging above their heads. The sky seemed to hang lower than usual, making her almost claustrophobic if she gave it too much thought.

"It's easy to be overcome with fear," said Gladys gently, eyeing the couple as if she could read their minds. "And rightfully so. The heavens opened up today with power so stupendous that it shifted the course of all our destinies. It is too omnipotent to combat."

"So, what can we do?" Jo said helplessly.

"We ride out the storm as best we can, child. The insignificant hands of man cannot match the forces of nature."

"I can't believe it's gone," Jo cried. "All of it. The whole city. There's no coming back from this. It will never be the same."

"I know it's not easy. But open your eyes. Look around. You will see that the worst circumstances bring out the best in people."

The idea that there could be good that comes out of this, in the end, was beyond comprehension. Surely if something this tragic and at this magnitude and scale could happen to this beautiful city, then there is an evil and vindictive power at work.

Gladys motioned with her eyes over to the next row of ramshackle setups. "Take a look around."

Jo took her cup of hot chocolate, along with Gladys's advice. She stood amid thousands of people of every imaginable nationality, all thrown together without any sense of order or reason. Though chaotic, there seemed to be a certain harmony.

An Italian family had set up nearly the entirety of their household's contents on the grassy field. How they transported it all here, Jo had no idea. As the parents walked away, probably to fetch another load, they left their baby behind, who screamed next to a neighboring German fiddle player improvising a melodic accompaniment.

An elderly white man sat under a wide umbrella, sharing it openly with a Chinese man half his age. This scene would have been unimaginable yesterday, but here they were, two men from different worlds coexisting.

Jo took a moment to take in the gravity. People of all possible backgrounds and statuses intermingled. Folks in nightclothes didn't seem to care about the matter as they sat next to children of all ages and dogs and cats and birds in cages.

Every person around her had lost something today, if not everything. It was an unfathomable loss, but the spirit of the camp was positive. Not happy, per se, but welcoming, accommodating, and supportive. This mass of people did not seem to see the lines of class or nationality as rigidly as before. It was odd, but it was wonderful.

Gladys came up behind Jo and tapped her shoulder lightly. "The Great Equalizer, they're already calling it. The quake left no one untouched. Every last one of us a victim. Every last one of us a survivor."

"I hate that word. Victim." The smell of the word was pungent as it rose from her lips. It sounded so helpless and cruel. And calling her a "survivor" seemed like a fancier way of saying prey.

"Now, child," she wagged her finger, "accepting you are a victim of circumstance does not carry the admission of powerlessness. If anything, it brings with it a certain level of strength."

"It's okay to admit you're a victim, Jo," Otto chimed in. "It doesn't mean anyone thinks any less of you."

Jo could not fathom how she had gotten to this place of being a victim, and she couldn't understand why someone like Gladys, or Otto for that matter, would bother taking a particular interest in helping her. Why her, out of everyone who needed help?

Since Papa's death, she had spent her entire life fading into the background, disappearing into the fog with the rest of humanity. She tried hard not to stand out. Every time she emerged, something terrible happened. Someone would scold her for doing something wrong; someone would tell her to do something differently.

After a while, the purpose behind this act of fading became a habit. Any day that passed without anyone saying hello was a good one. She didn't have to worry about what anyone else thought of her that day. She hadn't let anyone down for not meeting their expectations.

But the earthquake changed everything. Not only did she receive attention from others, but she wanted—no—craved it. For once, the idea of people being aware of her existence did not make her skin crawl. When Gladys looked out for her, Jo felt comforted.

"Take me, for example. Do I look like a victim?" Gladys turned to the side, tilted her chin up, and posed like a Roman statue.

Jo shook her head. "No, ma'am."

"I lost three babies by the time I was twenty-four. Problems with their hearts, the doctors said, each one of them. Believe me, it would have been easy to give up after that. To call it quits and take a long walk off a short pier." Gladys had a sadness in her eyes so deep that Jo worried she would forget to come up for air.

Jo realized at that moment that it wasn't about her. Not completely.

"But the way I see it, I'm standing before you today because I made a choice," Gladys continued. "I take the love I had for those three babies, and the love I can't give them as they grow older, and I use it in my work with the church. I care for all the tiny lost souls that cross my path."

Jo noticed the gold cross that hung on a thin chain around Gladys's neck. She felt sad about her losing her children. She couldn't even begin to imagine the pain.

"What you said about going on to help people when they need it, that's what happened to you, isn't it?" Jo asked. "You went through all you did so you could be strong enough when someone else needed it."

Gladys nodded. "And also to be able to recognize when someone else needs that help because we're not all accustomed to asking for it ourselves."

Jo thought of the story of the boy and his father—the story finally made sense. The boy had to call upon his father to utilize all his strength. Jo needed that help now, and Gladys needed Jo to accept it.

If she were to refuse the kindness, Gladys would feel unable to help. She imagined what it would be like to feel useless when you were in a position to be of use; she didn't want to be responsible for Gladys feeling that way. "May I have another cup of cocoa?" Jo asked.

Gladys beamed and refilled Jo's cup.

Chapter Twenty

Golden Gate Park, Wednesday, April 18, 1906, 4:47 p.m.

tto's head throbbed. The day's weight caught up with him, and his wound hurt more than he cared to admit aloud. He needed a break before his side split open. "Jo, I'm going to go sit for a minute."

"Is everything all right?" she asked.

"Yes, of course. I'm just tired. Why don't you find us a spot to spend the night? I'll look for you a bit later."

Jo's eyes narrowed in suspicion, but she didn't say anything.

"I promise." He settled himself in a quiet spot under the shade of a tree, and Jo walked away. Otto didn't feel much like himself. In a way, he felt more alive than he had his entire life. She had gotten under his skin like gunpowder. If given the right ignition source, he would surely explode at any moment.

He overheard people talking about the fires blazing through every corner of the city, obliterating everything they touched. It instilled a fear in him, but curiously not one of self-preservation—*it was about Jo*. She was all that mattered to him. Her safety, yes, but also the potential for something more after all of this was done and things went back to normal, whatever that meant. The pull toward her was like whales migrating south in springtime. It was built into his very being. To deny her would be to deny his very nature. He had to be with her, no matter the effort or the cost.

He thought of what had transpired at the Pavilion. He should never have let Jo be alone in deciding if Bernard would be left to die. The weight of that must be taking a toll on her. *It wasn't fair.* Now she had to live with that, and he had to live with his guilt for allowing it to happen. But not just that—he also felt responsible for everything that Bernard did to them both since saving him back at Alice's boarding house. If he hadn't played hero, they wouldn't be in this mess.

He wished he could take it all back. He wished he hadn't saved Bernard after the earthquake hit. He pondered how his compassionate action for another man's life could have come back to haunt him so much that he would wish him dead.

Regret was not something Otto knew well. He strived to live life as purposefully as possible. He never wanted to look back, only forward. But the weight of these last hours was so dense with disappointment he couldn't help but be angry with himself.

Otto awoke from a restless nap drenched in sweat and disoriented. He ambled to his feet and wandered in the direction that Jo had been before they parted. By the time he found her, the sky glowed orange as the setting sunlight passed through the thickest path of smoke. He expected to see fires pop up around the campsites until he remembered from the incident with Gladys that they were banned, not to mention probably a sore subject amongst the new fleet of vagrants.

Jo sat cross-legged on the ground in a circle with three smiling children, her long brown hair tickling the small of her back. A young girl with two missing front teeth spotted him looking in their direction. "Mister, you wanna play?" She pointed at the ground. "We didn't have a string, so we drew a circle in the dirt with a stick instead." The girl collected three brilliant marbles from outside the hand-sculpted boundaries of the game and placed them carefully in the lap of her dress.

Jo turned around to see the newest possible contender for their game. When she saw Otto, her eyes widened. "You found me." She clambered to her feet.

"I promised you I would. Did you wish I hadn't?" A wave of insecurity washed over him—another unfamiliar feeling. He was afraid that Jo didn't want him around.

"I don't know exactly." She sang as she teased her wavy locks. "I guess I wasn't sure you would want to."

"I'm sorry, I'll go." Otto winked before turning away to act a departure, but seeds of doubt crept in through the cracks. Had he misread Jo's signals? Maybe she wasn't interested in him at all. Maybe he had better stick to his original plan and leave the city forever. He knew the feeling well; he used to give up when things got complicated. Cut ties with everyone and everything and start anew. *Safer.*

He turned to check on her just as he felt a hand on his arm. There she was with her beautiful face right in front of him. He realized then how long her eyelashes were. Like butterflies. She bit the side of her lip and blinked so many times he thought she might take flight.

"Hey, Otter . . .?"

He imagined all the things she could possibly say to him. That he hoped she would say.

I missed you.

I'm glad you came back.

Never leave me again.

She looked up into space, apparently gathering her thoughts. But she said none of those things. "Where are you going, Paris?" she said with a sly smile.

"I don't know. I feel like this may not be the place for me," he said.

She pulled her hand back. "What . . . what do you mean?"

He couldn't tell her he had an indescribable pull to run away again. He couldn't admit that he was scared she didn't feel the same way and that it would be easier to leave. "What do you want me to say, kiddo? I can't stick around. There's nothing for me here."

"There you go again, being selfish."

That couldn't be further from the truth. "What do you mean, selfish?"

Jo's arms erupted toward the surrounding crowd. "Just look around," she hollered. "Look at all these people making the best of a crummy situation. They're helping one another. How could you be here and see all of this and still want to run away? Do you think you're better than us?"

Otto stared at his feet. The word "us" caught him by surprise as much as the accusation. He felt small. And frustrated with himself that Jo would think he didn't care. Did she think his privileged upbringing made him believe he was better than she was?

"I didn't come here for them, Jo. I came here for you. I was worried about you after what happened back there."

"There you go again, Otter, thinking I need to be saved."

"Don't you?"

Jo fumbled, tongue-tied. "Maybe—maybe I'm not worth it. Did you think about that?"

Otto couldn't help but be sad for her. She thought where she came from mattered to him. Maybe on some level, he had judged her based on what little he knew about her past.

Otto sounded an exaggerated sigh in Jo's direction. He calmed his tone and hoped that would calm her as well. "Hush, Josephine."

He extended his open hand. "Come here."

She accepted cautiously, and he walked with her in silence. He wanted to take her somewhere private where they could talk. He knew a place where they could go.

He led Jo into the heart of Golden Gate Park, where they crossed over a bridge to a path that swirled around and around a small funny island in the middle of Stow Lake. With every lap, they climbed higher. Otto winced with every step of increased elevation.

"I wonder if it survived the quake," Otto thought out loud.

"Wonder if what survived?" Jo panted heavily.

"Sweeny Observatory," he uttered as they approached the crest of Strawberry Hill and saw evidence of the wreckage. "Damn. What a shame."

The observatory had sat perched atop the hill, a distance from the rest of the park's hustle and bustle. The couple stumbled over the rubble of what once was a two-story colosseum-like structure.

"Best views of the city from up here, if you ask me," he said somberly.

They struggled to see what remained under the waning diffused sunlight. The panorama's crimson glow increased in intensity and distracted them from the collapsed structure before them.

"I remember my first time up here. I came with my parents for a picnic. My Pop and my Ma. It was before my sister was born. We took a carriage all the way up here and brought a slew of midday snacks we enjoyed in this little tucked-away world."

"Incredible," said Jo. "I've lived in San Francisco most of my life, but I've never been here before."

"It's a shame you couldn't see it before tonight." He tried to recall just how many times he had begged his father to return to this place. They never did. Not as a family.

The two circled the center of the derelict landmark, disbelieving the earthquake's toll, even up there. They sat together on one of the largest of the displaced observatory stones. It had cracked down the middle when it fell but wasn't quite split into two independent pieces.

"I used to come up here a lot to think and draw," Otto said.

"You draw?"

"Not very well. I mostly like to draw houses. The kind on Nob Hill and in Western Addition."

"The fancy ones with all the ornate details and all kinds of colors?"

"Yeah, those are the ones. Queen Annes, they're called."

"You've got a thing for buildings and stuff, don't you?"

"I guess so. I don't know what it is—I just love that no two buildings are alike. It's like each one has its own personality. Does that make sense?"

He wasn't exactly sure where his love for architecture came from, but he guessed it was from being exposed to the construction process of his family's home when he was growing up. Their home was one of several on Fillmore Street, built from the ground up by native Germans. All the gentlemen on his street had hired the same architect, yet each home had a unique design.

When Jo didn't say anything, Otto worried that he sounded crazy talking about buildings as living things.

"Actually, it does. That's how I feel about my maps," Jo flashed a smile but then glowered. "Well, felt."

"Yeah, those things were almost the death of you. Why do you love them so much?"

"It's like I have a bird's eye view of the city." She gazed at the shoreline from the Golden Gate to China Basin. "Each one has unique geography, topography, and placement in the world around it: the mountains, waterways, railways, even the monuments. You can see how all those elements come together and influence the street patterns and the orientation of the city centers and neighborhoods. You almost get a sense of the city's pulse."

Otto pondered this. He envisioned transforming into a bird and climbing higher and higher into the sky to see San Francisco from this new angle. When he saw it clearly in his mind's eye, he understood her perspective completely. He grew giddy and inched closer to Jo, then took her hands into his. "I understand perfectly! It's like the city itself has a heartbeat. A soul. That's precisely why I fell in love with painting."

"How is that?"

"There's a style called impressionism. If you stand really close to a painting by Claude Monet or Edgar Degas, you can appreciate it for all its detailed brushwork and careful blends of color. But it's not until you step back that you see the whole picture. It's impossible not to appreciate the absolute brilliance and mastery of it all. It's like—"

"—magic," Jo added.

"Exactly."

Otto gazed at her, enchanted. They found a deep and sturdy common ground, like a bedrock foundation engineered to withstand stronger quakes than the recent one. He was sure she felt the same way.

"Jo?"

"Yes, Otter?" her voice quivered.

"I don't think I'm better than you."

"Oh?" She blinked her butterfly wings at him again.

"Truth is . . ." he scooted in her direction, closing half the distance between them. "You inspire me."

"And you," she inched toward him until he felt her breath on his neck, "keep surprising me." She closed her eyes.

He licked his lips and turned his head to kiss her.

Then the earth rumbled. *Again.* It sent them sailing away from one another.

Chapter Twenty-One

Strawberry Hill, Golden Gate Park, 6:12 p.m.

Jo fell backward, gripping the stone platform wildly with open palms and splayed fingers. Her heartbeat sped like a horse entering a gallop, and she began to sweat. She tried to fight the urge to relive Papa's suicide, but she couldn't. She saw it as clearly as it was yesterday: Peter's crying. Blood and brain matter splattered all over Mama's face. Mama screaming at Jo to go back into her room.

When she caught her breath, Jo opened her eyes and saw Otto standing in front of her, his eyes to the darkening horizon.

"That was no earthquake, was it?" she shuddered. "It was an explosion."

"You're right, Jo. That's dynamite," said Otto. "Did the fire reach a stockpile or something? From a mining operation?"

There was another blast. Then another. And another.

"That doesn't sound like it hit something by accident," she said. "It would have gone all at once. Just listen."

They waited a moment. Then four more blasts in equal succession.

Otto's eyes got wide as he spun around toward her. "There's a pattern! Someone's doing this on purpose. What on Earth could they be destroying? Haven't the fires already done enough damage?"

Her being's every fiber wanted to send her into her dark place, but she shook some sense into herself. She needed to focus long enough to diagnose the explosions. Why would people be trying to tear down buildings? Was it malicious? Was it because they couldn't bear to see them burn, and they wanted the destruction to be on their terms?

Jo's realization sparked. "Oh my gosh. Are they—?"

More bangs came in quick succession and in sets of four, and although the sound echoed throughout the peninsula, they all sounded from the same location to the northeast.

"They're making a firebreak." Otto acknowledged.

Another series of detonations erupted into the city's abnormally warm smoke-filled air. Every bang brought a reminder of Papa and that night. Jo slammed her eyes shut and started to shake. "Go away. Go away." She heard herself say the words. "Papa!" she screamed. "Papa, no!" Her father's arms embraced her. *No, they weren't Papa's— they couldn't be. They were Otto's.* "I hate him! How could he leave us? Why would he leave me?"

Otto's arms tightened around her. Jo sobbed out of control. She wasn't looking for answers as much as finally accepting what had happened. It sank in that Papa had taken his own life, and the pain was as bad, if not worse, than when it happened. Never until this moment had she been angry with Papa. Sure, she had mourned and missed him but never blamed him. *Not until now.*

Jo opened her eyes—she sat with her knees tucked under her chin, her arms wrapped around her legs as she rocked and cried. Otto stretched one arm around her shoulders while placing the other gently on her wrists.

She had never felt this out of control before. A weight sat on her throat, cutting each breath short. If only she could come up for air, but she couldn't break free.

"Jo. Josephine." The echoing words swam toward her.

Otto shook her, and she bounded back into reality. He said, "Jo, tell me which one of your cities you would like to visit. Which one?"

That's stupid. Why think of something like that at a time like this?

"Jo, which city? Where do you want to go? Paris? Chicago? New York? Boston?"

She realized he was trying to distract her so that she would humor him. Jo swallowed a few big gulps of air, then nodded in response to him and wiped her eyes with her palms.

"Well," Otto hooted, "you have to pick one, silly. You can't just say yes to all of them and magically go everywhere at once. Who do you think I am, your fairy godmother?"

Jo snorted, and an unexpected laugh escaped. Otto laughed louder in response, and the two surrendered to the fit of hilarity. After their laughter died down, Otto's question still hung in the air.

"I'll go to whichever one you're running to."

He blushed and looked toward the sky. She faced the same direction—a few stars peeked through the veil of smoke, an eerie reminder that the normal world beyond kept moving on despite the one around them coming to a screeching halt. The stars still came out at night, despite her every feeling that the world had stopped spinning.

"Well, how about that." He whispered. She didn't know if he talked about the stars or what she said.

"Papa always said, *once you promise it to the stars, it must come true.*"

He jumped up to his feet. "Jo, I swear that nothing bad can happen as long as you're up here on this hill with me." He pointed to the brightest star. "I swear it to that star!" He pointed to another star. "And to that one. On this hill, you're safe. You're untouchable."

No one could promise any of those things. A person could never hide from tragedy. It had a way of seeping through the cracks or pouncing when least expected or deserved. But the purpose behind his words was what mattered most. He wanted her to feel safe. And at that moment, she did.

"Ow," he groaned, clutching his side. "I shouldn't have jumped like that."

She chuckled. "Yeah, Otto, you'd better rest."

"It's probably too late to head back to camp," he said, "Too dangerous to climb down the hill in the dark. Best sit tight here for the night."

Music to her ears. For once, she wasn't so upset that circumstance dictated her fate. If she stayed here tonight, alone on this island out of reach of the flames, it might as well be in his arms.

"Come here, you," he whispered, pulling her closer and kissing her on her forehead. She leaned into him and felt every muscle in her body relax.

"And do me a favor?" he added, putting his arm around her. "Don't call me Otto. It sounds weird coming from you."

Jo giggled. "You got it, Otter. Goodnight."

Jo awoke with a start; despite the warmth in the air, she shook in a fit of uncontrollable cold chills. Her teeth chattered, and she shivered so violently that she woke Otto.

"What's wrong?" he asked.

"So . . . cold," she muttered through the bone-chilling chattering. It was as if she had no control; her body was so stiff that she couldn't sit up.

"Jo, I've seen episodes like these before. My mother had them when she was pregnant with my sister."

"I'm f-f-f-fine!" She realized it was a stretch. She was so disoriented she barely knew where she was.

"Here," he said firmly. Instinctively, he took off his jacket and threw it around her shoulders.

When she finally could control her breathing, she tried to speak.

"I'm sorry. I'm so cold." She chattered between labored breaths.

"Bad dream?"

"I . . . don't know." Was she dreaming? She couldn't remember. She knew that she was still thinking about Papa and the shot. She heard another series of dynamite detonations. The memories came flooding back like a tidal wave slamming her against the jagged rocks of reality. She pushed her forehead down into her hands to try to keep them from pulling her below the surface.

"What's happening?"

Jo suddenly recalled details of the night Papa died that she had long forgotten. "The police commissioner showed up at the doorstep," she said, "And Mama was too shaken to answer the door. The officer said he received a neighbor's report of a loud bang. I led him upstairs, and Mama had baby Peter in her arms outside their bedroom, bouncing him violently to stop his crying. He was covered in blood. It was like something out of a nightmare. Mama's expression was vacant as if her soul escaped her body to float away in pursuit of Papa's ghost."

Jo twisted her neck to look up at the sky as if she were staring at a distant memory.

"I'm so sorry," Otto said pensively.

His pity made her fume, though how else could a person be expected to respond after what she had said? Still, she had more anger than she knew what to do with.

"It's Papa who should be sorry! He should have worked harder to keep the restaurant, but he didn't. He shouldn't have given up on finding a job, but he did. He failed us. And when he knew he had failed us, he gave up and killed himself. He didn't just leave us with nothing, he left us with less than nothing. My uncle forced me to work for him to repay Papa's debts. How could Papa have done that to me?"

Her anger shifted from Papa to herself. How could she be so ignorant for so long? She let her love for him blind her to think he was an innocent victim of circumstance when Papa was responsible for his fate all along.

"I'm so stupid." She exclaimed loud enough for Otto to hear. "I should have known better than to think he was infallible. He was just a man."

She got up and walked in circles because she needed an outlet for her negative energy, and moving was the only thing she could do. She tripped on a piece of the crumbled observatory and recovered with a less-than-graceful swivel.

"He may have been just a man, but he raised you, and you didn't turn out so bad." He gave her a sheepish smile—this man who twenty-four hours ago was a stranger. His grin thawed her from the inside out.

"Jo," he leaped to his feet, spun around, and grabbed her hands. "Leave with me. Let's go to New York or anywhere else you want. Let's get out of this God-forsaken city and explore the world. I was going to do it alone, but it would be so much more exciting with you by my side. Come with me."

Jo gasped and turned to Otto, who stared at her, eyes wide in hopeful anticipation. *He's not joking.* "I . . . couldn't possibly." *Preposterous.* Leaving San Francisco was too inconceivable to become a reality. But she realized that the sound of the judgmental voice was not her own; it was Aunt Rosalina's. Then she wondered why she should stay at all. Her city had betrayed her. It had taken everything she loved, destroyed what it could, and mangled the rest, leaving an unrecognizable oblivion. "Well, perhaps . . ."

"Well? What do you think?"

So many questions. "I just don't see how it would work. Where would we go? What would people think if they saw a young unmarried couple traveling together? How would I find and afford clothes suitable enough for travel?"

"Well, I could help with the—"

"And then there are the hundreds of questions I still have for Mama. I've come too far now to forget everything and leave. If I don't get answers now, it will haunt me for the rest of my life."

"So, what are you saying?"

"My mother," she said. "I have to find her."

"But you said she hasn't been there for you, that you never needed her before. You've been on your own for years. What difference would it make now?"

An eerie deep red glow, hinting of sun beyond the smoke, overtook their hilltop sanctuary while Jo paced and pondered for a moment. Maybe she *should* run away. Maybe it was worth letting her mother believe Jo was missing or worse. It served Mama right for not being there when Jo needed her.

"Besides," Otto continued, "you've got me now."

She tried so hard to hope this could be true, that she could have someone in her life who cared and wanted to be with her. But she had no guarantee that he would stay. He could get bored with her next week and leave her at a train station mid-country without a penny in her pocket. "What do you mean I *have you*?" she asked. "Who am I to be worthy of you making such grandiose promises? I'm nothing."

"Stop that." He cut her off. "You know better than to think you're nothing more than the bottom scum on someone's shoe. You've left me transfixed, Miss Josephine. You're like a shooting star. They're so spectacular that you can't look away when you see one. You have to get it into your thick skull that you're good enough." He put his finger under her chin. "More than enough, kiddo."

His words left her spinning. This was too good to be true. She had somehow found something extraordinary amongst the misery. Like hell she would let it go. "Let's do it, Otter. Let's run away."

Chapter Twenty-Two

Conservatory of Flowers, Golden Gate Park, Thursday,
April 19, 1906, 8:12 a.m.

They made their way back to what could pass for civilization. It had been a full day since the earthquake now, and, by the look of it, every living soul in the city made camp in the park the night before. Otto couldn't wait to get out of the city with Jo by his side. He wasn't sure yet which way they should go, but he had his money on the Ferry Building.

A small crowd gathered in front of the Conservatory of Flowers as disheveled paperboys who looked like they hadn't caught a wink in a week threw stacks of newspapers off a delivery truck. The domed glass of the Conservatory was miraculously still intact, and its delicate white steeples stood in stark contrast against the morning's smokey skies.

"What time is it?" asked Jo. "I promised Emi I'd meet her here at the Conservatory at eight."

"I'm not sure," said Otto. "My pocket watch went missing after the earthquake."

"Come on," said Jo. "We need to find her."

"Wait a minute, hang on." Otto was curious to see the earthquake coverage in the paper.

The Call=The Chronicle=Examiner was printed across the top, signaling an unprecedented collaboration. All journalistic rivalries ceased in an unprecedented camaraderie: a joint publication of presses from Oakland. Did that mean, he wondered, that the exquisite Call building had fallen?

EARTHQUAKE AND FIRE: SAN FRANCISCO IN RUINS

The headline spanned the entire width of the paper without any images whatsoever. Otto had to do a double-take. For some reason, seeing the event in print made what he had just lived through more legitimate.

The crowd chimed in with each of their calculations. "Forty-eight seconds, my behind," one man said, a cigarette dangling from his bottom lip. "That quake was over a minute, no doubt about it."

"Ninety seconds!"

"Nearly two minutes!"

One woman sang. "A full five minutes, the ground was trembling!" Everyone promptly ignored her blatant exaggeration. "Well, it felt like it," she muttered.

Otto picked up a copy. The dismal headlines read, *No Hope Left for Safety of Any Buildings, Whole City is Ablaze, Mayor Confers with Military and Citizens.*

He turned the page. "*At Least 500 Are Dead,* it says. Impossible!" He counted on his fingers as he did some quick mental arithmetic. "All those collapsed boarding houses, hotels, and apartment buildings we saw, there were at least 300 corpses alone. And that's just what we saw ourselves."

Jo's eyebrows did somersaults. "Who's reporting these numbers?"

He put the paper down a moment so he could see her. "This

number will get a lot bigger once it's all said and done; just you wait."

His eyes darted down the page. *Newspaper Row is Gutted.*

"Oh no," Otto nearly toppled. "It says the Examiner and Call buildings were completely devoured." The thought of those iconic architectural masterpieces gone simply broke his heart. What was San Francisco without its skyline?

Whispers of martial law reverberated among the throngs of the newly homeless, which had multiplied since the previous night.

"Has martial law been declared?" Otto asked a nearby gentleman who also held a paper.

"No word of a declaration from Roosevelt, but you wouldn't know it by the way they're patrolling the streets. Anyone with a uniform is getting away with murder."

"No kidding," said Jo to Otto.

"After that display at the drugstore with Bernard and the trigger-happy boy dressed as a soldier, I think we'd best steer clear of anyone in uniform."

Otto figured mayor Eugene Schmitz must have had a hand in the shoot-to-kill order that now seemed to be plastered on every tree and lamppost in the city. And now, he was certain that the guard handling the store hadn't been a real officer.

"Otter, we'd better find Emi."

"Emi?" Otto shouted through the crowd.

"Emi, where are you?" Jo cupped her hand over her eyes and stood on her toes, trying to see over everyone's heads.

A male voice boomed over the crowd. "Bully ruins, brick and wall, through the night, I've heard you call. Sort o' sorry for each other, 'cause you had to burn and fall!" The man's bravado struck Otto's eardrums and reverberated deep into his ribcage like a shell fired from a Winchester.

A congregation of men's and women's voices sprang up in response, "In those damnedest finest ruins, I would rather be a brick!"

The lead voice continued, "From the Ferry to Van Ness, you're a God-forsaken mess, but the damnedest finest ruins, nothing more or nothing less."

The troop wove their way through the crowd, hoisting poignant signs that sported phrases:

I'd rather be a brick!

I'd rather bore a hole than be an Oakland mole!

Otto turned in Jo's direction. He feared how she might react to the demonstration. If the words got in her head, she might want them to stay. Her eyes were fixated on the display, and he could tell from her steady gaze that she was taking it all in.

"Don't tell me you're listening to this hullabaloo." He spoke in a stronger tone than he had intended.

Jo folded her arms. "What's wrong with them not wanting to leave?"

"Nothing. The crowd can stay and wallow in the ruins. Makes no difference to me."

"Then what's your problem?"

Otto rubbed the nervous sweat from his brow as he paced. "I don't have a problem." He bought himself time as he tried to figure out what was bothering him so much.

"This is their *home*," she said. "This is *our* home."

"See, they're trying to make you feel guilty for leaving." Something had triggered his cynicism. These folks didn't just condone rebuilding the city; they wanted to condemn those who would leave to save their own lives. It was as if they didn't truly love San Francisco if they weren't willing to make a home out of the ash and brick.

"Do you think it means we're cowards if we leave?" Jo asked.

"It's not our responsibility to fix San Francisco. We've got our whole lives ahead of us. There's no opportunity here anymore, just desperation covered in cinders."

He wondered if he believed that, or maybe he was just trying to convince himself that there was nothing for him here anymore. It was true enough for him two days before the earthquake; why would it be any different now?

It was enough of a burden to take over his father's business. His father's high expectations for his craft and the perfection that came with it were too much—but assisting with rebuilding the greatest city in the West? How could he believe he would be capable, let alone qualified? The burden was too much to shoulder. The need to flee surged inside him like reflux. *He had to get out of there.*

"Let's hurry up and find Emi so we can go. We can get to the ferries before they fill their daily passenger limits if we hurry. Or we can get the train if it's running."

Jo looked torn. Her head oscillated between him and the crowd like an automaton. "I can't, Otto. I'm sorry. I need to see my mother. I'll never be able to live knowing I didn't confront her when I had the chance."

The rejection hit his gut like a cannonball. He felt betrayed, although he knew it wasn't about him. "I understand. What if we could do both?" he said.

"What do you mean?"

"I think I know a way that we could get your mother *and* get out of the city."

He had to keep Jo from staying behind and risk losing her forever. "I'll steal my father's car."

"What do you mean? Can't you just ask to borrow it?"

"I can't exactly expect him to say, 'Okay, Otto, we forgive you for running away and abandoning the family; now here's my most precious possession.'"

"Good point."

He could tell by Jo's expression that the wheels were turning. She was always in problem-solving mode, thinking of new ways to attack a problem. He was in awe of her for this.

"Maybe if you just explain yourself? You got scared, confused, a temporary lapse in judgment," she said.

"That's not good enough. My father doesn't accept weakness as an excuse. Pop would hold an entire trial as my judge, jury, and executioner. Don't worry about it. All I need to do is find a way into the garage where he keeps the car. I just hope it's there." Pop kept the Cadillac locked in the garage across from their home, Fillmore Street at Fulton. It would be easy to break in with the right tools, but he might need to get creative if he couldn't find any.

Jo rubbed the back of her neck as her head swooped in doubtful circles. "If it's so much of a hassle, don't worry about it. I don't mind walking to Mama's; it's less than five miles from the park. It will only take a few hours, considering the extra time to navigate the roadblocks. It's getting out of the city that's going to be tricky. The ferry terminal is supposed to be a circus, and I heard someone say the trains aren't running yet. Plus, I heard someone say that folks are hijacking automobiles."

"They, who?"

"Soldiers, police, and criminals."

"Jo, you know how dangerous it is out there. The fires are still burning. It may be less than five miles, but it is such a treacherous journey, it might as well be across the Pacific." The thought of her departing on her own was too much to bear. What kind of girl would go marching back into harm's way after everything she had gone through? *A girl as stubborn as he was, that's who.*

"I'll be fine, Otter. Trust me. I just can't sit around and wait for you to get a vehicle that may or may not be there. And I doubt the roads are clear enough to get to North Beach anyway."

Jo lifted her index finger as if she had an idea and searched the ground for something. She picked up a rock, drew an X in the dirt with it, then pointed. "This is Washington Square. It's on Montgomery Avenue." She drew a diagonal line and retraced it for emphasis.

Then she drew some wavey lines under the diagonal one. "These are the areas that are on fire. You're going to have to go the long way around. Take Van Ness north." She drew two parallel lines to the left of the fires. "It's so wide it should be a natural fire barrier, and there should be enough room for the Caddy. Then turn right on Bay Street to avoid going up Russian Hill with the car and another right here onto Montgomery. I'll be waiting for you at Washington Square this evening. If you can't make it there by morning, look for me at my mother's house."

"455 Green Street," he said, remembering the address from the envelope.

She nodded.

"Jo, are you sure about this?"

"Yes. I know these streets. You're the one who has to navigate places you don't know. You got it?"

"Yes, ma'am. And once I pick you up, then what? Where should we go from there?"

"We have family in San Jose; I bet we could leave Mama and Peter there with my uncle. He has a cattle ranch on Mount Hamilton. Then, we can go anywhere we want."

Chapter Twenty-Three

"JoJo!" Emi screamed as she ran up to Jo.

Jo swung her arms around the young girl and stroked her waist-length black hair. "Are you okay? Where's Fitz and Tilly?" While Jo asked the question, her old friend Fitz hobbled over, sweating profusely and carrying the cat under his arm like a Christmas ham.

"Mister Fitz says he's *exasperated*." Emi over-enunciated the s and t sounds. Jo thought Emi didn't know what the word meant, making her speech endearing. She hadn't realized how much she had missed her little friend.

Jo drew away from Emi and reached for the feline in Fitz's arms. She scooped Tilly and held her tightly against her face. "Oh, Tilly girl, I'm so happy to see you." The intensity of Tilly's purr penetrated Jo's heart and refreshed more than sleep ever could.

"Don't you two look like you have been through the wringer?" Fitz wiped his brow.

"Fitz, thank you so much for looking after Emi."

"Aye, my pleasure, Miss Josephine. Spending time with the little miss has been a pleasure."

Otto leaned over and whispered into Jo's ear. "Fitz looks like he's about to drop dead any minute."

He was right. Fitz began a coughing fit, doubling over and heaving on his shoes. She couldn't very well trust that Emi could stay within his care for long. Jo thought about how she could take Emi with her, but she would be leaving the city with no idea where she was going. And it would be impractical to drag her along with Tilly through the ruined streets to North Beach. But then—Jo had an idea. "Emi, I want to introduce you to a friend of mine."

The group meandered through the camp, following Jo's lead. Gladys puttered around her fire, nurturing a pot with whatever she had managed to scrounge up for breakfast. She twisted around, apparently looking for something misplaced, when she laid eyes on Jo.

"Jo, darling! How are you this fine morning?" Gladys squealed. "Oh, and you've brought friends. Could I interest you all in some porridge?"

A divine scent of apples and spices wafted through to Jo's nostrils. She peeked in the pot—not much there. "No, thank you, Gladys. I'm fine, but I'm sure my friend Emi here would enjoy some." The two exchanged a look, and Jo instantly knew Gladys understood: she wanted Gladys to care for Emi.

"Listen, Emi," Jo knelt and looked into the girl's eyes as she gulped down her meal. "I'm going away for a while. I don't know when I'll be back, so I need you to stay with Gladys here. And I need you to look after Tilly. She's yours now, you understand?"

Emi nodded. "Yes, JoJo, I understand. I'll take good care of her. Promise." Emi investigated her cup of porridge at the last morsel left and hesitated before setting it on the ground. She gently took Tilly from Jo's arms and sat her down next to the cup. Tilly sniffed it a moment, then lapped it up, purring loudly.

"Oh, don't worry dear, little Emi will be fine. I have some jobs around camp that I could use some help with." She turned to the orphan. "How would you like to give me a hand with some things to help the other children?"

Emi nodded enthusiastically. Giving her work to do to help others was probably the best way to keep her distracted and make her feel like her life had purpose after such a tragedy.

Jo reached over and gave her one last embrace. Emi was strong. Jo knew she would be okay, especially under Gladys's care. But it didn't stop the feeling—another piece of her heart was being ripped away.

Chapter Twenty-Four

arcasses of trunks lay scattered on Haight Street, abandoned in the extraordinary effort required to haul them uphill to the sanctuary of Golden Gate Park. Otto and Jo walked in silence, their tension ricocheting off each trunk like a ping-pong ball. When they got to the bottom of the hill, they would need to go separate ways—four more blocks.

As they marched closer to Fillmore Street, Otto thought about his future. He was never one for calculating. His future seemed uncertain, but he wanted Jo in his life. If there was any chance of her not wanting to leave town with him, he had to squelch it. That meant one thing—he had to tell her how he felt.

Otto didn't believe that he deserved to have anything good happen to him. Jo's landing in his lap was too good to be true. He had to tell her now in case he never saw her again. His insides resembled the porridge he'd just eaten.

Three more blocks.

"It's really something, isn't it?" Otto avoided looking at Jo.

"What is?"

The way I feel about you. Come on, say it.

A man and woman trudged past, each wearing multiple layers of clothing. Clearly, they had found a way around lugging their trunk up the road.

Jo stared expectingly at Otto, launching his thoughts into aerial acrobatics. "The destruction, of course. It's just so awful." He cursed at himself silently. Why couldn't he just say the right words?

"Oh, yes. Just horrendous," Jo agreed.

"Everything that we've grown accustomed to, it's completely gone. It almost doesn't feel like it's the same city."

Jo nodded solemnly, gazing up at the buildings and down at the rubble. "I know where I am, but none of it looks familiar. It's like I'm in a foreign country ravaged by war. I could get lost if I spun around a few times."

Yes, that's it! She made him dizzy with adoration, and he could fall in love with her any minute, about to tumble headfirst. *Tell her, you idiot.*

A warped piece of metal lay beside the street under a few bricks. *Something to break into the garage. That might do the trick.* He picked it up, reassured.

Two more blocks.

"I fear it will never be the same again, but I almost don't want it to," Otto said.

"You mean you're glad the earthquake happened?"

"In a way, yes. Is that bad?" He waited a moment for her to voice her understanding. But she seemed disconnected. *How could she not see it?*

The earthquake is what brought them together. Jo and Otto would have passed each other like ships in a storm without that tragic event. "It's about time for something new . . . something different."

"Are you referring to the City Beautiful notion everyone's talking about? It sure would be nice to rebuild the city according to that plan. More parks, instead of a grid, a spider-web of streets centered around cultural hubs, and a grand city center. It's an intriguing idea, but I'm afraid it's unrealistic—"

"Listen, kiddo . . . being around you makes me batty."

Jo froze in her tracks. "Excuse me?"

Not exactly how he intended it to come out. She looked as if she had just sucked on a lemon.

"You're . . . disorienting."

"What? Are you lost already? It's one more block."

Okay, it was not getting better.

"What I mean is, you threw me for a loop." He was out of breath, partially from not finding the words, partially from the walk down the steep hill.

"I don't know what you mean," she stared blankly.

"Christ, Jo, do I need to spell it out for you?"

Her long brown hair, slightly tangled from sleep with no hat to mask it, flipped defensively in front of her face.

"What? Am I too stupid to understand now?" she asked.

"No, no, that's not what I—shoot, Jo. You make me all jumpy."

"Out with it already; you're confusing me."

They reached the intersection, where he grabbed her hand.

"I'm trying to say you came out of nowhere. I wasn't expecting you, and I'm still not convinced you're real. Look, I'm unquestionably smitten with you."

"You're delirious. You must have hit your head when you trespassed into the print shop."

"You mean *rescued you.*" He wagged a finger in her face.

"If that's how you wish to see it," she smiled playfully.

He drew her hand to his lips and kissed it softly. "Don't worry, Jo. I'll find you. We'll get out of this hell hole and be together."

"I have no doubt you will. I can't seem to get rid of you as hard as I try."

He laughed with her, and every particle of his skin, muscle tissue, and bones pulled at him to kiss her. He neared her but then drew back. *It wouldn't be proper.*

Custom dictated he should appear at her door and present her with a calling card. They would attend social events while she flirted, and he strove to impress her. He had to bring her small tokens of his affection and only in the presence of her mother.

But she had no door and perhaps no mother. That remained to be seen. They would never hope to attend the same social events as they were from two different worlds.

"Jo, may I—?"

"Yes." She closed the distance between them and tipped her head back.

All the customs in the world seemed unimportant when the world was on fire. *What did they have to lose?*

Otto leaned into her, and his lips touched hers. He felt her push into him, and the ash that fell around them transformed into a flurry of falling stars.

Chapter Twenty-Five

*e kissed me.* Jo's lips tingled with the memory of Otto's more than ten minutes after he had left her standing in the middle of Lower Haight. She watched his faded silhouette disappear beyond the smoke-enveloped hill a block and a half north of her.

Jo looked to the east toward her direction of travel and took a careful sip from Gladys's flask. "Drink sparingly. Water is now a scarce commodity," Gladys had told her. She couldn't help but feel that she had sinned by having a flutter of happiness amid the devastation.

The day before, Jo was buried alive, lost her family and closest friend, was nearly kidnapped, and almost died more times than she could count. Yet, all she could think about was the kiss. The world around her disappeared for a moment, and she floated in the vivid memory of Otto's soft yet firm lips against hers. Happiness and hope had replaced her questions and fears, and hope was the only thing scarcer than water.

She had hope that Otto would succeed in borrowing–or stealing–his father's automobile. She also had hope that he would find her again at Mama's house on Green Street and that they would all be able to leave the city safe and sound together.

As Jo descended into Hayes Valley, families lined the streets outside their condemned homes. Many looked in fine spirits, so her guilt for the glee she felt lifted slightly. It was as if they were having a midmorning picnic surrounded by all their belongings as they awaited some sort of holiday parade that would never come.

Jo stepped over a boundary of rubble into the area where yesterday's fire had begun. People called it the Ham and Eggs fire since the blaze caught when a woman cooked breakfast on her gas stove.

When Jo turned left onto Market Street, the air became thicker, and she began to cough. Horror and disbelief from the devastation that surrounded her replaced her previous lightheartedness. Jo's heart ached, and her lungs burned. Hayes Valley, a beautiful district full of San Francisco's vital services and impressive cultural centers, was ravaged. Even though she had seen the destruction the day before, it surprised her. The Mechanics Pavilion, where the makeshift hospital had just been the day before—*gone. City Hall, even the post office. All of it—completely gone.*

Jo thought about Bernard stuck on that roof. He would have perished. She pushed the guilt down as far as she could. If she was going to hell for her sins, there was nothing she could do about it now.

She missed Otto. If only he could have come with her. *I'm on my own. I must keep going.* She repeated the words, mustering enough courage to take each step closer to North Beach, which was still at least an hour away. The smoldering ruins of Market Street taunted her. When she passed entire blocks and did not see another soul, she doubted her choice to traverse the city.

A large crowd gathered at Lotta's Fountain. What a surprise that the landmark was still standing. It now served as a gathering place where people reunited with loved ones or pleaded for their safe return. Layers of soot and debris were caked on top of its lion-head spigots and ornate embellishments. The cast-iron structure had some stories to tell.

As Jo looked up at the skyline, she saw two major fires burning. One was located to the southwest, likely the merging of many blazes in the neighborhoods south of the slot, including her house, and one to the northeast. She'd have to be careful not to get too close as she made her way north.

She took a breath and turned left onto Kearny Street. Gladys's words bounced in her head like a kitten playing with string. To be a survivor, you must first accept that you're a victim. Every step drew her closer to the fire. Each one tested her resolve.

Jo clambered over the wreckage of an indecipherable business. The partial skeleton of a cypress stood in front of her amongst the wreckage. She arched her neck in disbelief and examined the branches of this miracle tree, most of them somehow spared in the uncompromising firestorm. She reached out and touched its black trunk, and the flame-kissed bark left a dark, inky residue on her fingertips. She used to sit under a tree like that in the park by her house. It was probably gone. This tree should be gone, too. It should not have survived. Yet it stood there tall and strong.

Then a realization sparked in her mind, as sharp as the moon on a clear black night.

I am the tree.

She planted her feet firmly in the scorched earth.

"I am the tree," she said aloud though no one was there to hear her.

I am rooted. I am strong.

She thrust her chest forward, pulled her arms back, and put her hands into the air like branches. This position made her feel stronger. Confident. Unwavering.

"I am a victim."

There was another heart-stopping boom in the distance, but

she didn't lose her balance or cringe quite as much this time. The tree's branches stirred.

"The tree is me."

Damaged. Imperfect. Flawed.

She, like the tree, had weathered an unfair and furious storm, and it wasn't over yet. This was not too much for her to handle. She would make it.

Jo trudged farther north on Kearny through burnt wreckage, weaving among the soulless corpses of the mightiest buildings in the city. She passed by a once grand hotel, now a leveled graveyard for blackened clawfoot tubs.

The ever-present rumble grew louder, and Jo headed right toward the explosions. Fear bubbled up in her belly and settled in her chest. Her heartbeat rattled her entire body and shook her equilibrium. She might be hurled back into her dark place—she fought the familiar feeling.

Jo conjured joyful memories that would counter her dangerous surroundings. She thought of Otto and their kiss. She thought of his bravery to set out on his own and follow his dreams, and it reminded her of Papa's story of why he came to live in San Francisco. *Papa would have liked him.*

She tried to remember the last time she saw Papa happy. For some reason, she couldn't stir up the memory of the last time she saw him smile. Was she starting to forget? She could only see the anguish on her mother's face. She spun around in the desolation, made sure no one was watching, and screamed louder than ever.

"I hate you, Papa." She hollered toward the horizon, toward her father. Her anger sputtered like a *Bolognese* on high heat. "You were so selfish. You did this to me on purpose. You didn't even have the decency to off yourself in private. You had to leave us to clean up your mess!"

Her rage was cut short when a hailstorm of red-hot debris pelted her. Embers shot through a window of a nearby house, and the place lit up like a Christmas tree. Flames leaped and hissed as the familiar firestorm winds whipped around her.

She ran. Her ankle throbbed with pain which slowed her down. *They're making the fires worse.*

She tore through the doomed neighborhood, her hands covering her mouth and nose as best she could. She sped past folded buildings that leaned on their neighbors like they had too much to drink.

Do they even know what they were doing?

Jo tried to catch her breath between bouts of panic and anger. The air was too thick in all directions. She had managed to put herself in a precarious position, so she spiraled out of control again. She fought to center herself.

I am the tree.

Jo willed herself to be strong, to focus on the solution, the way out, instead of the problem at hand.

The tree is me.

The fire closed in on her from all angles. She had nowhere left to run.

Chapter Twenty-Six

Fillmore and Oak, 9:45 a.m.

tto made his way up the hill into Western Addition. People said there wasn't as much earthquake damage there, and it made sense since somebody built the area on solid bedrock. If his family's home was standing, his father, mother, and little sister were probably inside, and Pop's precious Caddy sat in the garage. If there was one thing Otto could count on, it was that his father was nearly as bullheaded as he was, and Pop would refuse to relocate unless the President himself gave the order.

Pop's Model F was like a member of the family. He had purchased it brand new last year for nine hundred and fifty dollars, and the four-passenger car was about all he ever talked about at the dinner table. If he didn't talk about work, that is.

He had let Otto drive the Caddy once and only once. "Don't do this" and "be careful about that" caused tension to coil up Otto's neck so tightly that it almost popped his hat clean off his head. The pressure Pop piled on top of Otto's own fear that he would crash the car was too great. Otto threw up his hands, jumped out of the car, and walked the rest of the way home. If Pop couldn't trust him with the Caddy, how could he possibly take over the company?

The street was oddly quiet, most families probably sleeping comfortably in their beds, grateful they weren't stuck in the dirt with the rest of the city.

Otto spotted the garage which held Pop's Caddy, located across the street from their three-story Victorian home. The dual sliding doors were padlocked, as was customary when securing the precious automobile. He hoped the car would be inside.

Otto pulled the long, twisted piece of metal out of the back of his pants, shoved it between the wooden garage door and the locking mechanism, and bent the metal like a crowbar. He popped out one of the four large screws fastening the plate to the door, and the screw landed on the ground. *Ding.*

Otto drew back, looking around to be sure no one heard him. *He was in plain view.* Anyone could walk by at any time. They would probably think he was a regular looter. That could be a good thing or a bad thing, depending on who spotted him and whether they were armed. He didn't feel like having another gun pointed at him.

He shoved the tool back into place, this time more determined, and pulled back harder. The wood splintered as another screw fell and clanged on the ground.

Otto adjusted the lever's position and angle, bending it until the last two screws evacuated their housings, sending the metal hinge flying forward and spinning across the ground. The doors released their hold and slid outward with minimal effort, though they squalled, announcing their widening gap, betraying his stealthy mission.

His prize sat before him proudly, a thin layer of dust shrouding its forest-green exterior. Either no one had driven it lately, or when the quake struck, the building shook just enough to redistribute some of the dirt from the rafters.

The riskiest part of the process lay ahead. The process of starting the car took time. He ran through the steps so he was sure not to forget anything. *No time to waste.* From the passenger side, he reached into the vehicle to set the spark. He pulled up on a lever next to the long bench seat upholstered with soft black leather. Then he reached across to the driver's side and shifted a handle under the wheel a little to the left to set the throttle. He found the small copper ignition switch embedded under the driver's seat, then turned it ninety degrees counterclockwise to switch it on.

Sweat trickled down the back of Otto's neck as he climbed into the car to pass through to the other side of the vehicle. He jumped out and reached for a small yellow handle, tickling the carburetor to flood it with fuel. *Almost done.* The last thing to do was attach the crank and turn it to start the engine. Otto opened the crank housing located next to the front left wheel, but it was empty. Pop sometimes put it on the floor in the back when he was in a hurry, so he peeked inside to look for it, but it wasn't there either. He searched the workbench and under the car.

"Looking for this?" His father's voice reverberated off the garage walls; his figure obstructed the doorway, a stoic silhouette in the smoke-diffused morning light. He was holding the starter crank.

Otto smacked his head against the chassis. "Pop, I—"

"I suspected you would try a stunt like this." His German accent thickened when anger was mixed in, like adding flour to schnitzel gravy. He held up the starter crank. "I felt it necessary to keep this with me at all times."

"I need the Caddy, Pop. It's my only way out of San Francisco."

"And what makes you think you need to leave the city? Is it so bad that it cannot be fixed?" Pop didn't pause to hear an answer before turning around and crossing the street. "Come inside; your mother is worried sick."

That was just it. Pop never seemed to care about Otto's feelings. Sure, he would ask, but he would never listen to hear what Otto had to say. Despite his misgivings, he followed his father obediently. He needed to set things right with his mother, at least.

While crossing the street, Otto assessed the exterior of their home for quake damage. The plaster casing on the bulkhead of their cathedral-style split staircase was cracked. Embellished with a triangular symbol and three half-circles, it stood bordering the sidewalk. Otto couldn't remember what the design meant, but it always reminded him of a triangular pool ball rack with the outlines of three balls on each of three sides.

Otto scaled the steps in silence. Every ornately accented arch and door frame seemed intact, a welcome exception from the city's theme. Not even chipped, the paint was a palate of green and purple with creamy white accents and gold embellishments. He couldn't help but wonder if his family knew how bad it was everywhere else.

His father thundered through the front door and up the last flight of stairs across the third-story foyer. "The city is in complete disarray," he announced as he stood next to the curved bay window in the parlor.

Otto looked out the eastern-facing window but could only see remnants of the collapsed city hall. The familiar perspective of the skyline was forever changed.

"Looters on every corner, they say!"

"For good reason, Pop. Those people aren't criminals. They're just trying to survive."

"Your mother is expecting you in the kitchen."

That's all Pop needed to say. Otto loved his mother; her getting hurt was an unfortunate byproduct of this business. He forced his knees to bend, reluctantly crossing the threshold into the rest of the house. He grew short of breath. Anticipating her disappointment, Otto swung open the door to the galley kitchen and entered a new kind of inferno, Pop following behind. His mother, puffy-eyed with ringlets of hair falling out of place, sat at the table tapping her foot.

His baby sister, Nella, played on the floor with blocks. She grinned and ran to Otto as soon as she noticed him.

Ma waited for a sign from Pop, who gave her a nod for permission to speak. Otto knew full well there was no slowing her down once she got started. A pile of broken dishes sat on the counter, but nothing was out of place other than that. Ma drew in a breath, her vacant gaze directed at her feet.

A full-winded tirade! This was going to be hard to swallow.

"Why on earth would you try to run away and get on a ferry? And then you had the nerve to come back to steal your father's Cadillac? Do you think we wouldn't notice? Or do not care? Or do you just think so little of this family that you would leave us stranded with no way to get anywhere?"

After taking a stunted breath, she continued. "You must have something to say for yourself. Your father and I—we." She tripped over her words; she had never done this. She was always so articulate and deliberate with how she phrased things. She took a stunted breath, then looked him in the eye for the first time, sinking deeper. "We're disappointed. You're better than this."

This came as a surprise. Otto had prepared for the anger, but her sadness struck him in a way he wasn't expecting. Guilt gnawed at him. He hated himself for leaving. He deserved every bit of wrath and misfortune that would rain down on him because of his actions.

Then, as if she were seeing him for the first time, she gasped and sprang to her feet. "Son, you're bleeding! What happened?" Her concern for his well-being was refreshing after laying into him so completely. He hated to disappoint her. It stung worse than saltwater on an open wound.

"I'm sorry, Ma. Really, I am. I didn't know what else to do. And I'm fine; it was nothing."

"You're sure? It doesn't look like nothing." She didn't look convinced but resumed her speech as though she had rehearsed it a hundred times. "It doesn't make sense, Otto. We've given you everything you could ever want. Your father came to San Francisco with nothing in his pockets but a chisel; he built his business and made a better life for you and your sister. And this is the thanks we get? A disappearing act and stealing your father's automobile from under our noses? Do you hate us that much?"

This open honesty was nothing Otto had ever heard from either parent. The earthquake must have shaken loose more than the fine china.

"Ma, I don't hate you." His voice cracked, and he swallowed before speaking again. He stretched out his arms toward his father's manufacturing shop on the corner of Golden Gate and Market Street. "But it's too much to ask for me to take over all of this someday."

"You don't know," Ma gasped and covered her mouth; she looked at Pop standing over her. "He doesn't know!"

Pop placed a comforting hand on her shoulder. "The shop, son. It's gone. Pile of burned-up rubble along with everything else downtown."

The news hit Otto like the recoil from a Winchester. "Everything is *gone?*"

Since he had thought his folks sat unsinged on the hill, he hadn't even thought about the shop. How foolish to believe they were invincible. These fires would surely leave no one unburned. Nothing was too sacred to avoid getting ripped out of existence.

"We're just lucky your father wasn't staying there that night like he sometimes does on weekdays." His mother seemed to be on a search for the silver lining.

He started to think about what it would have been like if Pop had been in the building when it shook and fell. Suddenly the fear of building billiard tables didn't seem so relevant or rational. What would they do if they had lost him? What if Otto had succeeded in leaving town and Pop was gone? How would his family survive?

Forget the *what-ifs*; what were they to do without a place of business? Or without any paying customers?

"What now?" It was all he could muster.

"Your mother and I have been discussing it," Pop said. "There's nothing for us here anymore. It will be years before saloons and hotels are rebuilt and operating again, let alone when somebody can rebuild the shop. And who knows if insurance will even cover it. We're better off leaving town. Not sure of where yet, but there may be the promise of a market somewhere up north."

His whole family uprooted like that, moving away—it seemed wrong. Even with the city in shambles, he understood the position of the Brickers. *Hell no, they couldn't leave.* San Francisco was their home. He had to make sure his family got back on their feet. *He had to stay.*

He imagined how he would tell Jo and how she would answer. Instead of dwelling on the problem, she would probably get him to think of a solution.

"No," he announced. "There must be another way."

"Oh, now look who suddenly thinks he has a say in the family business," Pop fired back.

"Now, now, August. Let the boy speak."

"There's opportunity out there. We can help rebuild the city." Otto had used the word *we*. The strange thing was, he didn't regret it. He could have a chance to make a real impact.

"What about your misgivings, son?" Ma asked.

"It's true. Pop's standards are impossible to live up to for anyone besides him; I didn't want to face it."

"Oh, I see," Ma shook her head knowingly. Maybe she was also aware of the pressure to perform at high standards. "What's different now, dear?"

"Up until now, I thought there were other things I wanted to do with my life. And that's still true."

"Your grandfather used to say that the hardest part about chasing your dreams is figuring out which way they're headed," Pop chimed in. He spoke about his grandfather so seldom that Otto sometimes forgot he ever had one.

"I can't stand by and watch everything Pop has worked for go up in smoke. I won't let that happen."

"There's nothing to be done now but start over somewhere new," Pop said.

"Now see, you're wrong. I've seen it out there. There are lots of people, good people, digging their heels into the ground and refusing to go anywhere. More than you'd think. They're stuck on rebuilding this God-forsaken city, and by golly, after seeing the fire in their bellies, I'd be surprised if she didn't come back better and brighter than she was the day before yesterday."

Otto paced, knowing that his parents might not receive his proposal very well. He wasn't entirely convinced himself. "What if we move the shop downstairs? We can run manufacturing out of the main floor, and the office from the second floor. That way, we can get up and running again right away."

Otto's father began to speak but paused, his mouth slightly agape. He mused for a moment, bringing his index finger and thumb to the unprecedented two-day stubble on his chin. "Hmm."

"We'll focus for a time on helping with the rebuilding. With our skilled labor in woodwork, we can be sure to rebuild the city with the class and elegance it deserves."

"Now, how about that? You were right, Marta. This son of yours has what it takes to be even better than his father."

"But first, I need to borrow the Caddy," Otto said.

Pop gripped the crank that he still held so tightly Otto swore he heard it yelp. "Why on earth if we're staying here?"

"I made a promise to someone. I have to bring them to safety. I'll bring the car right back, promise."

Pop glared but had a glimmer in his eye that, for a moment,

resembled pride. He and Ma exchanged a long look before turning back to face Otto. "No one but you drives her. And if you return her with so much as a scratch, it's your hide."

Otto could hardly believe his ears. "Yes, of course! Not a scratch."

Chapter Twenty-Seven

Kearny and Clay, 10:40 a.m.

The wall of flames growled with hungry anticipation no more than a block away in either direction from the southeast corner of Portsmouth Square. Jo felt like a dolt for venturing out this far into an active disaster area. Her throat burned again, triggering the same life-threatening panic she had felt in the print shop. She drank the last of her water and tossed the empty flask into the street with a *clang*.

Jo spotted a demolition crew dressed in army garb fleeing the scene of the Hall of Justice from where the fire was spreading. They disappeared into the smoke to the north. She was furious with them. They were idiots blowing up buildings without any reasonable tactics or strategy.

She hated Mama for moving so far away from home. North Beach might as well have been another planet. She hated feeling obligated to find her. But she needed answers. She needed to know why she had lied to her about Papa and what else she was keeping from her.

She sputtered a few steps north, but the smoke was so thick and the air so hot that it sent her stumbling backward. Then she tried passing east on Sacramento Street, but the way was blocked, so she pulled back south again. To her west, the precarious central spire from the Hall of Justice groaned in the hot wind, on the verge of collapse. She twirled in what resembled a drunken stupor. *There's no way out.* She picked up a piece of shrapnel from the ground, used it to rip a piece of cloth off her nightgown, and held it over her mouth and nose. She dove onto the ground, where she hoped to avoid most of the smoke as she tried to figure out an escape.

Think.

She was mad at Mama for putting her in this position—having to traverse the city only to find herself trapped by fire on all sides. But she couldn't focus on her anger now, only on her survival.

"Damn it, Mrs. Tucci, what do I do?" She spewed her question toward the infernal skies, took a big breath, and choked. *This hellscape would be her grave.* Her flesh would burn, and her unrecognizable bones would be found amongst the rubble. *Indistinguishable.*

At least then, she would accomplish what she always set out to do; she'd fade into the dust with nameless, faceless anonymity.

No. Think! Perspective . . .

If she couldn't escape the fire, she would need to seek shelter somewhere and wait for it to pass through and burn out. She couldn't run through the streets or into a building to get away from the flames or the smoke, but she could go down into the earth—*the cisterns.* Of course! She could climb into a cistern and wait until it was safe before traveling the rest of the six blocks to Mama. But where was the closest one?

She racked her brain to recall the red points on the cistern map that she knew. Where was she? Portsmouth Square meant she was just one block east of Chinatown. She knew the exact place to go—the intersection of Dupont Street and Washington Street just one block west of the park. But she had to figure out how to get there.

She blasted through the once carefully manicured park, ignored the paved pathways, and wove through abandoned tents and trunks that someone had rummaged through at the last minute.

Just one more block.

A line of massive, extravagant structures separated her and her target. Flames licked around the side of the farthest building to the right, a two-story residence pancaked by pieces of its taller assuming neighbor. The fire burned hot and thick, torching the masonwork like charcoal and forbidding a clear path.

Jo peeked intently beyond her makeshift handkerchief to inspect her options. Nestled between the collapsed three-story building and the California Chinese Mission, whose bell tower had caved in on itself, was a grand, intimidating manor. The top half of the four-story behemoth had crumbled and rendered it unrecoverable. She hoped the bottom floor was intact enough to pass through.

Jo ducked into the inset entry hall to escape the ash-filled winds, coughing and gasping for relief in the corner. The grandiose stained glass front door whined, opened, and shut sharply with a snap—a welcome, yet otherworldly, invitation to enter.

She barged into the entrance with a passing worry: a resident of the place could find her and accuse her of breaking in or burglary. This couldn't possibly be a home for one family. It was almost as big as City Hall. But the foyer's walls, lined with family portraits in decadent golden frames, said otherwise.

She wondered what any one family would do with this much room. They must have an entire floor of the house dedicated to fancy parties where they invite all the well-to-do people of the city over to talk about how much money they have, how they spent it, or how they plan to spend it.

But soon, everything these people owned would be lost, and everything they still had was what they could carry, the same as her. She imagined those fancy people sleeping in a tent in the park rather than in their soft fluffy beds. She didn't know why that made her feel good, but it did.

Jo's attention returned to her survival. The mansion ran the entire block's width, so she could see the street through the windows by the time she was at the other end of the house. But there was no door.

She grabbed a houseplant contained in a heavy ceramic vessel. She never understood the concept of having plants in the house. If anyone wanted to see a tree or flowers, they could go outside. She heaved the pot toward an oversized window, shattering the glass on impact.

She looked around to find something to set on top of the glass so she wouldn't cut herself and spotted a half-knit afghan from a basket next to a rocking chair. She snatched it and tossed it onto the windowsill.

Jo emerged into an alternate reality. It was her city, but different. Western references vanished behind oriental facades. Large signage scribbled with red or gold symbols punctuated decorative awnings with elaborate fringes. Doorways stood at attention, flanked with red paper lanterns almost as big as her uncle's fruit cart. This was Chinatown.

Jo dashed to the end of the block to confirm her theory of the cistern's location. She looked for an access point in the middle of the street.

Eureka! as the old-timey miners would say. She found it. In the center of the intersection of Washington and Dupont Streets sat an unassuming manhole whose cover had the raised letters "CISTERN S.F.F.D." printed on it. Her celebration was short-lived when she tried to wedge her fingers under the handle, but it didn't budge.

The reality was, short of locating the cistern, Jo had no actual plan for how to open it. The manhole cover was so heavy that there was no way she could lift it herself. She heard cries nearby. On a threshold, a Chinese woman stood dressed in long silky robes adorned with elaborate beadwork spiraled in mesmerizing patterns. Her stern face seemed resigned to her predicament.

The woman appeared to notice Jo, and when taking two shy steps forward to confirm her sighting, she revealed two small children who cowered behind, clutching one another. A boy and a girl. No more than seven or eight, the girl had on a blouse and a skirt, ringed with ribbons and embroidered designs. Her hair was pulled back into a braid that hung below her knees. In contrast, the boy, about twelve, wore a plain grey shirt and matching trousers. On his head, he had a round hat with a flat top lined in gold.

The boy looked up and spotted Jo, then jumped forward. She realized then that he wasn't cowering; he was trying to protect his sister. In unbroken English, he screamed, "Help us! Please!"

Jo couldn't believe her luck. Though she didn't wish these people were in harm's way, there was help when she needed it. She flailed her arms and beckoned for them to leave their shelter and join her in the street. The boy leaped toward Jo; his mother tried to grasp his garments as he flew by and screamed shrilly in Chinese, pleading with him to return. He stopped at the sidewalk and looked back at her.

"Help me lift this," Jo called to the boy.

He ran over to join her in the street, and they each took a handle, barely managing to lift the cistern cover two inches to clear the edge of the street. Jo dropped to the ground, rear first, edging the leaden metal disc forward with the heels of her boots. Every time she pushed, she scooted back twice as far. It took a few good shoves to move the disc so that it only slightly eclipsed the opening.

"Wow, what's down there?" the boy peeked into the dark cavern.

"If we're lucky, our lives." Jo peered over the edge. A refreshing wave of cool air wafted through the cistern opening. Hot red firelight from above illuminated the opening, and it was as she suspected—a brick-lined cavity. It reminded her of an old pizza oven. She prayed that it wouldn't heat up like one. She saw a dim reflection from the bottom, promising some level of water. She couldn't tell how much water was there, but it wasn't full, which meant there was a chance she wouldn't drown if she climbed inside. The only way to know for sure was to get down there somehow. And at this point, that was her and the young family's only option for survival.

There was at least a twelve-foot drop to the bottom. This wasn't a well, so there were no walls to shimmy down. And once inside, she wasn't sure if or how they would get out again. This wasn't like a sewer interconnected to an underground system. It was an independent water reservoir underneath the street that wasn't designed to have people climbing inside of it.

The boy's mother approached close enough to peer over the edge suspiciously.

"It's a cistern," said Jo. "We need to get inside, or we'll all die."

She stared blankly at Jo for a moment, then looked to her son, who instinctively translated Jo's request.

The woman looked frantic as she made stroking motions with her arms and shook her head.

"She can't swim," said the boy.

Jo hoped to God there wasn't much water in there, but she knew there was at least some—her mouth felt like a sandstorm in the middle of the Mojave Desert.

"Can you find rope?" Jo said to the boy and motioned for him to repeat the question to his mother.

The boy relayed the message, moving hand over hand in a motion that mimicked climbing.

His mother covered her face with her apron and ran in the other direction, disappearing into the thick smoke.

The girl began to cry, pleading for her mother to return. Thirty seconds passed, and she had not returned.

The boy left Jo's side and put his arm around his sister, who still cowered in the nearby building's threshold. Another full minute passed, and both children now had tears in their eyes as they watched the spot in the street where they had last seen her.

A moment later, she emerged with one hand over her mouth and the other holding a large, bright red lantern that brought with it a long string of more. She held them out proudly, coughing and remarking in Chinese.

The lanterns themselves were fragile, constructed of rippled red paper lined with twisted gold thread, and gold-painted Chinese lettering with hanging tassels from the bottom. But the attached rope was strong and likely long enough to reach the bottom of the cistern.

"Find something to tie it to!" Jo smacked her lips. Her mouth was so dry that she could barely speak loud enough for anyone to hear. Her throat was about to shrivel into a prune.

The boy translated, and they all searched for heavy objects that might support their weight. Fence posts, wagons, and barrels would not work. They were all too flammable or lightweight.

The only thing Jo could see was a lamppost. She didn't know for sure if it could be trusted, but at this point, it was their only option. The fire galloped forward, sending the house she had passed through earlier into a smoky surrender.

The boy helped Jo tie the end of the rope around the nearest lamppost, and Jo tossed the decorative lantern down into the damp chasm.

Jo pointed at herself, "I'll be the first one down. In case the rope doesn't hold." She motioned to the mother with both her hands in a snapping motion, then back to herself, and held up one finger to indicate she would go first. The woman nodded to indicate she understood. Jo couldn't live with herself if she were responsible for an innocent family getting hurt, or worse, because of her crazy plan.

The fire drew closer. Jo grabbed the rope with her hands and tightly pinched her boots together above one of the knots in the rope that secured a lantern. She clung to the edge of the street as the fire drew closer. She estimated they only had a few more minutes before it was on top of them. She shut her eyes tightly and held her breath as she lowered herself. When she felt that the rope would hold, she opened her eyes and drew in a large breath, relieved.

"I'm okay. It should hold. We just need to hope the fire doesn't burn it up, or else we won't have a way out."

Jo nervously descended to the next lantern rung. And then the next. The temperature dropped the farther she climbed. She prayed it wouldn't heat up as the fire reached them. She inched her way to each of the lantern footholds, which were about three feet apart. The boy gaped unblinking at her descent. Jo let go of the rope and jumped with a splash at the bottom, her boots submerged by only a few inches. The mostly empty water storage container was about fifteen feet deep and thirteen feet across and constructed of red bricks from top to bottom.

Jo waved frantically to signal that she was safe, and the next person could begin their climb down before she leaned over to drink up the water at her feet.

Jo cupped the water with her hands and funneled it into her mouth. Despite its tasting stale and chalky, she felt more refreshed with every drop. After a minute, she realized no one had followed her down the rope yet. Maybe something had gone wrong, but then the bare feet of the young girl appeared as her brother tried to coax her into putting all her weight onto the rope.

The girl's braid dangled as she lurched down to the next lantern, screaming at the loss of firm grip. Her mother and brother began to yell at her in Chinese. Jo didn't know what they were saying except for what must be her name, "Ling," because they kept repeating it frantically. The light behind their silhouettes began to flicker more than glow. The fire was nearly on top of them.

"Take it easy, Ling!" shouted Jo. "Take it nice and slow."

When Ling got about halfway, her brother got into position to begin his descent. Ling froze in panic and started to cry again.

"You're almost there! Just a little bit further. Only three more lanterns to go." Jo said.

Ling inched down until her naked toes reached the bottom. Jo hugged Ling. "Good job, Ling. That was very brave." They both waved to the opening. "Come on! Hurry, please!" Jo hoped they could see her better than she could see them. Ling held tightly to Jo as they watched for her brother to scale down toward them. Jo squeezed Ling's shoulder—the girl was safe, and soon, the rest of her family would be as well.

The boy exchanged words with his mother, then let go of the rope and vanished from view. He reappeared again a moment later and shouted down to them, but Jo couldn't understand what he said. He held up one finger before leaving yet again for what seemed like an eternity.

Finally, the mother and son appeared again, coughing violently. *Where had they gone?* The boy motioned his mother to go first, but she shook her head. Then as if recognizing he would be too stubborn to listen, she gave in and worked herself into a position to descend.

She secured the rope at the second lantern rung with the soles of her slippers when a snapping sound reverberated off the cylindrical basin, and Ling's mother, along with the rope of lanterns, jerked down a few inches.

"Mama!" Ling cried.

It wasn't clear if the rope had partially snapped, burned, or come loose somewhere, but the mother's pace quickened as her urgency intensified. At the next rung, her feet slipped, sending one of her slippers tumbling into the water with a splatter. She tried to regain her footing on one of the lanterns, but her feet kept getting caught in her long robes, forcing them to slip.

She kicked off her other slipper and then used her toes to grip the rope, inching her way down until she reached the bottom. The woman dropped her lips to the floor of the cistern, gulping water while reaching for her daughter. Above, the woman's son turned around, got on his knees, hung his feet over the edge, and got ready for his descent.

A loud explosion rumbled at surface level, sending the boy careening backward. He lost his grip on the rope and caught himself on the edge of the manhole opening with his arms as his body swung frantically.

"Quing!" his mother and sister screeched in unison. Quing coughed as he reached for the rope with his right arm, but it was on the opposite side of the hole, and he couldn't reach it. His body stopped swinging. He panted as he tried to hook the rope with his legs and missed. Again, it was too far to reach.

Quing loosened his grip with his arms and dropped, holding the sides of the opening with his hands. He howled and moaned as his legs oscillated freely, swinging closer to the dangling cord with each pass.

On his third attempt, he snagged the rope with his heel, slid down, and dismounted with a dancer's precision. His agility made Jo jealous. She could never even walk in a straight line without hitting a doorway with her shoulders. It's a miracle she'd made it this far in life without breaking a bone.

"What now?" asked Quing between slurps of mineral water.

"Now, we wait," Jo said, watching the lanterns churn in the air. "Wait for the fire to extinguish itself. And then maybe, hopefully, we still have a way out of here."

Chapter Twenty-Eight

Van Ness and McAllister, 1:10 p.m.

tto and the Cadillac crept through the streets, dodging every wayward stone and stick. He took Jo's advice and headed up Van Ness, knowing it would be his best bet to make it through since it was the widest thoroughfare in the city. He planned to take it all the way north to Bay Street before cutting over to Montgomery, which would lead him southeast to their rendezvous point at Washington Square. He kept getting out of the vehicle to move objects out of the way, making it a slow process.

Before long, he had burned half the day, and he still had most of the way to go. Fiery winds picked up from the east and blew hot on his already sweaty brow. The fire continued to spread and didn't show any sign of burning out yet. At least he had an opportunity at home to wash up a bit, fill his belly, and change into some clean clothes. He decided to keep the bowler hat he had found at the Palace Hotel.

Now that he intended to stay in San Francisco and help his family rebuild the business in their home, Otto worried about what Jo would say. He didn't know how she would react to his position shifting so drastically. Would she be angry with him? Or disappointed? Or maybe she would be relieved and decide to stay? No matter what, he wanted her by his side.

The Caddy puttered on. Otto spotted a demolition crew laying down detonation wire and preparing to blow some charges in one of the larger mansions along the west side of Van Ness. Men ran every which way, looking like someone had left the gate open on the chicken coop. Otto maneuvered the Caddy to give them enough room to work without disturbing them.

"You there," one of the men said gruffly, tossing Otto a glance. "Those look like some strong legs. Come over here a minute." He was covered in soot and sounded like he had swallowed a frog.

"Do you fellas need some help?" Otto wished he could grab the words and stuff them back in as soon as they slipped out of his throat. The last thing he needed was to volunteer for another task that would get him in a heap of trouble.

"Actually, son," he shouted over the sputtering motor. "We just might." Another man stepped out from behind a broken wagon full of explosives holding a rifle. The horse attached to the broken wagon neighed loudly and jumped every which way. A driver on the wagon tugged on its reins pulling its head back with the bit.

"Well, uh, actually, there's someplace I have to be," said Otto.

The man brandishing the firearm pointed it at Otto.

"I think you'll find that this is the only place you're meant to be," shouted the first man.

Shit, not again. Otto turned off the car and stepped out. Being on the wrong end of a gun barrel twice in twenty-four hours surely had to be some kind of record.

The explosives worker wiped his brow with his sleeve, but it did nothing but spread the smut around. In his other hand, he held a bundle of three sticks of dynamite. "This is official business. Direct orders from Mayer Schmitz. Our explosives team has been working nonstop since yesterday, blowing these buildings to build a firebreak."

He looked out over the hazy glow of the horizon with defiance. "We're blasting everything two blocks west of Van Ness: Franklin, Gough, all of it. Fire needs fuel to burn. We simply need to take it away, give it no place to catch."

Another worker approached, who wore an official-looking hat. "We can't let it win. We can't let it take the whole city."

"We won't, Captain," said the first worker. "We'll blast the place to hell before we let it take more from us."

"Whoa there, Hank." The captain held up his palms to slow him down. "We're trying to save the city, not blow it all to kingdom come."

Otto wasn't sure if there was anything the men could do to stop it. He had witnessed firsthand the unyielding fury behind the flames. They were relentless and all-consuming. Plus, people said the explosions were adding to the flames rather than preventing them. "Won't it just make the fires worse? If you blow things up and something catches, it will only mean more fire."

The man who still pointed the gun at Otto coughed and read-justed the grip on the trigger to be sure Otto saw he wasn't off the hook.

Otto put his hands in the air. "Easy, fellas, it's only a question."

The captain said, "That's only if it isn't handled properly. It takes a certain kind of explosive in a very precise quantity, strategically placed. The damn Presidio sent the wrong kind of explosive: gunpowder, of all things! It won't level a building; it will just make a mess."

He pointed an accusatory finger in the direction of the smoke plumes. "And that fool John Bermingham, a so-called explosives *expert,* was dense enough to use it. Jagged off his heinie, he is. I can't make sense of the strategy. Just making it worse and risking people's lives."

"So, what do you need me for?" asked Otto.

"Our dynamite runner over there, Thomas, just gone and broke his leg—chimney went and fell on him. Crushed him like a snail. The men were just barely able to drag him out. We need a new runner. Someone nimble enough to place the charges and safely make it out in time for it to blow. Plus," he licked his lips and salivated, "that auto-mobeelie of yours could sure help us haul our load. That damn horse is scared shitless."

"Can't any of your other men do it?"

One of his men who had been hurt and was nursing his wounds shouted in their direction, "Oy, Hank! We need to get this done! It's getting closer, and the wind is picking up."

Panic flooded Hank's gaunt cheekbones. "They're weary and sleep-deprived. They'd be better off manning the charges on the ground and clearing the scene. Fresh legs would do a world of good for morale."

The area had been evacuated for the most part, and not many able-bodied men could be found. By then, the entirety of the brigade was at a stand-still, near death, and pleading with hopeful, tired eyes.

Otto thought of Jo, her mother, and her brother waiting for him in Washington Square. "I understand you need help, but I really ought to get going," Otto told Hank and the captain.

Hank grabbed Otto's shirt and pulled him close. "Listen here," he growled while his eyes pleaded. "My men need this. I need this. I'm desperate."

Shit. "Fine. One hour. Two at the most," Otto told him.

Hank nodded.

Otto reached for the bundle of dynamite.

The rifleman threw down the gun, dropped to his knees, and made the sign of the cross.

"Easy!" Hank held the explosives away from Otto. "You fool, you'll kill yourself before we can even get you into a building. We're creating firebreaks, not passing a baton in the Olympics."

"What am I supposed to do with it then?" Otto asked, irritated. First, Hank asked for his help; then, he couldn't go five seconds without saying he was doing it wrong. It's just how it was with Pop.

Hank rolled his hands forward slowly like he was kneading dough. "Easy, boy. Just take it easy. Go slow; this stuff is volatile as all hell. Damn," he muttered, "I wish Sullivan were here."

"Who's Sullivan?"

"Dennis Sullivan, the fire chief. Poor bastard."

"Where is he? What happened to him?"

"It was his idea to use dynamite in the first place come the event of a big fire, but the unfortunate soul was one of the quake's first casualties. He was over at the firehouse on Bush when the hotel next door collapsed on top of his wife's room. He ran to save her but fell two stories, where he was scalded by steam from a boiler."

"Is he dead?"

"Unconscious, but the docs aren't holding out much hope. They've got their hands full with patients who have a fighting chance."

No wonder the city was under such frantic turmoil, Otto thought. If major players were either incapacitated or worse, and we were relying on bench hitters, no wonder we were losing the game. But maybe if he helped, they didn't have to lose the war.

The distant destination attracted Otto's gaze, then he turned. "Okay, so what do I do?"

"It's delicate work, so pay attention. You have to gain access to the lowest floor in the building so you can set the charges. If the base of the structure is evenly hit, the rest will pancake. Do you follow?"

Otto nodded—the realization hit him. How much danger was he in? How much time would this take before someone relieved him? Would he get to Jo in time?

Hank showed him how to set the fuse and gave him tips on positioning the explosives without making any fatal missteps.

Otto asked, "This is until your men have rested up a bit and can take over for me, right? An hour or two?"

"Sure, kid. Now let's go. Four drops, remember. One in each corner. Then run back here as fast as you can."

Otto took the bundle of explosives and collected three more from an open truck bed nearby. He made his way into the front door of a large home where he imagined an oil baron or railroad owner lived. His family's home could probably fit inside this one six times over. He wondered if four charges would be enough to bring the building down.

He tried hard not to pay attention to the beautiful architecture that would soon be laid waste. It felt so wrong to be responsible for destroying such a work of art. Every last structure on this stretch of road was a testament to San Francisco's great Victorian age. And it was all disappearing before his eyes.

A man handed him an axe on his way into the already busted-down door. He made his way through the house as quickly as possible, trying to find access to the basement. Once he did, it was dark enough that he had to feel his way through the halls to place the charges, one at a time, then he made his way out again. As soon as the men saw him exit, they started the countdown.

"Five! Four! Three!" Otto didn't realize just how little time he would have. He ran faster, wincing as he clutched his side and dove behind the men working the detonator's plunger. They were uncomfortably close to the blast area. *It didn't make any sense.*

"Two! One!"

Rubble and timber rained down on them and the nearby vicinity. Dust exploded into Otto's face, and he cried out. "Why are your men so close to the building? Can't you stretch the fuse across the street to be safer?" He shouted at them as debris continued to fall around them.

"These lead wires are all we have!"

Every time they blew a building, the lead wires got shorter.

Before long, they were going to run out.

Otto saw red. This entire operation, which was supposedly the city's last line of defense, was being run by careless and incompetent men. "What is your plan for when it's too short to be any use? Are we going to blow ourselves up with the houses and pray the angels carry us to safety?"

"We haven't figured that out yet." The man who pushed the plunger growled as he sneered at Hank.

"Well, we're going to have to sooner or later," Otto fired back. There seemed to be a lack of clear leadership here. Nobody was prepared to make any tough decisions, and the time for those had come.

Otto thought about Jo again and what she would do in this situation. He wiped the sweat and dust off his forehead with his sleeve and took a look around with a fresh perspective. There had to be a way to set off the charges after the lines ran out. If not, they would never clear enough houses to build an effective fireline, and they would lose it all.

A bright spark caught Otto's attention out of the corner of his eye. Half a block over, downed poles from street wires jumped like pistons in a combustion engine. Then it came to him—he could use the street wire for detonation. "What about that wire?" Otto pointed down the block.

"Dagnabbit, boy, you're a real sort of genius!"

Hank sent Otto and one other man to retrieve the wires. They had to scale the poles and carefully cut the wires using sheers whose handles were wrapped in coats to insulate them from the electricity. It was unclear why the wires were live since power was out throughout the whole city. Fire down the line somewhere must have caused them to carry a charge.

They repeated this pattern for several hours. They blasted about ten homes, then harvested more street wire. Over and over again.

The air was thick as milk with the impending hellfire that crawled nearer. Otto had to run back and forth to the Caddy to move it up the street and check that his belongings were secured. Meanwhile, he kept up with the demolition crew's progress. Though he allowed the crew to use the car to carry supplies, he strove to abide by his father's wishes by not letting anyone else drive it. The evening was getting late, and he itched to leave and continue on his way. No one knew if the work they had done was enough.

Otto ran into a new building, his arms loaded with explosives and his axe, but he struggled to see anything in the darkness. The thick cloud of smoke had enveloped their location, and it was as if he was wearing a blindfold. His muscles ached. His shirt was completely drenched in sweat and felt like a heavy weight pulling him down. He couldn't access the basement. He reached down to place the dynamite off to the side carefully, then yanked a rug off the floor in the foyer. After taking the axe, he thrust it directly into the floorboards.

He struck repeatedly until he made a hole large enough to fit. He scooped up the artillery and leaped into the dark abyss, readying his stance to soften the impact of the ground, but then the mangled edge of an outstretched nail bit into his thigh. He hit the floor, lost his grip on the explosives, and heard a stick of dynamite land with a splash. The basement held an inch or two of water, probably from a burst pipe.

Otto's leg stung. He got onto his feet okay. Warm blood ran down his leg and pooled in his shoe. He couldn't tell how bad it was. He took the weight off his good leg to take a step and lost his balance. He cursed to himself, deciding that after he laid down these charges, he was done. The whole crew should hang their hats up and quit if they knew what was good for them. He hadn't intended on spending this long helping, but what could he do? Walk away and let the city continue to burn?

Otto quickly spotted the fallen stick of dynamite. It was soaked through, and he wondered if it would still work. His mind shifted: he could actually *see* again. A red-orange glow emanated from the hole above him. *The house was on fire.*

He limped his way to the back corners of the house in the fire's direction. Maybe he would have more time to escape along the side that wasn't already aflame. He moved at half his normal speed. Though trembling from the pain, he had a deeply seeded worry: What if he didn't make it? What if he never saw Jo again?

He made his way to the front corner of the house and laid the third charge without finding a stairwell. There was no way he would make it back out through the hole he made. He imagined what Jo might think if he never came for her. She might never guess he had gotten himself trapped in an exploding building. She would probably think he left without her. The latest in a long line of people who abandoned her. He couldn't bear to think of her feeling that he would do that to her.

On his way to the final corner of the house, Otto finally spotted the staircase. It was already ablaze. He had taken too long. He took the fourth and final charge, dried it off quickly on his shirt, and set it.

Otto began to think he was a fool to fall for a girl like Jo. The risk of his hurting her was too great. She had already lost so much the last couple of days, and he knew it was against her better judgment to get attached to someone new, least of all him.

All he could do was swear that he would get to her. All he wanted to do was hold her close, run his fingers through her long brown hair, and tell her tenderly that he would never leave her again. "No matter what, I will find you," He swore it to the sparks that swirled through the air like falling stars. "Because once you make a promise to the stars, it must come true." Tears streamed down his face uncontrollably. "I pledge to you this night, Jo. I will get back to you."

Chapter Twenty-Nine

Dupont and Washington, 3:25 p.m.

"Can we go *now?*" It was only the thirty-seventh time Ling had asked Jo since they managed to climb safely into the cistern. Despite the extreme temperatures, the Chinese lantern rope seemed to hold, but she wasn't overly confident.

"Yes, Ling. I think enough time has passed. We should be safe."

She had gotten to know the family a bit in the time they spent sequestered from the world in this underground sanctuary. The woman, Su, and her husband had moved here from a small village in China north of Hong Kong a day after they were married. He had been promised a job on the California railroad, only to find that they did not need him when he arrived. He took a job at a laundromat and eventually inherited the business. Su, Ling, and Quing helped out with the family business.

Jo figured it was late afternoon or early evening on Thursday, as best she could tell. She still hoped to reach her destination, Washington Square, the park in the heart of North Beach, before dark. However, that thought was silly since an unrelenting shroud of smoggy darkness covered the whole city.

"May I go first?" asked Quing, his black eyebrows pleading for the honor. It made no difference to her, but other people looked to her for approval, and this unfamiliar responsibility of leadership made her uncomfortable. Modesty could be life-threatening in certain situations, so she saved her humility for later. She continued to worry the rope would not hold, and she didn't want to risk Quing's life, but if the rope snapped, they were dead anyway. She prayed this brick-lined cavern that spared their lives would not become their tomb.

"Ask your Ma. It's fine with me." She tried to sound chipper.

After his mother's nod, Quing scaled the rope with ease, propelling his tiny body upward several feet with every push from each lamp knot. He made it look easy. The rope held—that was the critical part. And it continued to hold, so each of them climbed out of the cistern, one at a time. Once on ground level, Jo inspected the rope closely. It was charred black in places but not burned through. "I can't believe this held."

A smile washed over Su's face, exposing many crooked or missing teeth. Then the children giggled in unison.

Was Jo missing something? "What is it?"

"Laundry soap!" exclaimed Quing. "Mama had some in her pockets left over."

Jo was confused. What about laundry detergent made them so happy? And why on earth would someone always keep some in their clothing?

"Left over from what?"

Su's hands dipped into her pockets and pulled out a dusting of chunky white powder. She spat a few times into her palm and rubbed her hands together until the powder turned into a milky paste. Then she rubbed it onto the rope first and then on her clothes, looking up to make sure Jo saw and understood.

"Left over from what she rubbed all over us to protect us from flying embers."

Jo nodded. "So, the laundry soap makes it fireproof?"

"Not fireproof exactly, but more resistant if licked by flames," Quing translated.

"Fascinating." Jo surmised that since the rope was in the road and not surrounded by anything else, it probably was spared being exposed to any large direct flames. The coating must have been enough to prevent the rope from catching fire.

Jo could only imagine what would have happened to her if the family had not been there. She would have had a more challenging time accessing the cistern, and she might never have found a way back out. "Su, you saved our lives. I don't know how to thank you."

"If you hadn't come along when you did," Quing translated, "we would have been *wándàn*, finished."

Jo and Su embraced, and for a moment, Jo felt as if she were in Mrs. Tucci's arms. She wept at the strange familiarity.

Around them, flammable pieces of buildings smoldered, exposing twisted steel skeletons. While the worst had passed, the fire lingered like circling vultures.

It was late afternoon when she finally made it to Washington Square with her new companions; they seemed to be out of the grasp of the spreading flames. But the wind had shifted again and now blew eastward, which put North Beach directly in the path of the flames. Just as she began to think luck had returned to her, the universe changed its mind. She wasn't surprised—at this point, she would believe anything was possible, even the most horrific and impossible thing imaginable.

"The wind is blowing it all back in this direction. At this rate, the entire city will be gone in no time." She was emotionless in her prediction. She had to disconnect the feeling part of her brain from the thinking part. It was the only way to not break down into tears in front of her new friends.

"Do you think we'll be safe here?" asked Quing.

Jo didn't know how to answer right now. She had only gut feelings and survival instincts. Everyone was in a heightened sense of adrenaline-driven self-preservation. It was their best tool for making it out alive. "I think so, for now anyway. Why don't you find a place to rest for the night? I need to find my mother."

Quing ran over to Jo and gave her an unexpected embrace. The gesture brought another tear to her eye. *So much for those feelings being cordoned off completely.*

"Good luck, Quing. Continue to be brave and protect your Ma and your sister."

Su and her children disappeared into the fog of bodies. Hundreds of people gathered in the park that spanned one city block. Many had camped out the night before, squeezed together like sardines in a tin can.

Saints Peter and Paul Church sat east of the park. You could barely see its triangular spires from where Jo stood on the grass. She had been there once before for her brother's christening. The beautiful but humble building showcased a pair of grand stained-glass windows above an arched entrance. A bell tower adorned with a golden cross sat above the grand doorway.

An Italian Catholic priest in tattered dusty robes ran frantically from the wooden cathedral carrying an armful of books as thick as her head. He sailed toward her. "Young lady, would you give me a hand?" he asked in a panicked tone, his accent thick with old country inflections. "Hold these for me, would you?"

"What are those?" Jo asked.

"Church records," he said. "Irreplaceable archives that document births, marriages, and deaths." He didn't even wait before thrusting the giant ledgers toward her. Soon she held four heavy volumes of records that spanned decades.

The Father pulled out a shovel he had hidden in his robes and started frantically digging a hole while grumbling, *"Mannaggia!"* repeatedly. It reminded her of Papa whenever he would wash dishes after one of Mama's big meals. *"Mannaggia tutto,"* he would mutter repeatedly after Mama used every pot in the kitchen.

Once the hole was big enough, he reached into his robes and pulled out what looked like a purple tablecloth, probably from Lenten services. While Jo wondered what else he could have hidden in there, he lined the hole gingerly with the cloth, took the records from her, then placed them carefully inside, covering them with the fabric's corners.

She helped him scoop the dirt back into the hole to cover the treasures.

He said, "Now, *ragazza*, find some rocks. We must mark the spot where they are buried."

Jo complied, fetching several large rocks.

"There," the Father clapped the dirt off his hands. "Safe and sound underground."

"Do you really think the flames will reach us here?" Jo realized that anything was possible with this fire. She'd seen it up close. *No one was safe.*

"Josephina!" A familiar voice rang out from the conglomeration in the park. "Oh, Josephina, do my eyes deceive me?"

"Mama?"

Chapter Thirty

Van Ness and Broadway, 5:30 p.m.

team hissed through the thick air as Otto threw water onto the fire on the stairs. He hadn't been able to gather much water in the bucket he found, but it was enough to make the fire dissipate enough to pass. He ascended the stairs, broke through a window, and ran as quickly as his injuries would allow while brushing shattered glass from his hat.

Otto's eyes met with Hank's, whose look of relief lit the night more brightly than the fire on top of them. "Oy, blow it!" One of the men pushed the plunger and set off three out of the four explosives, which brought down the building's remains. Debris rained on the crew as they took shelter underneath their shovels and coats full of burn holes.

"Was worried about you for a minute there, kid." Hank slapped Otto on the back. "You did a great job in there."

Otto's posture grew taller with pride. He may have really made a difference. He couldn't wait to get back to Jo and tell her that he may have helped stop the fires. One of the sparks that hadn't extinguished on impact landed squarely on the Cadillac beside the fuel tank. "No!" Otto deflated and ran toward the car, watching the spark eat through the tank. There was nothing he could do. The subsequent explosion blew back everything within a fifty-foot radius, including Otto.

"Let's get out of here!" Hank picked himself up and shook off the surprise. "Now, all we can do is run and pray."

Otto's head swirled as he screamed at the naked chassis of Pop's Cadillac. What a foolish move—he had brought the car into the fire's path at the edge of Armageddon. He wondered if it would now cost them their lives. Otto swallowed his guilt and focused on moving forward. "I hope all our efforts prove worth it." He was drenched in sweat and caked in sludge.

"Me too, son. If the firebreak holds and the rest of the city is spared, then it will be."

"Good luck out there," Otto said.

Otto trudged up Van Ness and stopped when he reached the intersection of Green Street. He wondered if he should head east now to see if he could get all the way through to North Beach since he no longer had to maneuver with an automobile, but he saw smoke rising from the hill. The eastern winds started to shift, and the usual northwesterly winds fought to take back control, sending swift gusts cutting through the broken skyline. This was good news for the fireline at Van Ness. It meant the western part of the city would likely be spared, and his and the demolition team's efforts might be successful. But it painted a different picture for Russian Hill, Nob Hill, North Beach, and the waterfront. *It was headed straight for Jo.* It was as if the fire was metallic, and Otto was a magnet drawing the inferno closer no matter where he intended to go.

Otto was devastated they no longer had their ticket out of the city.

But after finding out what was at stake with his father's company, he had to stay. He still didn't know how he would break the news to Jo.

He envisioned the new shop. They could put the workbenches for carving in the front room so that the rounded bay window would flood the space with natural light. Initially, they would carve architectural decorations: corbels, gable boards, or keystones.

They could use the middle bedrooms as storage for lumber and other supplies, the study for staining or painting, and the back kitchen for assembly and shipping. Since they already had a good reputation for quality detailed woodwork, Otto would convince builders to hire his team. He would use integrity and class to help rebuild the city.

Otto trekked north on foot; the heat of the fires licked his tailbone until he got several blocks away. It must be near evening, but the sun thought it clever to remain hidden behind the thick veil of smoke shrouding the peninsula. He barely remembered the smell of fresh air. A permanent scratch in his throat made his eyes water.

He reached Bay Street, where Jo said he should have taken the turn with the Cadillac. His stomach roared—he hadn't eaten a lick since morning. Ma had insisted he throw some provisions into the back seat before leaving. *So much for that.* Otto decided it best to veer all the way north to Fort Mason. The soldiers there must have food and water to spare. He would have to push his luck and hope Jo would still be waiting for him in Washington Square come morning. It would also do him good to get some rest.

The urban landscape turned rural, and nearing the seaside, Otto descended to the area on a dirt path, curving downhill to the left into an open clearing. He wasn't alone. As the evening drew to a close, Fort Mason's entrance was thick with people, wheels, and dust, the crowd having the same idea as he had. Thankfully the fort was some distance from the flames, and the winds now blew them in the opposite direction. The closer he got to the coastline, the more he could breathe something that resembled air again. It was like surfacing from the sea after holding your breath for two minutes.

Makeshift tents and lean-tos made of scrap wood peppered the landscape, similar to Golden Gate Park, but with more military presence since it served as U.S. Army Headquarters. A long refugee line stretched at least a hundred yards. At the front, the crowd funneled through a food station: a semicircle of boxes piled on top of crates that held fruits, vegetables, and some unidentifiable rations. At the stations, flanked by cannons, Army officers divvied up the food. The threatening cannons seemed to say, "Take more than your share at your own risk."

Otto grew uncomfortable. Maybe the cannons' forbidding nature made his skin crawl, but he felt something distinctively menacing. Perhaps someone was following him.

"Never Try Frei!" In the unfamiliar, blistering landscape, a familiar voice shot up his spine and turned it to ice.

Cecil Miller. *The bastard.* Otto braced for what would surely be an unpleasant conversation. "Cecil, what are you doing here?"

"Being a post-apocalyptic shoulder to cry on for any young dame in need, if you catch my drift?" He exaggerated a wink to punctuate the innuendo. "Some Italian birds wandered down here from North Beach. They may not be too bright, but boy, can they carry a tune, if you know what I mean." Cecil swept his arm in the shape of a big 'S,' once again winking at Otto.

"Watch your mouth, Miller. Those are fine ladies you're talking about."

"Woah, Frei, I was just playing. What's gotten into you? Say, you look like you crawled through the underbelly of hell to get here. What happened to you?" Otto noticed Miller's smug words. *Great—he wouldn't let this go.*

"Was helping the demolition crews down on Van Ness," Otto said.

"Well, look at the good Samaritan over here!" He spun around, holding out his arms as if introducing a three-ring circus and shouting to whoever would listen.

"Knock it off." Otto knew he'd get a reaction from Cecil, *but this production was worse than expected.*

"Saving the city from the red devil himself. What bravery! What selflessness! Oh, let us all thank our hero, Otto Frei! Without him, we would all surely be doomed."

Bastard. "Give it a rest, Miller."

"What are you even still doing here? I thought you had left town for good."

Otto had no idea how Cecil found out that he left since he hadn't told a soul other than leaving his family a note. Best he could figure, word must have gotten out when he wasn't seen after the earthquake.

Then, just like every time he finished pushing Otto's buttons, Cecil reeled it back and said, "Take it easy! I'm just pulling your leg, *freund.*"

He never let Cecil get to him, but this time was different. The bastard had struck a nerve. Otto wondered why he ever tried to fit into the socialite group of self-absorbed aristocrats who expected everyone around them to do what they say and cater to their every whim, no matter the cost to their dignity. He wondered why he had ever tried to meet his father's expectations when he knew he never would; why he tried to be friends with people like Cecil, whom he genuinely didn't like and who didn't like him. He couldn't think of a good answer to that question: *why?*

The best answer he could figure was that it was either a matter of pride, power, or fear. It always seemed to be one or the other that motivated people in a position of power to do whatever they wanted—or, heaven forbid, all three at once. It drove him crazy to think that he wasn't in charge of his destiny; that someone else of greater influence was pulling the strings. He felt an urge before the earthquake to do something about that feeling of powerlessness;

something that made him feel like he was calling the shots in his own life. That's why he had chosen to leave.

But since the earthquake, everything had changed. Since Jo. Since the promise of a future with Pop's company that he had agency over. He no longer felt like leaving was his only choice. And surprisingly, that didn't make him feel trapped. It was his choice to remain in San Francisco. His honest-to-God decision was to stay put and build a future that hopefully included Jo. Starting fresh in a reborn city made him feel like anything was possible. It made him feel free.

"You hear me?" Cecil waved his hand an inch from Otto's face. "Looks like your departure was another big bumble by Never Try Frei!"

Cecil's burn stung, but Otto let it roll off his back and into the mud at his feet. "Actually, I decided not to go. Turns out there's more for me here than I realized. What's the situation here?" Otto felt proud of being the bigger man and changing the course of the conversation rather than feeding into his taunts.

Cecil took an exaggerated, off-balance step back, visibly jarred by Otto's quick change of subject. He practically foamed at the mouth with anticipation to take more jabs at Otto's character, but he played along. Otto knew Cecil was waiting for another opening.

Cecil said, "Oh, they're evacuating people by the hundreds, thousands even, taking them north to Sausalito and Tiburon. There has been an entire flotilla of rescue ships going in and out all day."

It made sense. People probably couldn't traverse the city to reach the main ferry terminal, so passenger ships came to them anywhere they could find an accessible pier.

Otto looked toward the bay from the military outpost on a hill about eighty feet above the sea. Beyond the field trampled by thousands of homeless, past the Army Hospital and hundreds more temporary shelters he saw two large ships docked, clew lines drawn in, tightly concealing sails in its yard. "Are they forcing everyone to evacuate?" he asked.

"Not really, but since they don't have enough supplies yet to feed and shelter everyone, they're encouraging it. I'm planning on grabbing the next one myself. Probably catch a ride over to Oakland the first chance I get and wait for the city to draw its final breath."

"She's not going to die!" Otto shouted, startling the people around him, who must have thought he was talking about a person.

"W-w-whoa, buddy! What are you, married to San Francisco? A few days ago, you were about to leave her at the altar. Open your eyes, my friend." Cecil snuck up real close and whispered into Otto's ear louder than his regular speaking voice. Otto smelled the hot stink of Cecil's bitter breath.

"Watch it, Miller." Otto felt heat rise up his neck and settle in his cheekbones.

"There's nothing for you here," Cecil spat. "Whatever life-changing bullshit happened to you to make you a sudden saint won't change the fact that even in its current state of rubble and bones, this place is still too good for you. You ain't worth its smoldering carcass, Frei."

Otto liked to think he had grown as a person, but all those thoughts went out the window. The heat in his temples shot down the veins of his forearm and pulsated as his right fist tightened.

Cecil shrank and barely squeaked out a "Take it easy!" before Otto's fist arced across the sky—his swift right hook met Cecil's left mandible with a satisfying *crunch*.

Chapter Thirty-One

Washington Square, 5:48 p.m.

Mama clawed her way through the thickest part of the crowd to get to Jo. Her eyes widened, and she made the sign of the cross as she emerged. "I have been so worried about you. Thank heavens you are safe, my darling." She fell to her knees and embraced Jo, weeping before the dystopian backdrop.

Jo struggled to cling to her resentment as tightly as Mama held onto her and fought the urge to return her embrace. If she gave in now, everything she intended to tell Mama threatened to float away like burnt paper on the wind. She had spent too long being angry and hurt; too long believing she knew what happened to Papa, only to realize it was all a lie.

Mama pulled back and looked her up and down. "My daughter. My sweet daughter, I was so worried about you." Her brown eyes twinkled with tears.

Jo recalled a similar vision of her mother from when she was about eight years old and playing in the street. A rancher drove his herd through the city and lost control of one of the heifers. The

NOTHING LEFT BUT DUST

cow stormed straight toward Jo, and Mama scooped her up by the armpits and carried her to safety. She knelt and held her then, the same as she did now.

Jo snapped her eyelids shut tight as raw clamshells to hold in her tears. "Mama," she choked, "I'm here." That was about all she could manage.

"I'm fine, Mama," Jo reassured. Her mother stroked her hair with her long fingers, now more calloused than she remembered. "Where's Peter?"

As soon as she asked, a bright-eyed little boy bounded his way into Mama's arms. He dressed as if ready for Sunday school, somehow clean as a whistle.

"He has no idea what's happening," Mama said. "It's all a game. He loved camping in the park last night."

"I can't believe how much he's grown. The last I saw him, he was still in diapers."

"He's nearly four already. It all happens so quickly . . ."

"Mama, the fires are still burning, and the winds are changing. We should leave. I'm afraid we're not safe here."

"No, Josephina, we should be safe. We got word that they are letting us back into our homes. Please, come with us. You can stay with us tonight."

Jo hesitated. "I'm supposed to meet someone here at the park." She popped her head up and looked around for Otto or a Cadillac parked on the street but saw nothing. "He should be here any minute."

"Will he leave without you if he sees you're not here?"

"No, I don't think so." Jo didn't want to give any sort of voice to the doubt she had inside that Otto might change his mind and leave her behind. *He wouldn't.* And besides, he knew Mama's address, just in case. "All right, let's go."

They walked two blocks over past Dupont to the servant's

quarters that occupied the ground floor of 455 Green Street. They approached the front door, and Jo felt as if someone were watching them. She turned around and hoped to see Otto, but he wasn't there. *He would find her soon.*

The place was smaller than Papa's bistro and smelled a bit musky from the fires. But it was not enough to overtake the familiar aroma from her childhood of coffee and currant jelly. Cookbooks littered the kitchen countertop; Mama must use them when cooking meals for the family she served.

Jo didn't know much about Mama's life here. While Jo was living with her aunt and uncle, Mama had sent her letters every month for a year after Papa died. But she never read them. She didn't want to hear whatever excuses Mama had or her empty promises to one day be a family again. Mama must have stopped writing those letters after she never heard anything back, or Aunt Rosalina stopped giving them to her.

Jo waited for the right time before mentioning Mama's letters to Mrs. Tucci and the secret they contained about Papa's suicide.

She watched Mama's dress swing back and forth as she rummaged through the cupboards and scrounged up some food. She found half a loaf of bread and a few tomatoes that she sliced up and dressed with olive oil, salt, a little garlic, and dried oregano. Fires were still outlawed, and without the use of the stove, options were limited. She split it between three plates and set all but one of them at a tiny bistro-sized table in the kitchen. Peter jumped into one of the two chairs, grabbed a fork, and began to eat. Mama nibbled hers while she stood at the counter.

Jo had to credit her mother this much—Mama was a good cook. No one could make pasta like she could: slightly past *al dente* with the right amount of salt to enhance the natural flavor of the sauce drizzled on it. "Your pasta water should always taste like the sea; that's what your Nonna taught me." Jo craved her pasta from time to time, mixed with a little olive oil and parmesan or with a thick Bolognese on a cold night.

But right now, Jo didn't care. She sat down and gobbled up the bread and tomatoes as if she hadn't had a morsel in a week.

Mama let her finish eating before she spoke. "Where are Rosalina and Giuseppe?"

She had nearly forgotten. It seemed like so long ago that the house collapsed upon them. "They . . . they didn't make it, Mama. The whole neighborhood toppled, then went up in smoke before anyone could figure out what was happening."

Mama looked over at Peter, who held his plate vertically with both hands while oil and vinegar raced to the bottom edge. "Ah, ah, ah!" she tsk-tsked.

Peter's eyes glanced over to Mama without turning his head, flopped his tongue out of his mouth, and took three quick licks.

Mama pointed, and without saying a word, Peter put the plate down and ran into the bedroom, giggling.

Jo realized Mama might not have wanted Peter to hear about family members having died, but he didn't seem to understand.

Mama sat in Peter's vacant chair and looked at Jo. "Oh dear, I'm so sorry."

"We also lost Mrs. Tucci." Jo teared up again. The mention of her name aloud and declaring what happened made her loss tangible.

"*Dio mio*, Josephina, you poor thing." Mama placed her hand on Jo's knee. "I know how much she meant to you. And you to her."

Mama composed herself before getting up and walking to a secretary's desk in the corner of the small apartment. She pulled open the large door, folding it down to reveal piles of papers and a small stack of books. Her mother drew out a stack of twine-wrapped envelopes. After untying them, she spread them out on the table for Jo to see.

A stamped return address with *V.T. Press* in large print was in the top left corner of each of a dozen envelopes.

"Are those from Mrs. Tucci?" Jo asked.

"Yes. Starting about a year after Papa . . . since I came to work here. When you didn't answer my letters, I reached out to her. It's how I always knew that you were okay. Mrs. Tucci, bless her soul, was a gift from God. She loved you dearly and thought so highly of you. I trusted her to look after you."

Jo let her fingertips dance across the fanned-out envelopes. Her whimsical handwriting spelling out Mama's name and address was enough to comfort her. She opened one of the letters.

Dearest Alma,

Josephine is doing well. She spends most days upstairs in my office, studying each map that comes out of production. I know she dreams of where she can go and what she can do, which is healthy for a young girl to imagine at her age. She's a bright one too. Your daughter has quite a brilliant future ahead of her. The girl just needs to learn how to break out of the familiar and go out into the world. She needs to live a great life instead of just yearning for one. In time I know she will be ready. She is still hurting. She lets her fear have too great an agency over her. Her eyes get a faraway look, and I know she misses her father. In time, she will be ready to know the truth. Once she understands, she'll be prepared to come to you. She has a lot of pain to work through, but I know she'll find her way back.

Sincerely,

Vittoria Tucci

Mrs. Tucci's last words rang in Jo's mind like a bell. "You can't see the full picture," she had said. "You are in your own way." Jo wept, wiping her uninvited tears away with the palm of her hand. This letter was a key to Jo's understanding of how badly Mama wanted to fix things. How much Mama loved her.

Mrs. Tucci never intended for Jo to inherit her shop. She didn't plan to lock Jo into a career in printing. At least not before she rekindled her relationship with her mother and knew that's where she wanted to be.

But that didn't change the fact that Mrs. Tucci and her mother had deceived her with a hidden relationship. Jo gripped the hand-written evidence of their duplicity, crunching its edges and fighting the urge to throw it in Mama's face, run out the door, and never speak to her again.

But then a curious thing happened. Fury overwhelmed her instinct to avoid the confrontation. That anger bubbled up, and a new, unfamiliar voice took control. "How could you?" Jo asked. The words seemed to escape of their own accord.

Mama gasped. "Whatever do you mean?"

"You lied to me." Jo held firm and refused to allow any salty tears to betray the severity of her accusation.

Mama gasped. "I did no such thing, child."

Jo threw up her arms. "I know what happened to Papa. What *really* happened. I know he killed himself."

"Josephine, you are tired. Not another word. We will discuss this in the morning. Now get some rest."

They had nothing else to say to one another. Mama retreated to her bedroom, and Jo made hers on the sofa.

Peter peeked his head out of the sole bedroom in the place. He looked at Jo like she was a stranger. "Here," he said. "You can have my bed." He pointed in the direction of a tiny bed in the corner of the bedroom he shared with Mama. She looked at her brother, whom she barely knew.

"That's okay, kiddo." She remembered Otto had called her by the same nickname. "I'm okay here on the sofa. But you get some rest. Tomorrow's going to be a big day."

Peter hopped off to his room. Jo tried her best to sleep, but she struggled, knowing the world was on fire outside and that a different sort of disaster between her and Mama was left unresolved. Her mother said she wasn't worried about the flames, that they were too far to pose a threat. But Jo knew better. Conditions could change quickly.

Night trudged into morning, and Jo didn't feel like she had gotten any rest. Maybe ten minutes here and fifteen there; at any given time, she had no idea what time it was or if she was awake or asleep. She had woken up twice in torment with chills, wishing Otto were there to hold her in place of the unfinished afghan that was one foot shy of covering her whole body.

When the house was eerily quiet, she lay awake, imagining where Otto was and worrying if he would show up this morning. He could change his mind, or something could happen on the way with the state of the fires and changing conditions. It was impossible to say. She thought she heard a knock at the door once, but when she got up to check, she realized it must have been a dream.

Mama emerged from her bedroom and behaved chipper and well-rested. She searched for something to eat and settled on oats and dried fruits. She separated them into three servings and set two of them on the table. Peter clambered into his chair, wearing his outfit from yesterday.

"Why have you never come to visit us here?" Mama asked matter-of-factly. Jo reacted by swallowing too soon, causing a mouthful of oats to get stuck. It sent her into a coughing fit. Mama seemed genuinely unaware of the answer, but Jo was certain that she knew why. Her mother was taunting her with guilt. That didn't take long to understand.

Jo had carried her anger all the way from South of Market. When she opened her mouth, her words turned to polenta globbing off a spoon. "I can't explain, Mama. I just didn't feel like I should be the one to chase after you when you were the one that left *me*."

She let the words marinate in Mama's ears for a minute. Her family was not usually this forward, typically dancing around a sore topic like ballet dancers. It was considered, at the very least rude, if not unquestionably unladylike, to present one's distaste so frankly. Italians were notorious for holding grudges, especially when it came to family.

Her mother stared, seeming bewildered. Since she had begun ripping the bandage off, she might as well continue. *It was now or never.*

Jo said, "When Papa died, I needed you. But you left. I was stuck serving Uncle Giuseppe like an indentured servant. I had to leave school. He was about to see me married off; he didn't care what I wanted. Not like Papa."

"Your father was an exceptional man."

Jo looked at Peter. "Hey, kiddo. Why don't you go finish your food in your room."

"But Mama says I'm not supposed to eat in . . ."

"Go on. Just this once," said Mama, and her brother obeyed.

"Mama," said Jo. "If Papa was so exceptional, why did he kill himself?"

Mama grimaced as if a horse had kicked the wind out of her. "What do you mean? Where did you even hear that?"

"In your letter to Mrs. Tucci. You said you were keeping it from me. I saw the article."

"*O, accidenti!*"

"Why did he do it? Why did he give up? Why did he shoot himself in the damn head?"

"Josephina! I ought to wash your mouth out with soap," Mama leaped up from the table and scurried about the kitchen, cleaning things that didn't need cleaning. "Your father was sick."

Jo jumped up from the table and shouted, accenting her frustration with a flip of both wrists into a double-finger purse. "He wasn't sick. He was perfectly healthy. Why would you say that?"

"I don't mean physically. It took me a while to see the truth myself. Your father was a wonderful man, but he was not well. He had *demoni*."

"What do you mean, demons?"

"They haunted him every day. They told him he wasn't a good husband or a good father, a provider. In the end, those demons had voices louder than the love he had for his family. It took me a long time to understand this. For years I blamed myself. But the correspondence I had with Vittoria—Mrs. Tucci—she helped me see that it was not my fault. There was nothing I could have done to help your father. Nothing anyone could have done."

Jo couldn't hold back anymore and spun into a tizzy of tears. "So that's it. Papa was sick, and you blamed yourself. That's why you left. And that whole time, you didn't think to tell me?"

"I didn't want to burden you with the memory that he was anything less than a wonderful father. And he was. He was so good to you. He loved you so much. And you were so young, *Passerotta*."

"No! You don't get to call me that."

Mama, still holding her dishtowel, planted her hands on Jo's shoulders and yanked her back to the surface of the Earth.

"My little *cannoli*," she said. She hadn't called her that in years. She used to say when Jo was born, she was no bigger than a cannoli. "Listen to me carefully. Your father may not have been perfect, but he loved you dearly. You were his lighthouse on the foggiest of days."

"But it wasn't enough. In the end, I didn't matter enough for him to choose to live."

Mama put her hands on her hips and plucked her words carefully from the rafters. "Sometimes, Josephina, when things get impossibly hard, we can't always see the end of the pain. We spin like we're underwater, and we don't know which direction to swim for a breath of air. We all have moments when life becomes too heavy for us to carry on our own. Your father was so lost he couldn't get to the surface to breathe."

Jo had found that to be true in the last two days. If Papa's daily mindset was anything close to hers, she couldn't imagine how she would carry that burden on her own. *Poor Papa. He must have felt so crippled. So scared and alone.*

"Your father lost sight of this. And perhaps, for a time, so did I. I blamed myself when I thought what happened should have been within my control. I took responsibility for all his pain and then for all your anger and discontentment. I couldn't face you. I felt that I had ruined you. And my not being in your life would be your best chance for success. I thought you would be happier with your aunt and uncle."

Jo didn't buy it for a second. *There was more to the story.* "You expect me to believe that, Mama?"

Mama brought her palms together in prayer and gulped a mouthful of air like it was minestrone. "*Ti prego,* Josephina. The truth," she stuttered. "The *truth* is—"

A trumpet blared from just outside their door, and the women jolted in surprise. A forceful knock preceded a flurry of indecipherable demands. Jo froze. Mama smoothed out her apron, walked to the door, and opened it slowly.

The man at the door pushed it open the rest of the way. His gruff voice belted, "Get out now! We're going to blow this place for the sake of the firebreak."

A uniformed man waved his arms wildly in the street, motioning for everyone to vacate their homes. Again, a trumpet sounded, now a few houses away. "What does that mean?" she asked Mama.

Mama turned as white as a sheet.

"It means to move along or be shot."

Jo was nearly knocked off her feet by a gust of wind so strong it carried pieces of charred paper from miles away. The winds had changed direction entirely and were now coming from the northwest, sealing the fate of everyone in North Beach.

Soldiers escorted families up and down the street, where there was an eerie sense of calm. The evacuees reacted in a similar perplexing way. They gathered a few belongings, went out into the street, looked up, and shrugged as if to say, "Oh well, I guess that's it."

Mama yelled, "Peter, get your things. We're going back to the park."

Jo ran up the sloped hill of Green Street, where she found a better vantage point over the valley. The once-distant firestorm churned below, producing a spinning groundswell of orange flames that roared and whirled upward. The heavens opened up above the swell, and clouds mixed with dark smoke arched into a tornado of fiery bedevilment three times the size of the tallest building.

The vortex conjured a tremendous wave of heat that hit Jo full force with the intensity of a tidal wave, knocking her backward. The ferocious funnel howled promises of complete and unbounded annihilation. San Francisco was doomed.

They had to get out.

Jo scrambled to plot an escape route in her mind. Her city street maps might be gone, but she studied the patterns engraved into her mind. She surmised that they had two options: go up to the top of Telegraph Hill, which had no guarantee of being out of the danger zone, or head for the waterfront and hope a ship was there to carry them away. Worst case scenario, they could wade into the frigid waters and hope the flames died down before they froze to death. *That was the better option.*

Jo ran back to the house and found Mama inside, racing around the place and throwing what she found into a trunk.

"How are you going to carry that?" Jo asked.

Mama stopped and stared at all her belongings spilling out of the trunk. She smacked her forehead with her palm, apparently realizing that she had not thought that far ahead.

A man burst into the basement apartment; his arms filled with sticks of dynamite. "Ma'am, you have to go! Now!" he yelled.

Mama was scared stiff, just staring at her belongings in the trunk. Jo knew what was happening—her mind wasn't working right. *She needed to do something.*

"Here, put this on," Jo grabbed a dress and threw it at her. "And this." She grabbed another dress and a coat. Then Jo took two of each and put them on.

The man laying the final charge looked at them as if they were two nickels short of a dollar.

Jo grabbed an armful of Peter's clothing, and Mama stuffed a cookbook in her bodice before grabbing Peter's hand and dragging him out the door. They hadn't yet reached the far side of the street when the whole line of houses behind them exploded, sending bricks and pieces of flaming timber shooting outward in every direction. They ducked behind a carriage and avoided being hit by blast material.

The vehicle they hid behind was not so lucky. Shards stuck out of its side, and one of the barrels the carriage held had a hole going straight through. Black metallic sand was pouring out. *Gunpowder.* Jo noticed a few particulates had struck the cart and were on fire.

"Run!" she shouted to her family. They scrambled to their feet and took off up the hill as the flames reached the cart and rose to lick the barrels full of gunpowder. The sky flashed, and a shockwave pulsed through the air; all three of them flew forward onto their hands and knees.

Jo got up and brushed the dirt off her legs. Her knee felt like it was bleeding, but she couldn't tell from all the layers she wore.

"Josephina! You're on fire!" Peter shouted.

Jo slapped her chest and arms frantically with her hands, spinning uselessly in a circle. The heat radiated through the clothing to her back. It didn't hurt, but she could feel the warmth spreading between her shoulder blades.

Mama began to beat Jo's back with her hat before struggling to take off Jo's outer layer coat. She threw it on the ground and danced on it like she was doing the Turkey Trot. She spun around, popped her chin up, and smiled at Jo. "There. Now where to?"

Jo took a moment to catch her breath. Her mother had just saved her life. She did it with such calculated showmanship that she could have been part of a Vaudeville act.

The family had to get somewhere safe, and fast. At this rate, these imbeciles handling the gunpowder would spread it faster and farther than ever. They could either seek high ground and hope the fires would lose steam or get to the wharf and hope a ship would be there to board. The thought of leaving the city without Otto left a fistful of olive pits in her stomach. *It was almost too much to bear.*

"Up there," Jo pointed to the top of Telegraph Hill, where two stuck-together mounds of earth, one slightly shorter than the other, were ornamented with precariously placed houses on stilts spread far apart. Maybe they would be far enough above everything up there, a natural firebreak.

"Are you sure, Cannoli? We might be better off just going to the piers and trying to get a boat."

"We can't leave!" Jo bit back like a snake that someone had stepped on.

Mama shut her mouth and started walking.

As they walked, Jo couldn't shake the feeling that someone again was watching her. "Otto?" she called into the street below. No one answered.

Chapter Thirty-Two

Fort Mason, Friday, April 20th, 1906, 6:00 a.m.

y daybreak, the southwest winds steadily pushed all the smoke from the encroaching fireline in Otto's direction on the waterfront. The city to the south, including Russian Hill, was in full blaze.

Desperate refugees migrated toward the pier on the west side of the harbor, hoping to board a ship to carry them to safety. The incoming smoke, thick with burning cinders, brought a new wave of thousands of people seeking a way out of the damned hellscape.

A protected U.S. Navy cruiser glided into the harbor.

"The U.S.S. Chicago!" Men shouted proudly. "Flagship of the Pacific Squadron! God bless the U.S. Navy!"

Otto ran eastward along the bluff, with hundreds of others itching to see the dazzling vessel pull into the harbor. She was magnificent. This beauty was built for speed and maneuverability between the two-stack steam engines and the triple masts. The artillery battery penetrating the thick armor of gun shields showed she meant business.

Otto reached the wharf as about two hundred officers disembarked and began to bring order to the crowd.

"How many can it hold?" One rough-edged gentleman asked.

An officer in a blue uniform, adorned with double-breasted gold buttons and frilly shoulder epaulets, responded to the crowd. "Thousands. With her and the rest of the fleet, we can move about twenty thousand souls."

Otto approximated that at least that number were taking refuge at Fort Mason. An evacuation that size would easily be the largest in history.

The crowd around Otto grew denser. "If you want to come aboard, you'll need to get in line along with these fine folks." The sailor motioned toward a growing line of people. "You'll be safe and sound in Tiburon by this afternoon."

The queue started in front of the ship and stretched far down the coastline, almost reaching the beach. Pairs of men and women teamed up to drag their trunks and miscellany up to the ramps of the awaiting ship.

"No belongings aboard the boat," the sailor announced. "We need the room for as many souls as it can hold!"

Otto looked at the disappointed and heartbroken faces of all the waiting people surrounded by personal items. How they managed to get their things to the piers was a mystery to Otto. The boarding queue stretched farther than he could make out. Officers repeated, "Limited space available. Please bring only what you can carry."

"You boarding, son?" one of the officers asked Otto.

Otto looked toward the burning city. The flames were close enough to again feel the heat. Boarding the ship would be the sensible thing to do. *But he couldn't leave. Not before finding Jo.* "No," he told the officer. "I can't."

The route back to Bay Street looked to be aflame. Otto didn't know which direction to go to get to their meeting spot. He turned to the waiting crowd. "Excuse me," he announced. "Does anyone know how to get to Washington Square?"

A hunched-over Italian man stepped out of line, carrying a lamp in one arm and what must have been his wife's hatbox in the other. "Just go there to Montgomery and take it up, *ehhh*, about eight blocks," he pointed to a nearby street. "But, *ehhh*, we just came from *thatta* way and *ees* all full of smoke. They are blowing up our homes to save the city."

"Oh no," Otto exclaimed.

"*Itta don't make-ah no sense!*" He pushed his pointed fists in the air to emphasize the unacceptable situation.

"Johnny, *devi calmarti! Rilassati.*" His wife slapped her hands together audibly in pleading prayer.

"*Oi Maria, aspetta, aspetta,*" Johnny put his palms up to say *wait a minute, don't tell me what to do.*

"*You-ah,* could go *arounda. Sticka* to the sea wall and find a *nuovo percorso. Ehhh,* a new path."

Johnny's wife grabbed him by the ear and pulled him back in line.

"Thank you for your help." Otto distanced himself from the happy couple arguing in Italian as if in the privacy of their own home.

The wind began to shift again. Gusts began to blow in from the west, which meant the ocean air would soon send the fire back from where it came, assuring it would soon consume everything lucky enough to have survived the first pass. *Mother nature had written the city a death sentence.*

The wind shift also meant that the people in North Beach who thought they were safe were now directly in the path of the firestorm. *Jo was likely one of them.*

He saw two choices. The first would be to stay where he was and hope that Jo made it out okay, praying their paths would intersect. The second was to go back into the belly of the beast, hoping he could traverse the streets of the collapsed infrastructure and locate a single soul. It would be reckless and damn near impossible. But had he a choice? He had come this far; he wasn't about to abandon Jo.

He sighed as he looked inland at the glow of the fire against Russian Hill. The fires were closer than they had been the night before. He was exhausted and dehydrated. He hadn't gotten much rest, although the soldiers had been able to provide him with a blanket. A shooting pain spread from his arm up to his neck every time he moved. As a result, he fought a severe headache.

Otto decided to try his luck at passing on Montgomery. Long strides propelled him further down the crowded boulevard that ran diagonally to the rest of the road grid—droves of people headed in the opposite direction. Their instincts told them to run away from the fire. Of course, that's what any sane person would do. But here he was again, running into danger rather than away from it. *Was he brave, or did he have a death wish?* More buildings fell to the flames.
Shit.

When he got within a couple of blocks of the park, he climbed on top of an abandoned trunk to get a better look. He scanned hundreds of faces, but none of them were Jo's.

And then something shifted. More people headed back the other way, appearing to ricochet off an invisible wall. They shouted, "Go back! The flames have blocked us off! There's no way through!"

"It's made it all the way to the water at Montgomery!" Another voice came.

Otto had to see it to believe it. He ached to get a better view from the top of the trunk, then climbed higher onto a nearby abandoned wagon. Sure enough, the smoke plumes reached the north of their location. In the last two hours, the fires had swept through an area populated with countless people and cut off an entire corner of the city. There was no way to escape to the west. He and the rest of these people were trapped like rats with only one way to go: east toward the bay.

He forced down a lump in his throat—a voice in his head tried to tell him that Jo was either dead or had left without him. Either one of those meant he would never see her again. He gathered himself and looked in the opposite direction of the flames. *She's smart. She would know what to do.* He tried to imagine where her journey might have taken her and where she might be.

He remembered her mother's address—455 Green Street. He remembered passing it on his way north after separating from the demolition crew, but he hadn't seen it yet. It had to be farther inland. He tried to recall the specifics of the crude dirt map that Jo had drawn for him. It must be a couple of blocks away. He imagined that she knew the fires were spreading to the east, which meant she would try to flee to a safe spot without leaving the city, so she would either be on the waterfront or . . . Otto's gaze plotted her trajectory toward the top of Telegraph Hill. *That had to be it.*

The way forward was impassable. But he remembered the old Italian man's advice to follow the sea wall. He would have to try and get there another way. He scrounged up every last bit of *oomph* he had and took off in a run to the north up Mason Street.

He would find her, she would be safe, and he would never let her out of his sight again.

Chapter Thirty-Three

Green and Dupont, Friday, April 20th, 1906, 8:30 a.m.

Jo, Mama, and Peter trudged up Green Street, the slope becoming more vertical the closer they got to the southeastern crest of Telegraph Hill. Mama panted as Jo swallowed gulps of air and sweat formed underneath the weight of her multi-layered fabric fortress. They caught their breath at Kearny, a level cross street, where Jo could see the crest of the hill half a block in front of them.

"Almost there," Jo huffed.

"Not quite," Mama pointed to the left where the hill gained ground.

They reached the end of the block, where they could see the bay below buzzing with the traffic of rescue vessels cutting through the smoke. Jo hoped she'd feel a blast of cool air off the water, but instead felt the heat on her back from the fires in the valley below. She turned around and watched as the blaze swept its way across the valley, claiming North Beach and the parts of Chinatown it missed on its first pass before the winds shifted.

"I'm tired, Mama," said Peter. "I want to go home."

"Not yet, little one," Mama said calmly. "We've got to race to the top of the hill first." Mama cleared her throat when Peter skipped ahead out of earshot. Before them stood a near-vertical climb up the side of a cliff.

Jo wiped the sweat from her brow with Mama's furs. "All right, let's go."

"Josephina, I think it's time you know more about your Papa and me."

"What do you mean?"

Jo continued up the road, whose sidewalks were so steep they gave way to wooden steps, huffing under the weight of her multiple coats and frocks. She didn't look up as she concentrated on where she was stepping, hoping not to tip over.

"I need you to know that I was afraid," Mama whispered.

"What were you afraid of?"

"What you didn't see, what your father and I kept from you, is how much we fought. It was quite a bit. He would come home at night and be unhappy with how few customers he had that day, and how your uncle was putting his nose where it didn't belong with the business. It would put him over the edge.

"It would escalate into how unhappy he was with his life. He was dissatisfied with the neighborhood where we lived and felt frustrated that he couldn't do anything to give us a better life, no matter how hard he worked.

"When your brother came along, it made it more challenging. You were probably too young to notice, but he grew short with Peter. He couldn't tolerate it when he cried. 'It's like a thousand knives piercing my soul,' he would say. And he blamed me. That was the hardest part.

"He was so lost in his ocean of despair that he didn't see he was sick. He blamed his feelings of helplessness on me. Whenever I tried to help, he told me I made it worse. He warned me that I would drive him to suicide one day. I didn't believe him. That is—"

"—until it happened." Jo couldn't breathe. She stopped in her tracks. Panting heavily, she stripped back down layer by layer until she was in her nightgown.

"I was afraid you would blame me for what happened, Josephine. Just like your Papa did. I couldn't have you find out that I was responsible for what happened to Papa. And I couldn't fail you as I did him."

Jo bent over to catch her breath as her heart pounded heavily in her chest. She could feel it beating like a drum and thought she might keel over any minute. Everything she knew to be true, knew to be her reality, was wrong. Her love and hate for her mother and father swirled and bubbled, boiling in frothy, messy uncertainty.

Could her happy, pure memories of Papa still endure knowing how imperfect he was? How poorly he treated Mama? Were all the lessons he taught her, every ideal she held herself to, still valid, knowing now that he was sick? Could he still be her hero, or was all of that tarnished because of his fatal flaws?

A thick film of doubt and doom shrouded every happy memory she had of him. "Papa always taught me to see the beauty in life. How can I see any of that now? Now that I know the dark veil he lived under?"

Mama said, "*Figlia*, life is never black and white. Sometimes, you must try hard to see in color in the grays. Other times life's so bright and beautiful you almost have to look away, or you'll go blind. It's the blessing and the curse that is life. I'm sad every day your Papa left us, but instead of letting it consume me, I choose to remember him for the color he brought to my life."

Mama looked ahead to Peter, kicking a tin can down the steps and singing. She smiled. "You and your brother are the brightest stars in my sky."

Jo bent over and picked up her mother's clothes that she had scattered around her and continued climbing.

When they reached the intersection at Union Street, an older woman with gray hair and a hump on her back, probably from laboring over countless stews and sauces, came out of her front door and hobbled to meet them.

She spoke in Italian, "Is it here?"

Jo could make it out from hearing Papa and Mama speak Italian when she was little, but they never wanted her to speak it herself for fear of sounding foreign. Mama explained to the woman that the fire was indeed close. She couldn't confidently say they were safe on the hill, but she wanted to believe they would be.

Jo, Mama, and Peter walked down a side street that brought them close to the edge of an open embankment. There, they had an unobstructed view of the smoldering ruins of downtown and could see fires approaching from the west. More and more neighbors emerged from their homes, joining them at the vantage point. They looked together at the raging inferno headed their way. The fire began to climb in elevation above the base of the hill, eating its way through North Beach. Jo watched in horror as the flames consumed Saints Peter and Paul Church. She wondered if all the records she had helped bury in Washington Park would survive.

Jo turned away to assess their surroundings for escape routes. Decades of dynamite blasts had sculpted the eastern side of Telegraph Hill, forming jagged cliffs and a rockslide-prone landscape. They stood at the edge of a drop-off into a massive quarry that spanned the length of the hill. A series of dirt paths and precarious steps meandered through a network of ramshackle two and three-story cottages and led down to the docks. Two hundred feet of primitive stairway separated them from sea level. If they were forced to evacuate the high ground, it would take them a very long time to retreat.

Otto. If he were still coming and still had the automobile, there was no way for him to reach her. Jo's heart sank. It would be impossible for him to get to her, and he had no idea where she was. *She may never see him again.*

Embers flew up in the draft, latched onto bushes and fence posts, and nibbled away at them. Several shirtless, barrel-chested men, muscles built for dock work, threw buckets of water on every spark in sight before it could make a full meal of its target.

Jo approached a girl who was watching the men at work. She was near Jo's age with hair like the glow of sunset. "What's going on?"

"Oh, you see, they've been workin' all mornin' on saving *tha* hill. Firemen been workin' for three days straight, they *ave*." The girl's Irish accent was nearly incomprehensible. She pointed at the firehose running down the side of the steps.

"It runs for *'alf* a mile, it does, down to the *wa'er!* They were able ta get it *ta* work some, but it doesn't look good now."

A single fireman manned the hose nozzle as saltwater trickled out in a line thinner than spit. Another group of men gathered around a stove mid-street, and they ate food they had no doubt "borrowed" from a corner store. Their faces were long as they stared into space, not speaking a word to one another as they drank ale from one of two nearby kegs. An axe leaned up next to the open keg.

Suddenly, a solid stream of bay water erupted through the end of the hose and then slowed down to a moderate flow. "Boy, howdy!" The fireman holding the hose shouted as if waking from a meditative state. The increased water pressure gave the firefighters a second wind. It was just in time, too, because embers swirled in the air, hunting for something combustible.

Jo traced the hose path back to the stairs to see what caused the change in water pressure. Otto was at the top of the steps, walking sluggishly toward her, drenched in sweat and filth, but smiling ear-to-ear.

tto tipped his hat toward the firefighters as they scattered like balls on a billiards table struggling to gain control of the water-filled hose.

"Tell me, what'd you do?" One of the gruff, half-drunk men asked Otto.

"There was a kink in the line a little way down," Otto panted. "I figured it probably wasn't meant to be tied up in a knot."

"You may have just saved us the hill." The man rasped before getting back to work.

When Otto turned back to face Jo, she was running toward him with a look that screamed relief and exasperation.

"Hey, Jo." He opened his arms to her, but she drew near, raised her right hand, and clocked him on the cheek. He had never felt a sweeter sting.

"I've been worried sick. Where on earth have you been? How did you get here? Are you okay? Where's the Cadillac?" Jo rattled off the whole series of questions in one breath before drawing in another. She exhaled. "Oh, never mind, it doesn't matter."

She grabbed him so tightly that he thought his heart would stop. She began to sob. Her body writhed against him, and her intensity muffled the dynamite blast reverberation. He closed his eyes and held her close.

"You okay, kiddo?"

Jo forced herself to take slow breaths to regain composure, "I told you not to call me that." She beamed as she wiped her glistening eyes with her open palms.

They looked on together as the city below them burned. Well, it wasn't much of a city anymore. It wasn't much of anything. Just a bunch of bricks, bones, and smoldering ruins. *A liquefied hell.*

Jo led Otto to the other side of the hilltop. She introduced him to her mother and brother, who stood at an overlook watching the rescue ships maneuver around Goat Island.

"Careful, Peter. Stay away from the edge," Mama warned. Peter's foot slipped from under him as a piece of rock tumbled down the hill into the quarry below. He recovered his balance and scurried to the safety of his mother's dress skirt.

Otto peered over the edge. The quake appeared to have compromised the structural integrity of the rock retaining wall. While most of the surface was covered with small plants, some of its boulders had fallen, taking the ground cover with it, and crashing into the siding of the buildings at the bottom of the hill.

He wanted to tell Jo about what happened at home, about the revelation with his father. He needed to tell her that he had changed his mind and intended to stay in San Francisco. As he looked south toward the tragic state of downtown, he saw no obvious sign of hope. Countless buildings no longer stood; boarding houses, hospitals, churches, and libraries. The Call Building and Palace Hotel were empty, smoldering shells. Yet he knew that if enough people were like him and saw the potential for what San Francisco could become, it wouldn't take long for the clouds to lift. Once the flames went

NOTHING LEFT BUT DUST

out, the work would begin. They would rebuild.

"It's awful, isn't it?" Jo reflected, hugging herself.

"Yes, but I see it now for more than that."

"What do you mean?"

"There will be a rebirth." He motioned toward the alien land-scape with his open hand. "A new renaissance. It will sweep through the streets and erect beautiful buildings; homes and businesses will leave the hopelessness of this day long forgotten."

Jo squinted critically into the distance. "It's hard to see beyond the grief and the devastation." She looked up at him with a soft calmness. "But after seeing the unbroken spirit of the people who live here, I believe you. We San Franciscans are a mulish bunch."

A feeling of ease washed over Otto. They looked out over their city, his arm around her shoulders. They had been through so much, independently and together; nothing could tear them apart. He felt, at last, he could stop running. "Jo, I have something to tell you. I'm—"

From about a block up the hill, the firefighters started hurling expletives as far as they could shout. Otto looked their way. The flow of water had stopped entirely. The firefighter operating the nozzle side of the hose shook it, then banged it against his boot to no avail.

"What happened?" shouted Otto.

"Don't know," one of the men shouted back. He ran toward them in a panic. "This is bad. Even if we can get this to work again, it's only putting out a trickle. Not good enough."

Otto exchanged a look with Jo; they understood what would come next. Just when they thought they had finally found safe ground, they would have to run again.

The helpless firefighter sulked back to the dry hose, crouched to the ground, and put his head in his hands.

"Where are we going to go?" she asked.

"I . . . well." Otto looked around at the surrounding landscape on the hill. The fire enclosed them on three sides. The only way out was to go down the eastern steps and to the water. But the steps were wooden. So, it was only a matter of time before that was no longer an option.

Neurotic laughter echoed from behind the back of the hill. A hooded figure emerged and hobbled toward them, compensating for a limp with the knob of the fire crew's axe.

"Are you crazy, old man? Why would you cut off our only water supply? Who are you?" the fire chief demanded.

"Oh, *he* knows very well who I am." He pointed a boney finger in Otto's direction. "Don't you, boy?"

Jo gasped. "Bernard. It can't be. You should be dead."

"Ah, the curiosity of things that appear to be. The moment you look away, they could become anything at all." He punctuated this remark with an ornery giggle and reached up to slide back his tattered hood, revealing his shadowed face. As he placed the hood behind his neck, the action revealed a grotesque burn on the entire right side of his face. The bright red open sore was peppered with black charred bits that hung from his bones like overcooked pork knuckle.

Otto and Jo drew back. Otto positioned himself between Bernard and Jo, their backs to the crumbling embankment.

Otto wondered what had become of Bernard after they locked the door, trapping him on the roof of the Mechanics Pavilion. At least they knew the answer, though it spelled doom for them and everyone else in this humble neighborhood on Telegraph Hill.

"How did you find us?" Otto asked. "Have you been following me this whole time?"

"Yer sweetheart had her dear sweet mother's address tucked into her boot. After ye left me for dead, I knew you'd make yer way there eventually."

"How did you know I'd come?"

Bernard waved the axe in the air. "'Cause folks be predictable when ye find out what they most desire. They be greedy and shortsighted when they be focused on feeding their ego." He pointed the butt of the axe at Jo. "And yer ego be hungry fer *doxy*."

Otto shook his head to deflect the insults and readjusted his footing between Bernard and Jo. "I'm not going to let you rile me up, old man." He sensed the danger of the cliff behind them, so he sidestepped to the right and forward.

Bernard swayed his hips and moved his feet to counter Otto's position, inching himself closer to the edge. He chuckled as he continued pointing in Jo's direction with the axe before letting its weight overcome his limb. His arm fell and swung like a pendulum. "You underestimate my cleverness, boy. Though to yer credit, folks 'av been doin' so since my rear was barely out of nappies. My Pa could 'av easily gotten three times what that grifter paid him."

"Your father *sold* you?" Jo crept out from her hiding place behind Otto. He reached for her to push her safely back behind him, but she held her hand up without breaking eye contact with the disfigured pursuer. "Bernard, I'm sorry. Leaving you on that rooftop was wrong; I realize that now."

"Oh, deary, of course you do. Ye at least owed me a blinker; I'll give ye that." He sang the overripe, sarcastic words. "But the fate ye sealed me, cursin' me to lay down me fork and knife, was unfairly dealt, even for a knave like me."

"I know, I'm sorry," Jo stepped forward so that she was even with Otto, her eyebrows arched in genuine empathy. "I was just trying to protect myself. To protect both of us. I've been wracked with guilt ever since."

"Jo! What are you doing?" Otto whisper-yelled at her, but she paid no mind. He couldn't tell if she was sympathetic toward Bernard or if she attempted to draw his attention. He watched her closely for a hint of intention.

"Oh deary, no, don't worry your pretty little head. Lucky your assassination attempt was planned by a wooden spoon." He glared at Otto and wagged his finger at him. "Or else you wouldn't have this once-in-a-lifetime opportunity to learn a little something."

"I never should have saved your life, you scoundrel." The words dripped from Otto's teeth like venom.

"Now that, *boy*, be the smartest words that've ever come lurching out of yer *hoity-toity* mouth."

"Have your beef with me—that's fair— but why risk the lives of all these people? What did they ever do to you?"

Bernard lit up like the fiery glow behind him. "I'm not doing this to them; *you* are, boy. It's due course for defying me! This could have been so much easier, but you had to be selfish and rattlebrained."

"What are you talking about? I'm not the one that doomed us all."

"Aye, but ye did, lad. When ye were foolish enough to get shot instead of coming quietly, fer instance—*Selfish*. Ye had many chances to act honorably and give me what was due."

"You're a crimp and a kidnapper!" Jo's voice cracked as she roared. She looked at Otto and took two defensive steps back.

"It's not an honest living, so to speak," Bernard swung his hips, "but it's a respectable one all the same. Somebody's got to teach these young, spoiled *boys* how to be men."

That was the only signal Otto needed. "You're the least respectable person I've ever met." He lunged forward, half ready to knock Bernard's block off, but he stopped. He recalled what Bernard said about his father selling him to a criminal as a boy. This sad little man lashed out because he didn't have the love in his life that Otto had. If Otto reacted to Bernard's verbal jabs out of detest or revenge, he wouldn't be much better of a man. Otto flung his arms above his head and flicked his wrists. "Shoo! Get out of here! Leave us alone!"

Bernard recoiled and took half a step, his eyes wide. "And yer so perfect, young *prince*, chasing your princess all over town. *Selfish!*"

Otto grabbed Jo's hand and stepped away from the edge. "Come

on, Jo. This poor old fool isn't worth another minute of our time."
He broke eye contact with the seething criminal and aimed toward
the empty street behind him.

Then, he heard a strike and a sizzle. Otto turned around and
saw Bernard's face aglow.

"No!" Jo shrieked.

Bernard wiped spittle from his chin with his tattered sleeve, then
pointed at Jo with a shaky hand, delicately pinching a lit match. "Yer
always getting what yer little heart desires, aren't ye now, young
prince? Just another notch in yer bedpost."

"Are you insane? Put that out!"

Bernard tucked the axe into his belt, drew out a half-smoked
cigarette, and placed it between his bone-dry lips. "Don't act like
yer a knight in sheeny armor come to save the *I-talian* princess."
The cigarette bounced between his lips as the flame ate through
the matchstick. "Ye know as soon as ye's bagged the lass, ye'll send
'er on 'er way."

"That's not true," Otto growled, pulling his fingers into tight
fists at his sides.

Bernard looked down at Otto's hands and smiled maniacally as
he steadied the cigarette with his lips. He cupped his hand around
the lit match and puffed.

"Now listen here, charlatan." Otto pointed at Bernard. "That's
no way to speak about a lady!"

Jo tugged his arm. "Stop him," she whispered.

Otto pushed his shoulders back, thrust his chest out, and broke
loose from Jo's grasp. "And what are you trying to do, doom the
whole hill? There's still hope they can save it!"

"Hope!" Bernard removed the lit cigarette from his mouth
and spat toward the block of homes across from the cliff's edge.
He spun to face the houses, restoring the cigarette to his lips, and
muttered. "Hope be an *illusion.* All that transpires be from either

spite or dumb luck."

"We're losing ground!" A firefighter shouted, kicking dirt on a flare-up while trying to extinguish it. "We must fall back! Everyone, get your things. We need to leave now."

"All hope is lost." An older Irish woman wailed. "Our homes are as good as gone." Bernard cackled and slapped his knee as if someone had just told a joke.

"See? Bad luck. Now, come 'ere, *boy*." He motioned for Otto to follow as he sauntered closer to a blue and white Gothic Revival-style house with delicately carved trim under the eaves, characteristic of an Italianate facade.

"Ye lost the moment ye decided ta come up this 'ere hill." He pounded the axe head on the ground twice in quick succession.

"No, Bernard. You are the one who has lost."

Otto leaped toward Bernard. He landed on Bernard with his entire body weight, tossing him onto his back with an audible *crunch* of his spine. They dropped on the dirt road a couple of feet from a ramshackle picket fence that encircled the Italianate house. *Thud.* The axe landed in the dirt between Bernard and the ledge.

Bernard wriggled like a fish under Otto, kicking up dust and rocks. Otto pushed himself up and shielded his face as he looked for the cigarette. He spotted it in Bernard's fingers.

"Spite," Bernard hissed.

Flick.

Otto dove after the burning butt; his open palm swiped the air. The cigarette smoldered for a moment in the weeds next to a fence post. Then, a spark flared up and clung to a broken picket. He reached for the cigarette hopelessly, then pounded his fist into the dirt. "Shit!"

Otto couldn't fight Bernard and squelch the flames at the same time—impossible. Then, he remembered Jo's story about the little boy and his father. He knew his reach was far greater than it seemed.

He had only to call upon it.

"Jo," Otto bleated. "Please help."

Jo ran up to the fence and kicked at the dirt as more smoke rose from the pickets.

Bernard grabbed Otto's shirt from behind and pulled, flipping him over like a pancake. Though Bernard was not powerful, he had leverage and the element of surprise. He sat on top of Otto's stomach, pinned him to the ground, then grabbed his neck and squeezed.

Otto tried to inhale but could not get any air. As more smoke rose from the nearby fence, he coughed, pushing at Bernard's chest and arms, but he couldn't break the man's grasp. Otto swung his free legs to get momentum and rolled to his side, taking Bernard with him.

Bernard wriggled beneath Otto; his movements scooted them closer to the edge of the retaining wall above the quarry. Bernard tried to imitate Otto's rolling move but failed. His face contorted as he reached out in desperation.

"Otto," Jo screamed. Her mother stood beside her as small flames gathered height behind their legs. "Look out!"

Otto only caught a glimpse of the axe swinging toward him before—*whack!* It struck the side of his skull.

Otto screamed in searing pain, his palms hit the gravel, and he saw nothing but red. He pictured the world around him spinning into an abyss of hazy havoc. Bernard's guffaws commingled with Jo's and her mother's shrieks. Otto heard a clink and thud of the axe as it dropped into the dirt, and boney hands locked around his ankles and tugged.

His center of gravity shifted, causing his chin to hit the ground when his arms could no longer support the weight of his upper torso. He blinked away the stars in enough time to look toward his feet and noticed they were mere inches away from the cliff's edge.

"Beg." Bernard's demented voice rose out of the cloud of chaos. "Beg for your life, *boy.*"

"I won't," Otto muttered, his eyes half-closed as he struggled to retain consciousness. Bernard's blurry figure hunched against the smoky sky above the embankment. Otto felt himself being dragged a few inches further.

"Beg, *boy*," Bernard spat on Otto's legs which he held suspended over the quarry. "Tell me why you deserve to live."

Maybe it was the intense pain or feeling close to certain death, but Otto pondered this existential plight. Did he deserve to live? Or was he no better than the likes of Bernard in the end? He had left Bernard on the roof of the Pavilion to die after all. Had he just become the same trash he hated in people like Cecil? After all, he had punched that bastard in the face instead of walking away.

"Otter, don't listen to him." Jo pleaded. She had abandoned the spreading fire and stood closer to him in the middle of the road. "He's trying to trick you."

No. Otto wouldn't let the scumbag win. He knew why life was worth living. "Hold on," Jo said. Her sparkling eyes brimmed with pleading tears.

She was his *why*. And so were Pop, Ma, and Nella. "Love," he shuddered.

Chapter Thirty-Five

Jo couldn't believe her ears. Had Otto just confessed to being in love with her? She couldn't think about that now. This was her chance to gain an advantage against Bernard.

Mama screamed from the house. "Help! *Aiuto!* Arsonist! *Incendiario!*" She pounded at a portion of the flames using one of the frocks she'd removed. But no one came.

"Love?" Bernard howled, doubling over with laughter. He lost his grip on Otto's ankles as he coughed and wheezed. "Love is a fool's errand, boy. Ain't no decent man's life been saved by *love*."

Otto's feet dropped over the edge, and he kicked at the air to try and propel himself back to the safety of solid ground. It didn't work.

Bernard took his boot and perched it on top of Otto's behind, holding him down. "Love will never teach ye the value of hard work and the duty a man has to his family." Bernard pushed his foot against Otto's hip, turning him over face up and shoving the rest of his body within inches of the quarry's edge.

Bernard pressed his heel into Otto's stomach so hard he winced. "'Tis a shame ye wound up missing yer boat to China, *boy*. A missed opportunity to learn a thing or two. Now I be forced to take extreme measures."

Jo spotted the axe a few feet away from her, where Bernard dropped it after he struck Otto. A bloody streak beneath the axe led to Otto's head lying face up in the dirt.

"Josephine," Mama called from the smoldering fence line. "Don't do anything foolish." Jo ignored her mother's cries and sprang for the axe.

"Jo!" Otto held his head up and gasped.

Jo picked up the bloodied axe and clutched it with both hands. She had never held one before. The handle was rough wood, and the axe was top-heavy. She raised it above her head, blade forward toward Bernard. "Get back!" she screamed at Bernard.

"And why would I want to do that, *deary?*" he asked with a smirk and a high-pitched inflection.

"Just leave us alone!"

Bernard shrugged and looked at Otto. "But then your friend here wouldn't learn his lesson, would he?"

"What lesson? What are you trying to teach him?"

"That he can't just abandon his kin on a whim!"

Otto coughed, managing to prop his head up with his elbows. "You have no idea what you're talking about, old man."

There was no reasoning with this man. What was his plan? To somehow teach Otto about loyalty by dangling him over a cliff? His grip on reality was so far removed from theirs that there was only one way to get to him—force.

Jo ignored the chaos of the scene: men running every which way trying to get the hose to work again, women coordinating bucket brigades that went down to the bay to fetch saltwater, and Mama throwing frock after frock on top of the flames. Jo focused only on Bernard—the only thing that stood between her and her future with Otto. As she watched him bend down to grab Otto by the shirt collar, she knew her feelings for Otto were real. She was certain. She could not stand back and watch as he got dragged to his death. *She loved him.*

Jo took the axe in her right hand and adjusted her grip. She swung it behind her shoulder, took four running steps forward, and aimed with all her might at Bernard. He stood and watched her, slack-jawed and speechless. He ducked to her left, evading the strike and causing the axe to swipe across her whole body to her left. The swipe had countered her forward momentum enough for her to balance her weight on her right foot, inches from the edge. She caught the axe with her left hand and swung it back to her right with the force of both of her arms, landing the butt end squarely onto Bernard's gut. He inhaled sharply, followed by a low, guttural moan.

The strike's velocity knocked him back a step, and the rock from the quarry's edge crumbled under his feet. Jo let go of the axe that tumbled along with Bernard down the side of the cliff.

Jo covered her mouth with both hands to muffle a scream at the sight of Bernard's fall. The sound was drowned out by the cracking of heavy boulders pounding against the hillside. *Had she really just done that?*

She looked down at Otto, propped up on his elbows beside her, bloodied and panting as if he had just swum across the bay and back. He looked up at her and sighed before collapsing onto his back and rubbing his eyes. Jo reached out to him, and he grabbed her arm and pulled himself up.

"Are you okay?" He wiped his face with his sleeve. There he was again, more concerned about her when he looked like he'd just gotten in a fight with a heavyweight champion and lost.

"I ... I was scared." She put her arm around him and helped him stand. "I was so afraid I was going to lose you. I had to do something."

"It'll take more than a blow to the noggin to get rid of me, kiddo." Otto smiled at her with bloody teeth and took her by both hands. His joyful expression melted into a serious one. "But really, though, I couldn't have gotten out of that one alone. Thank you, Jo. You did the right thing."

"I know."

She felt something that she didn't feel after leaving Bernard on the rooftop. She felt relief.

"Jo? I—"

A raspy laugh came from over the edge. Jo let go of one of Otto's hands and took a step toward it. A white-knuckled Bernard clutched the middle of the axe handle that had caught on rocks on each end. The toes of his boots clung to an outcropping.

"No! It can't be!" Jo stared.

Bernard groaned as he kicked his left leg up a couple of times, found a foothold, and tried to pull himself up.

Before Jo could step away, Bernard reached up over the cliff edge with his left hand and grabbed Jo's boot, his fingers clutching its laces. Jo screamed as she lost her grip on Otto's hand and collapsed under Bernard's pulling force.

"Jo!" Otto threw himself on her torso and held her in place against Bernard's weight. He reached for her leg and tugged at the knot in her bootlaces.

Bernard mustered enough leverage to release his other hand from the axe handle. He grabbed one of the thick-rooted succulents growing from the cliff's edge. Then with both hands and his left leg secured in the foothold, he gathered enough momentum to swing his left foot up to the top of the ledge.

"Got it!" exclaimed Otto.

Jo felt her boot loosen and slide off her foot. She watched as it sailed out of Bernard's grasp, over his head, and into the embankment.

Bernard wailed as he slid back. The fingers of his left hand scratched at the bare rock as he dangled between the roots of the succulent with his right hand and the heel of his left boot on the edge.

Jo clambered to her feet and watched as Bernard clung to the edge of the crumbling retaining wall and hollered.

"Just take one step forward . . ." the voice of The Pull sang its siren song.

"Shut. Up." Jo said.

Otto put his arm around her and held her tightly as he pulled her back and away from where Bernard kicked at the side of the quarry wall with his frayed right boot. He drew her close to him. She buried her face in his chest, and they struggled to catch their breath.

Bernard gave them a crooked grin as he panted like a dog. "Aww, sweet prince and princess, life is no fairytale. Happiness be an illusion."

Jo looked at Otto. "No, it's not."

He grinned back at her. "But what do we do about him? He's never going to stop trying to hurt us or everyone else here."

"Mama, help!" she yelled. She saw Mama crouched in front of the fence, her arms around Peter. The flames were gone.

"It will all end in tears and misery, it will." Bernard heaved, struggling to pull himself up the rest of the way. "Mark me words!"

Mama grabbed something off the ground, stood up, and ran toward Jo. "Josephina!" She threw the object, a half-burned portion of a fence post, in Bernard's direction with all her might.

The post twirled in the air and landed against Bernard's forehead. His hands lost their grip on the rocks and foliage and flew up as Bernard plummeted backward. He wailed with shrill surprise, vanishing into the smoke-filled quarry below.

Jo swallowed gulps of air as she ran to hug Mama. They both peered over the quarry's long drop. She didn't see his body, but no one could have survived that fall. She didn't know what to feel other than relief and gratitude that Mama had been there to help them.

"*Va bene,* Cannoli, it's okay. You're safe now. *Sei al sicuro.* You're both safe." Mama held her tight and rocked her.

Otto took heavy breaths and looked at Jo with tearful eyes as if he finally allowed himself to feel. He said, "For a moment, I thought—" Jo let go of Mama and put a hand on his cheek to tell him she understood. She knew he was trying to say that he was scared he might lose her, just as she had been scared about losing him.

"We have each other now," she said. "None of what that lunatic said was true." She wanted to ask him what he meant when he mentioned love, but she wasn't sure what to say. She knew she loved him but had no idea how to tell him.

"What I said before ..."

"Yes?" This might be it. He was going to say it, so she wouldn't have to.

Jo was overcome with an undeniable desire for him. Though building for so long, she had pushed the feeling aside and held onto anger instead. Now her defenses were obliterated.

"Josephina?" Mama spoke in a discreet tone. "What do we do now?"

Jo turned toward her mother and saw the love in her eyes. She felt grateful to be surrounded by so much love but foolish for not seeing what was in front of her this whole time.

For too long, she had let her misunderstandings of the past keep her from having the relationship she wanted with her mother. Resentment was the true hell, and self-pity was the devil in disguise. How foolish to think she was the sole victim of Papa's suicide. All she wanted to do was find a way to move forward.

"Mama, I'm so sorry. For everything."

"Don't worry about it another second, Cannoli. We are together now. That's all that matters." Mama grabbed her, kissed her on the mouth, then did the same to Otto.

Chapter Thirty-Six

The fire was closer now. Though it lost steam going up the hill, it spawned spot fires in unassuming places that went unnoticed. The firefighters had fallen back, and men working on the hill shouted for everyone to retreat to the eastern side.

The side of Otto's head throbbed, and his body, still unrecovered from the gunshot and blow to the head, begged him to rest. "Jo, I can't keep going like this." He retrieved a handkerchief from his pocket and pressed it against his head.

"All right. Let's find somewhere to sit for a moment."

"Here," Jo's Mama said. "Let's see if someone's home." She opened the gate to the Italianate, went up the stairs to the front door, and knocked.

Almost immediately, an old Italian woman with a hunchback wearing an apron opened the door. She held a torn white dishtowel that twirled around in the air as she spoke. Occasionally she would gesture in his and Jo's direction and frown disapprovingly. Jo's Mama would return a gesture that appeared calming in nature.

After the two women were done talking, they embraced one

another like old friends. Jo's Mama waved them all forward.

Jo slowed her pace to accommodate Otto, and Peter ran ahead. Signora Antonietta DeLuca welcomed them into her home, where they rested on worn, dusty furniture and calculated their next move. They covered their noses and mouths with handkerchiefs that helped block the dusty smoke but did not mask the heavy perfume of fermenting wine wafting up from the basement.

"I don't think we have a choice now. We have to leave and try to find a boat out of here," Jo said as her Mama helped her bandage up Otto's head so the bandage covered most of his right eye.

"Thanks, Mrs. . . . uh . . . hmm. I just realized I don't know your last name."

"Moreci. Mrs. Alma Moreci." The woman bowed slightly, a twinkle in her eye. "Thank you for saving my daughter's life, Mr.—"

"Otto Frei. And I do believe that was the third time. Or was it the fourth?"

"Watch it, Otter." Jo grinned.

After some time feeling pressure from the bandages, his head felt surprisingly better. "Now, that means you too, Signora DeLuca."

"This neighborhood is so close," Signora DeLuca explained as Mrs. Moreci translated. "And it's full of salt of the earth, hard-working folks who would rather lay down their lives than sacrifice this small piece of the world they proudly call home."

"I don't know what to say, Signora DeLuca. We just can't stay here. It's not safe," Otto said. "Explain to her how dangerous it is."

Mrs. Moreci spoke more with Signora DeLuca, then explained that she would rather walk down to the bay and carry back buckets of seawater than let her home burn without a fight. She was foolish, but her wild devotion made Otto want to help.

"I don't know if there's anything we can do, Cannoli, but I'll tell you what, this smell is getting to me," Mrs. Moreci said.

"I've almost gotten used to the smoke," said Jo, "I know that's not good to say."

"No, not the smoke. The *vino*! All I can think about is how I want a glass."

"The wine," Otto shouted. "Of course!"

"You're not ready to give up that quickly, are you?" asked Jo.

"No, that's not what I mean. How much wine is in the cellar, Signora?"

Mrs. Moreci translated, and Signora DeLuca became very chipper, bragging about her wine cellar. "Signora says she doesn't know exactly how many bottles, but numerous. She says about all the Italian families ferment wine in their basements."

"We can use the wine to squelch the flames," Otto explained. "Hurry, down to the basement. Mrs. Moreci, could you spread the word since you speak Italian? Tell everyone to break into their barrels by any means necessary."

Otto scrambled excitedly out of the house with Jo to get to the cellar entrance. He looked around for something to use to open it. He found a crowbar tucked beside the stoop.

"*Aspetta, aspetta,*" Signora DeLuca muttered, waddling a large distance behind them and signaling with both hands to wait.

Otto felt impatient and tried to pry open the cellar door but found it locked. He pushed on the crowbar repeatedly, but it did not budge.

"*Aspetta, te l'ho detto!*" She slapped one hand against the air and revealed a key; then, she fumbled to fit it into the lock. It was like watching a drunk thread a needle.

Otto couldn't watch. He put his palm to his bandaged forehead and turned away. He felt Jo's hand touch his back.

The door creaked open, and a sweet perfume of fruits and tannins drifted out from the basement cellar. Otto spun around, and warm light grew inside as Signora DeLuca turned the key on a lantern tucked into a shelf to the left of the rickety stairwell. She picked up the lantern and toddled further into the room, revealing six large oak barrels sitting in a row in the center, bookended by two support beams. She reached up to put the handle over a hook attached to the closest beam, pushing her five-foot-tall body onto her toes to reach it.

No time to waste. Otto approached the farthest barrel, raised the crowbar above his head with his right arm, and adjusted his grip the best he could. "Here goes nothing. Stand back, Jo."

Jo took a step back as Otto's arm swung and missed the barrel completely. Then he tripped over his feet and nearly toppled over.

"My depth perception is off," Otto pointed at his eye, partially covered by the bandage.

"How embarrassing for you," Jo teased. "Here, let me see that."

Otto reluctantly handed Jo the crowbar as he pushed humiliation aside. He felt like a ballplayer taking a swing against Rube Waddell's sharp-breaking curveball only to strike out.

Jo held the metal bar in both hands and forced it behind her back as far as it would go. She grunted as she spun it in a magnificent arc and made contact with her target, denting the barrel's head hoop and piercing the wood on the top. A second swing sent wood splintering in every direction as wine splashed out of the top of the barrel.

"Grab buckets! Any you can find," she directed him. Then she turned to the older woman. "Do you have any blankets—um—*coperte?*"

Signora DeLuca nodded and went upstairs to fetch some.

"Why the blankets?" Otto asked.

"To soak up the wine."

"Okay." Otto wasn't satisfied with the vague response, but instead of questioning her, he grabbed a rusty metal bucket from the corner that held a mop, which he tossed aside. Jo left the cellar for a moment and reappeared with a watering can from the garden. The two got to work filling them.

They ran outside to find Jo's mother and started pouring wine on small flames that reached the crest of the hill half a block up. Mrs. Moreci gathered some of the neighbors and explained what they were doing. Everyone watched as white steam hissed and the flames were extinguished.

Cheering and singing erupted from the crowd as everyone scrambled back to their homes. Some returned with various household items containing wine from their supplies—vases, bowls, even a bedpan. Some of the Irish with no wine barrels grabbed any vessel they could and trudged down the Filbert Steps to retrieve seawater. Every single person was doing anything they could. They had an advantage in this battle at last, and they would take it.

Jo ran back to Signora DeLuca's house and retrieved the wine-soaked blankets. She assessed the surrounding structures.

"Which one is closest, do you think?"

"That one over there," Otto pointed to a modest two-story down from the top of the hill. The Irish girl hung over her front porch railing; she held the top layer of her dress over her mouth and nose as smoke swirled menacingly behind her.

Jo turned toward him, arms full of wine-soaked bedspread that stained the ground red as it dripped at her feet. Her nightgown would be discolored permanently as well. She looked as if she had so much to tell him, but her drawn-out silence said she didn't know where to start. "Otter, if this doesn't work . . ." Tears welled in her eyes again.

"It will, kiddo. We'll keep fighting. You're so strong. You know that, right?"

She shook her head. "I'm just stubborn. Never know when to give up. It's my biggest fault."

"It takes a lot of guts to admit you're not perfect. But you need to know something."

"What's that?" Jo blinked, fanning her long, lush eyelashes in his direction. He couldn't tell if she knew what he was about to say.

"To me, you're perfect. See, I don't see you as stubborn at all. I see you as tenacious, persistent, and determined."

He paused, waiting for a response, but he didn't get anything more than stunned silence. For the first time, Jo didn't have anything to say. "Geez, Jo, I'm trying to say I love you."

Chapter Thirty-Seven

"o, did you hear me? I said I love you."

A million thoughts rippled through Jo's mind like waves on the ocean. *Otto loved* her. He loved her. He loved *her*.

This is the best thing that has ever happened to me.

I can be happy.

The reflection left her elated, but it carried momentum as the idea's wave drew closer. By the time the wave reached her, its force knocked her off her feet and left her drenched and cold.

It's too good to be true.

I don't deserve it.

I'll never make him happy.

It's just heartbreak waiting to happen.

Her instinct told her to fight. *Don't let Otto in.* Say something cold and cruel to drive him away so she wouldn't have to take the risk and put all her cards on the table.

There was a look of softness and hope on his face.

But she couldn't even take the time to feel right now. They were in danger. She wasn't allowed to be selfish right now. "I need to go." Jo ran over to the Irish girl's house and asked her to help get blankets on the roof.

"Da!" The girl called, and her father and brothers came running from the back of the house.

"Here," Jo thrust the blanket into their arms. "Put these on your roof."

She watched as the men ran into the house and emerged from a window in the attic. They clambered onto the roof and spread the blankets over the flammable shingles to snuff out a spot that had begun to smolder above one of the bedroom windows.

When the winds changed yet again and began to blow in from the east, they knew they had a chance.

After countless trips back and forth to assist more neighbors in the fight, the group had over half a dozen homes with wine-drenched bedding draped over roofs, fences, and steps. They had to keep trying, to keep hauling water in bucket brigades to dump on the flames until the fire had nothing else to cling to and died out.

And that's exactly what happened. The flames eventually hit their limit and went no further. Jo, Otto, Mama, Peter, and the residents of Telegraph Hill had faced a cataclysmic inferno, one that had consumed nearly an entire city, and won.

"I'm afraid I have some bad news, Jo." Otto sat on the ground next to Jo at the cliff's edge and watched the sunrise over San Francisco Bay. He clutched his wounded shoulder as he stared drowsily off into the distance. The flames subsided quietly as gentle showers began to fall on San Francisco.

Jo's mind raced. She couldn't think of anything else that could possibly have gone wrong after today. "What is it?"

"I lost the Caddy. It sort of exploded."

Jo had forgotten about the car. It seemed like ages ago that it was the most important thing in her life. She laughed. Otto looked perplexed. "It doesn't matter, Otto. We did it. After all of that, after everything, we're still here."

Otto exhaled. "You're right, kiddo. We survived."

They *had* survived.

She was a survivor.

She couldn't have said that four days ago. The Jo from four days ago, the one who was too afraid to face her fears and challenge herself, the one who lived in a fantasy world where she worshiped Papa and vilified Mama, was gone. She no longer wished to disappear into the background. She no longer believed she didn't deserve happiness.

It was funny; in a way, she was grateful for having to go through so much because, in the end, she knew herself and trusted herself more than ever before.

"So, now what?" Otto turned to face her and his bangs fell in into his face. He swiped them out of the way with his hand, revealing his blue-eyed thoughtful gaze that punched a hole in her armor.

She reached for his hand and squeezed it tightly. "Now, we move forward." *No matter what happened, they would always have this moment.*

Otto reached out and put his arm around the small of her back.

"Come here, you." He whispered words barely audible for her to hear as he drew her into him. His breath warmed her cheek, and she bent in to meet his lips in a kiss.

They sat there together in silence as a slight mist formed and developed into showers. The rain cleansed them and fell forgivingly upon their new, unfamiliar city. As the smoky air cleared, she saw what she needed to do. "I am so grateful that I met you, Otter."

"Me too, Jo. You truly changed my life. I wish I could say that I can still run away with you, but after everything that happened and working things out with my father, I decided I need to stay."

"That's great news." She was already a million miles away as the words slipped out, hovering over the Arc de Triomphe in Paris. She had trouble reeling herself back in. "But I can't."

"You can't stay? What do you mean?" He tried to clamber to his feet but struggled to find his balance.

She looked over at Mama, sitting under one of the neighbor's porches on a rocking chair. She had Peter in her arms, who was fast asleep. Her eyes were closed, but she rocked back and forth.

Jo rose to her feet, grabbed Otto by the hands, and sighed as she deliberated over what she was about to say. "I have spent the last several years pushing my family away when I should have been working on letting them in. I only realize that now, after everything. It's a shame Mrs. Tucci and my aunt and uncle had to die for me to see it. My mama has been there for me all along. I just didn't see it. Now it's time for me to be there for her. I need to get to know her again, and I want to be there for Peter as he grows up. I'm moving with them to San Jose."

"I . . . I don't know what to say, Jo. I finally found you. I want us to be together."

"I want that, too. I'm in love with you, Otto, but it cannot be right now. I will be back. One day. She's my city just as much as she's yours."

"Promise me."

"I promise to the stars," she smiled at the sincerity of her pledge. "I'll tell you what. Meet me back on Strawberry Hill, where we spent that first night, where you promised me that we were invincible. On the first anniversary of the earthquake."

"Okay, deal. April 18, 1907." He reached out his hand to shake it. Jo returned the gesture. "Don't make me chase after you, Jo. You know I always find you."

"I'm counting on it."

He pulled her toward him, and they held each other in perfect silence, all their pain forgotten, all their differences turned to dust and swept away like ashes in the rain.

Author's Note

This book is a work of historical fiction.

The Great Earthquake and fires of 1906, however, were very real. On April 18, 1906, at 5:12 a.m., an earthquake that today would measure 7.9 on the Richter scale hit San Francisco and the greater Bay Area. The shaking lasted about 45 seconds. It brought down many poorly-built buildings, damaged the water system, and ruptured gas lines.

It's estimated that 90 percent of the damage done was not by the earthquake itself but by the resulting fires. Without access to water, there was no way to put out the fires. In the end, the fires lasted three days, 80 percent of the city of San Francisco was completely destroyed, and over three thousand souls lost their lives.

Growing up in San Jose, California, my great-grandmother Josephine DeMaria told stories about the earthquake from when she was a little girl living in San Francisco. Nana reminisced about living in a tent city before being loaded up on the back of a wagon to live with her uncles on a cattle ranch on Mount Hamilton.

When I got older, I spent a year living in San Francisco in the second-story flat of an old Victorian on Fillmore Street, which was built before the earthquake. I participated in documenting the restoration of its exterior, dazzled by each handcrafted detail uncovered with every removed layer of lead paint.

I fell in love with the city because of that house, the eclectic multicultural residents, the vibrant nightlife, and the rich history that surrounded me. When I researched the house's history, I found that it had been built by August Jungblut, a German billiards table manufacturer, along with the house next door. After the earthquake, he moved his business operations to his home, which eventually became occupied by his son, Otto.

While Jo, Otto, and the rest of my characters are fictional, I'd like to think that they, in some way, pay homage to the spirit of the individuals that sparked my inspiration and eventually took on a life all their own.

The story behind the story could stop there, but it doesn't. Two years after I began writing this book, I experienced my own natural disaster. On October 9, 2017, I lost my home to a California wildfire. Everything about that experience—the terror of being caught in the middle of a firestorm, the uncertainty of how to process the trauma of the loss, and the resulting resilience—helped me sharpen my skills, refine the details of the scenes, and drive the main themes of the story.

I hope, dear reader, that you take something away from this story and carry it with you. I hope it helps you to be strong when you need to conjure the strength. I hope it inspires empathy for those struck by disaster as we each process things in our own way. And I hope it offers a gentle reminder to be prepared. Disaster can strike anyone at any time. Have a plan, and be safe.

I invite you to join me each year on the anniversary of the 1906 earthquake and fires. You'll find me at Lotta's Fountain dark and early, carrying on the tradition as did generations before me: remember not just all that we lost that day, but everything we gained because of it. Learn more at melissageissinger.com/1906.

Resources

I enjoyed researching the earthquake just as much as writing about it. Here is a list of publications and resources that both informed and inspired me during this process.

BOOKS

A Crack in the Edge of the World: America and the Great California Earthquake of 1906 by Simon Winchester

Among the Ruins: Arnold Genthe's Photographs of the 1906 San Francisco Earthquake and Firestorm by Karin Breuer

The Barbary Coast: An Informal History of the San Francisco Underworld by Herbert Asbury

Complete Story of the San Francisco Earthquake and Other Great Disasters by Marshall Everette

Denial of Disaster by Gladys Hansen and Emmet Condon

The Great Earthquake and Firestorms of 1906: How San Francisco Nearly Destroyed Itself by Philip L. Fradkin

Historic San Francisco: A Concise History and Guide by Rand Richards

Saving San Francisco: Relief and Recovery after the 1906 Disaster by Andrea Rees Davies

Slang: To-day and Yesterday by Eric Partridge

Three Fearful Days: San Francisco Memoirs of the 1906 Earthquake & Fire by Malcolm E. Barker

MAPS AND OTHER RESOURCES

1905 San Francisco Sanborn Insurance Atlas, Sanborn-Perris Map

Company, David Rumsey Map Collection at davidrumsey.com

Ancestry.com

Archived editions of *The San Francisco Call,* California Digital Newspaper Collection at cdnc.ucr.edu

"Water Works," a project by Scott Kildall that mapped all of San Francisco's water infrastructure, including a beautiful interactive cistern map

MUSEUMS

Museum of the City of San Francisco at sfmuseum.org

San Francisco Fire Department Museum

VIDEOS

"1906 Refugees at Ferry Building, San Francisco," YouTube video by tuckergperry, July 15, 2009

"Exploded Gas Tanks, U.S. Mint, Emporium and Spreckel's Bld'g," YouTube video by Library of Congress, July 29, 2010

"In The Shade Of The Old Apple Tree," YouTube video by Georgia English, December 18, 2013

"San Francisco Earthquake Aftermath: Riding Down Market Street 1906," YouTube video by A/V Geeks, February 27, 2014

"San Francisco Earthquake and Fire, April 18, 1906," YouTube video by Library of Congress, July 29, 2010

"Scenes in San Francisco, [no.2]," YouTube video by Library of Congress, July 29, 2010

"A Trip Down Market Street Before the Fire," YouTube video by Library of Congress, July 28, 2010

Acknowledgments

What a long road.

I'm going to do something unconventional here and acknowledge my own impulsiveness. Though it occasionally gets me into trouble, it was responsible for me moving to San Francisco on a whim in 2008. It was there that I opened myself up to strange and unfamiliar experiences, became inspired, and first began to identify as a storyteller.

Thank you to my Nana, Josephine Moreci DeMaria, for sharing your childhood stories that sparked my curiosity and bolstered my personal relationship with the history of the earthquake.

Thank you to Nancy Austin, the kind stranger who planted the seed that I could one day write a novel about San Francisco's history.

I was lucky enough to run into my writing coach, Eric Elfman, at a party years ago. Eric helped me get my sea legs. I'll be forever grateful to Jan for forcing us to talk to one another.

I'm grateful for my early readers and beta crew. Keith Fleming, your bottomless support and enthusiasm has been exceptional. Tom Kelly, this story wouldn't have come out quite the same if it weren't for our serendipitous encounter at San Francisco Writers Conference (SFWC).

Jude, thank you for your ridiculous banter and unwavering friendship going back over 20 years. You're kind of my rock, dude.

Lance and Barbara Cottrell, you've been there for me through it all. There's no one else I'd rather play D&D with, bounce ideas off of, or have a boot-kicking session with. Evacuation buddies for life.

Cole, this project may have lasted longer than our marriage, but I am grateful to you for always making me feel that my dreams were worth seeing through.

Mom, thanks for letting me share this whole process with you. I love how much this book's journey brought us closer to our roots and gifted us with experiences and new traditions that will last lifetimes.

Dad, thanks for raising me to work hard and set big goals. Kenny, I appreciate your brutally honest feedback.

Thank you to every agent that told me no, but took the time to validate my skills and commitment.

To my editor, Gini Grossenbacher, and my proofreader, Laureen Urey. Working with both of you has been a gift. You each really know your craft, and you've made me a better writer and storyteller. Thank you for all you do!

Scott, being with you has been the biggest adventure of my life. It's an honor to be as big of a fan of you as you are of me. You're my Strawberry Hill.

And Apollo. This book was for you even before I knew you. I hope it reminds you to be strong, love fearlessly, and keep going no matter what. Resilience is in your blood. I'm so proud that I get to be your mom.

MELISSA GEISSINGER is descended from survivors of the 1906 San Francisco earthquake and is herself a wildfire survivor. A neuro-divergent optimist, Melissa is predisposed to following her dreams as well as every shiny side quest along the way. She lives in the San Francisco Bay Area with her partner, her five-year-old heart warrior son, and a menagerie of fur kids. She enjoys the outdoors, soaking up knowledge, and connecting with other passionate creators. *Nothing Left But Dust* is her first novel.

You can follow her writing at melissageissinger.com
or on Instagram
@melissageissinger